THE DEVIL'S HARVEST

CHRONICLES OF THE SUPERNATURAL BOOK THREE

J M HART

First published by JMH World Publishing in 2020
This edition published in 2020 by JMH World Publishing
Copyright © JM Hart 2020
www.jmhartwriter.com
The moral right of the author has been asserted.

All the characters in this book are fictitious, and any resemblance to actual persons living or dead is purely coincidental.

The Devil's Harvest: Chronicles of The Supernatural: Book Three

EPUB: 978-0-6450396-1-0
ISBN: 978-0-6450396-2-7

PROLOGUE

The Emerald Tablet was returned to the Tomb of Thoth. But the world is a very different place, with few survivors. The friends are about to embark on separate journeys to find survivors. Chronicles of the Supernatural Book Three: *The Devil's Harvest*, is Shaun and Rachel's story as they continue to move along a timeline that appears to be set by the gods and which they are yet to recognize and accept. Things are not as they appear to be and time is short.

BEFORE THE APOCALYPSE, HELPING OTHERS WASN'T SHAUN'S forte, but he was gradually getting used to being part of a community, and helping. There are only seventeen people at Casey's estate, so it feels like one big extended family now.

During the past six months, Shaun has gotten to know

Rachel intimately, and he'd do anything for her. Rachel is free spirited, and strong-willed, and he knows she's determined to return to Israel to find her family. Kevin, at sixteen years old, is a very cool guy and their portal master; although, for the past six months he's been unable to open a portal because of emotional blockages – mainly due to the loss of Alex, his brother – and the effects of the whiteout. This situation means not one of them has been able to travel beyond the east coast of the United Kingdom, so it's been easy for Shaun to play along with Rachel and listen to her talk about returning to Israel, knowing it's not possible. But things have changed and Kevin has his mojo back, which is probably all to do with Jade ... they're as nerdy as each other and belong together.

So now Kevin is ready and willing to open a portal for Rachel. Shaun has grown comfortable with the routines on Casey's estate and doesn't care if he never gets home. There's nothing there for him: everything he needs is right here. But he gets it that Rachel needs to go home; she needs to find her brother and mother. She knows he will go with her; that he would die for her. Shaun thinks she is making a mistake, and they will not return here with her mother or brother, but he knows he has to let her try. If they do find her family, he can only hope they won't hold the death of Rachel's father against him.

Rachel is the only other person who knows everything Shaun's father did, because she was there. It seems like a lifetime ago when his father released the virus and blew up the cave with Rachel's dad and the archaeology team inside. It is Rachel who sees a side of Shaun that nobody else does; she once said he was her knight in shining armor, and she always believed one day he would return for her when she needed him the most. And he did, eleven years later – by accident. He had thought she died all those years ago, in the explosion, with her father. Shaun had only been seven years old at the time of the explosion, and had no way to know she survived. Shaun doesn't believe he is any kind of knight, because growing up he bullied, teased, lied, and stole. He destroyed property and dreams. But he has changed for the better because of Rachel.

And the world has changed, but not for the better – nothing is as it should be.

1

It was a frosty spring morning at Casey's estate. Shaun watched Rachel and Jade make a pact to both return to the estate with their loved ones, because Jade and Kevin will go to the United States of America to find Jade's father after Kevin has opened a portal for Shaun and Rachel to go to Israel. To Jerusalem.

"You ready for this?" Kevin asked, slapping Shaun on the back.

"Always!" Shaun said, hiding his apprehension.

Rachel, walking with Jade and Sophia, presented herself to Kevin. "Ready when you are maestro," she said with a cheeky bow.

They were minutes away from leaving. Shaun imagined Israel to be hot, but he couldn't remember what it was like when he was a kid. And when they returned from the Emerald

Tablet journey over six months ago, in the dead of night, in a fiery tomb, doesn't count for remembering details.

Shaun stuffed his hands in his pockets to keep warm and to feel for his favorite gemstone in its pouch, and panicked.

"What's wrong?" Casey asked.

"I'm missing a stone," Shaun said, taking the pouch out of his pocket and pouring the sacred stones into his palm.

"You placed it on Alex's grave, for keepsake," Casey said.

As soon as Kevin's brother's name was mentioned, Shaun remembered and felt foolish. "Cheers," he said to Casey, putting the stones back. He kept the icosahedron sapphire in his hand and rolled the edges around his fingers like a coin.

"Let's do this," Rachel said.

Shaun squeezed the icosahedron, feeling the pointed edges dig into his palm. He dropped it into the pouch in his pocket before it drew blood. The sacred geometric gemstones gave him a sense of comfort he wasn't willing to admit to others.

Kevin gently placed his fingers on Rachel's temples to access her memories. He took his time as it had been months since he had opened a portal. Their friends standing nearby watched in awe. Shaun rubbed his hands together in anticipation, and shifted his weight ... he couldn't remember feeling this nervous.

Silver sparks and swirls of green, blue and purple energy circled Kevin and Rachel when Kevin created the portal, his actions enabled by Rachel's emotionally charged memories of her home in Israel.

"We'll catch up with you on Saturday, four days from now," Casey said, "when you return." Casey, over the last six months, has grown an inch over six foot, and towers over twenty-year-old Rachel.

Casey slapped Shaun on the shoulder. "Make sure you're back at the portal with Rachel's family when Kevin returns to collect you."

"Will do," Shaun replied, knowing Casey was just trying to get a sense of how he was feeling.

Shaun looked at Rachel. She had her bowie knife strapped to her thigh, and he could see she was itching to go. He moved to stand at Rachel's side and took her hand. The trio stepped into the sparkling color energy.

It looked like liquid to Shaun, and it always surprised him when he didn't get wet. He lost himself in the portal's serene energy and all his worries dissolved. He felt Rachel beside him, and there was nothing else he needed in the world.

THEY STEPPED FROM THE PORTAL INTO STIFLING HEAT AND HARSH winds. The sky was a smoky, dirty brown, and the air smelled of death. Shaun put his sunglasses on and pulled his blue neck gaiter up to cover his mouth and nose. *Where are all the trees? The land's so barren. The rocks were white and, from where he stood, the city of Jerusalem was rubble.*

"It looks like an earthquake has rippled through the town," Kevin said.

"A big one," Shaun said.

"We live on a fault line. It's only a matter of time until we have another one like the Jericho earthquake," Rachel said, scanning the destroyed buildings. "This makes little sense, though. The sky should be clear. Perhaps there's been a sandstorm?"

"Do you want to go back?" Kevin shouted. "Or I could stay? You might need the help. I can take Jade to find her dad after we find your family."

"We'll be fine," Shaun said. "Go back and help the nerd find her dad."

Rachel lightly backhanded Shaun on the arm. "You're the only portal master, go back and help the others," Rachel said, stepping away from the portal's swirling energy.

Shaun heard crackling static electricity over the wind: the sparks of swirling energy turning to liquid power that he knows as the opening and closing of the portal. Shaun thought about how much had changed since he had left Kevin for dead in the bushfires last summer. Ashamed of his past actions, Shaun looked down and busied himself in retying his bootlaces. If it hadn't been for Kevin, he never would have found Rachel; he never would've found his new family; he never would've found out his father wasn't crazy; that there is a place where all heals. Kevin is the key.

Kevin would be returning in four days to this very spot, so they needed to be back with Rachel's family ready to go. Shaun stood tall and patted Kevin on the back. "Cheers." Shaun wanted to say more, he wanted to thank him, to say sorry, but he just didn't know how. So he gave him a manly slap on the back. "You're all right."

Rachel took hold of Shaun's forearm and pulled him toward

her, before pulling her purple neck gaiter over her mouth and nose.

"You've got to remember I can feel people's emotions, and you're no exception." Kevin raised his eyebrows.

"I think it's about time you left," Shaun said, ignoring Kevin's comment.

"See you soon," Rachel said.

"Four days," Kevin said, holding up four fingers on his right hand while walking backward to the portal.

Shaun turned his back on Kevin, knowing he was about to step into the portal and disappear along with their only means of transportation back to Casey's estate. He knows Kevin senses people's emotions, including Shaun's, and that will have to do for now. One day he might be able to apologize, but somehow, with Kevin, he didn't think he had to.

Every time he looked into Rachel's green eyes, he remembered the day he met her when he was seven. She wore a lilac dress and gumboots. That was over eleven years ago. That day his life, and the world, changed forever. She still loves her purple colors though, and she's still full of gumption, passion, tenacity, confidence and emotions. For the past seven months, it's like they had never been apart for eleven years. He's mesmerized by her strength, joy, quick wit, and caring nature. Rachel got along with everyone at the estate, she was good at everything except controlling her fiery emotions. Rachel could shoot a rifle and throw a knife with skill, and she could punch like the best of them, but she was also a soft, gentle, beautiful woman. Two months ago, she had cut her long wavy hair short, and still looked like a goddess.

Rachel, squinting, trying to avoid the sand blowing into her eyes, yells, "What are you thinking?"

He also had to shout over the wind. "Is this what you imagined?"

Rachel shook her head, looking around in dismay. "This is not how I remember my hometown. This isn't the street I lived on, but it is the street I picked for us to exit the portal. I never imagined such destruction." Clouds of smoke hovered just above the city, unmoving in the air, although the wind should be driving it westward. "This way," she said. They walked a little then switched to a light jog.

Shaun halted briefly. The popping sound of gunfire came from a few streets away.

"Gunfire," Rachel said. "People!" Rachel jogged faster. She stopped at a narrow crossroad and listened. The gunfire had stopped. She ran on.

Shaun kept pace as she climbed over broken terrace walls to knock on the doors of the few homes still standing.

"Joseph, Michael, Ruth, anybody home?" she called out.

"Nobody is here. Listen, the gunfire stopped." He felt the wind die down, and the streets echoed the sudden silence and he wondered if the people with the guns had heard their voices?

Rachel rammed her shoulder against the blue door of a white semi-detached house. Shaun helped her, but the door wouldn't budge.

"Let's keep moving," Rachel said, leaving the property.

"Slow down, Rachel."

Rachel continued to run and jump over walls and peer through windows. "Stay low."

"Is this your family home?" he asked when she slowed to look through windows and scan rubble.

"Two blocks away. But this is the home of my cousins."

Shaun was having trouble keeping up with her. "I need a minute to catch my breath," he said.

THE AIR WAS FILLED WITH DEATH AND SMELLED OF RUBBISH AND decay. Shaun had expected it to be a ghost town, so he wasn't surprised they didn't find any people, but there was obviously someone running around with a gun.

He kept pace with Rachel, matching her stamina, climbing over broken rendered stonework to enter a narrow laneway. "What is that smell?" he said.

"Maybe sewage."

The odor of decay was filtering through his gaiter. "It smells more like rotting garbage, but there are no visible signs of the source."

As they got closer to the city, they were finding more buildings with minor damage. The city couldn't have been the epicenter for an earthquake, or a bomb. Left untouched by the devastation was a row of homes.

Rachel stood in front of a black iron gate surrounding the front courtyard of a two-story terrace house.

"What is it? Is this your home?" Shaun asked.

Rachel didn't move. "Yes."

"Do you want me to go in first?"

She gazed up to the second-floor windows. "No," she said.

The gate squeaked as Rachel entered the courtyard. She looked calm, focused, as she pressed her palm against the front door, trying to feel for the vibrations of movement and life behind it. Frustrated, she banged her fists against the door. She stood back, her eyes pooling with tears. "Eema ... eema! David! Kick the door, Shaun, help me kick it in!"

He stepped back and rammed the sealed door, to no avail. They both jimmied their bowie knives between the door and the frame. The wooden frame splintered. Shaun searched the street for a metal wire to pick the lock. He found a piece and went back to the door.

The sound of shattering glass startled him, and he ducked. Rachel was already trying to climb through the window she had smashed in and jagged glass was still stuck in the frame.

"Stop, wait a minute," he said abandoning the wire hanging out of the lock. Quickly, he cleared the shards of glass from the edges of the window with his knife. She scrambled through the window as soon as he stepped back.

Shaun finished picking the front door lock in seconds and went inside. He stood in a small entrance that had a picture on the wall of an old man, and on the opposite side a row of hooks for coats and hats. The hooks were empty.

Rachel ran from the front room into the hall and up the stairs calling out, "Eema! David!"

Shaun stayed to search the lower level of the terrace. He walked into the front room where glass and a massive rock lay on the floor. Besides Rachel's mess of broken glass, the house was in perfect order: books were neat on the shelves, the remote control for the TV on a coffee table next to a pile of coasters. Everything was in order as if Rachel's mom had just stepped out. He trailed his finger along the furniture, catching a light film of dust. He opened the refrigerator, and found it empty, as empty as the fruit bowl on the kitchen bench. The plates were in the cupboard; the glasses washed – they would have at least fallen or shattered if there had been a quake. It felt like nobody had been in the house for a while.

RACHEL WAS STORMING THROUGH THE UPPER ROOMS, CALLING out, "Eema! David!"

Shaun went upstairs to help her. It was very tidy and there was a sense of calmness. He found Rachel in her brother's room, staring at a folded pile of clothes placed on the end of the bed. A burst of gunfire filled the street below. Shaun looked out the window into the street, but it was empty.

Rachel suddenly threw herself into his arms. Choking back tears, she said, "They're not here, all their things are here, but they're not." She pushed back from Shaun's arms as quickly as she had entered them and started ranting, waving her arms in the air as she talked. She was a fireball of frustration. When she got like this, she spoke in Hebrew and he didn't understand what she was saying, which he thought might be a good thing. He didn't know how to handle her or what to say. Her vulnerability was scaring him.

"Calm down, Rachel," he said and her eyes widened. By the

murderous expression on her face, telling her to calm down may not have been the smartest thing to say. "Look at this place. They left, but weren't in a panic. The place is clean, there're no signs of chaos. Everything is in perfect order. They must be somewhere safe."

"I'm afraid they're dead like everyone else. We must find someone. Come, we must find whoever is shooting. There must be others alive too. There must be more survivors." She was off again, rushing down the stairs, out into the street screaming, "Hello?"

She ran to the next window, the next street, until she found a door slightly ajar.

"Slow down, what if you run into whoever has the gun." Shaun pulled her back from entering the building. "Wait!"

"Let go of me!"

He let go of her arm. "You're no good to your family if you're dead."

She took a few breaths, getting herself under control. "You're right. I need to get control of my emotions." She nodded, thinking and processing.

"I'll go in first. Stay with me until we know it's safe."

"Okay."

The home had rotten food on the kitchen floor, furniture was overturned, and the air was filled with dust. Rachel was stealth like as they entered each room of the house together, then she moved toward the stairs. Shaun stood in the entranceway to the living room. A cup lay at his feet, surrounded by a dry coffee stain. Whoever lived here had departed in a mad rush, voluntarily or forced he couldn't tell.

Rachel went upstairs, her knife drawn. Shaun moved into the living room and out to the kitchen. A child's sandal with a daisy on the toe-strap lay on the kitchen floor by the back door, as if it had fallen off in a tussle. Shaun looked out the door and saw what looked like human remains, the aftermath of a savage dog attack. He was quick to shut and bolt the door, then went to the refrigerator. It was full of rotten food.

Rachel was stomping above him, searching every room. "Clear!" she yelled. "No one is here!" she said walking down the stairs.

"There's no one down here," Shaun said. He didn't think there was any point mentioning the sandal or possible human remains.

It was hard to tell if people were forced to leave their homes, or if they had left of their own accord in a panic during the apocalypse. Amalgamated swarms of micro shape shifting beasts could have destroyed the town with ease.

Rachael's hometown reminded him of images he had seen at school of a terrible nuclear disaster in Russia, at Chernobyl. It happened before he was born, and it was still contaminated. "Maybe there was a nuclear explosion here, and that's why the sky is such a strange color. We need survivors to tell us what happened."

"It's six months since we've been here. If there was a nuclear explosion, there would still be fallout from a small ten kiloton surface explosion, but it depends on how close we are to ground zero. Chernobyl was equivalent to two thousand times greater than a ten kiloton surface explosion," Rachel said, pulling her neck gaiter over the back of her head and around her mouth, creating a balaclava. "We'd better move fast."

THEY WERE NEARING THE TOWN CENTER. RACHEL GUIDED THEM down narrow streets and up alleyways. Shaun's senses were on high alert; he felt like he was being hunted. The gunfire had stopped. He saw an odd shadow of a deformed dog: against the building wall the shadow's muzzle looked elongated, like an alligator. It convinced Shaun they were being followed. Rachel stepped into the town square before his "Wait!" could stop her. On the other side of the space, a piece of corrugated metal sheeting that was covering a pizza shop window, moved. There was a dark pedestrian tunnel at two o'clock. He felt whoever was stalking them was close. His skin crawled. "Hide, now!"

Rachel ducked down behind a dried up water fountain.

Shaun studied the darkness of the tunnel: a dozen red dots were getting closer. The corrugated sheeting moved again. The stones in his pocket warmed up and he could see them glow through the material, which they'd never done before.

Rachel peeked around the fountain and saw the sheeting move. "Hello," she yelled.

Claps of thunder, then the pop, pop of gunshots echoed from the dark pedestrian tunnel. Instinctively, Rachel and Shaun ducked down.

A boy, only about eight, ran from the tunnels firing a gun. He was heading toward the corrugated sheeting. An elderly woman pushed the sheeting out, urging the boy to hurry. The boy ducked under her arm into the safety of the pizza shop. The woman spotted Shaun and quickly pulled the iron sheeting closed. Strange red-eyed creatures galloped from the tunnel on four legs as the shadow stalking Shaun and Rachel revealed itself to be the same as these creatures. They had a lion's mane, an upper muscular body, the snout of an alligator, and the hind legs of a hippopotamus, and they were as tall as a small horse. The creatures skidded to a stop as the one stalking Shaun and Rachel joined them. They sniffed the air with their elongated snouts. The beasts opened their mouths and roared, revealing their razor-sharp teeth.

"Run, Rachel, run." Shaun bolted into the open, racing with Rachel to the pizza shop.

Rachel banged on the metal. "I know you're in there. Please! Let us in."

Shaun positioned himself between Rachel and the charging creatures. The gemstones were burning in his pocket, so he took them out. The pouch was cool in his hand, and a brilliant blue light radiated from his clenched fist into his body. He'd seen Sophia and Casey hurl energy balls and blast cars and trucks to kingdom come a hundred times, but it wasn't something Shaun knew how to do. Clutching the pouch, he thrust his fist forward as if punching the air. Like a photon blast, thunderbolts of lightning shot from his hands, hitting the first creature on its reptilian snout, sending it tumbling backward, knocking the other beasts over like skittles.

The creatures were on their feet in seconds and heading straight for them again. Rachel screamed and bashed her other fist against the corrugated iron. In an insane fiery voice, she yelled in Hebrew, and the woman lifted the corrugated sheeting just enough for them to squeeze inside.

The power was exhilarating and Shaun fired one last bolt of lightning from his hand before sealing the iron sheeting. The light disappeared back into the pouch of gemstones as quickly as it had appeared, but his hand was tingling from the energy. He tucked the leather pouch back into the pocket of his jeans, wondering which crystal had generated the power, or if it was a combined force.

The deformed creatures' outside rammed into the corrugated sheeting. It slightly buckled, but held strong.

2

Shaun quickly scanned the pizza shop. Someone had stacked tables and chairs as a barricade. The walls had autographed pictures of the elderly woman with celebrities who had dined at the restaurant.

The woman, sitting on a chair next to a square table, muttered something in Hebrew and crossed her arms over her chest.

"Will it hold? What the hell are those things?" Rachel said.

"They cannot smell us through metal."

"What are they?" Shaun asked.

"They're called Ammit." The old lady spoke English, staring at Rachel. "They are creatures from the world of the dead. Ammit roamed in ancient times judging and eating the physical, impure hearts of men before devouring their souls, condemning them to horrors worse than death. They returned to the world of the living on the night of judgment, six months ago, and for six months they have fed on the dead bodies of the infected. They should have returned to the realm of the dead, yet they are still here. They are hungry and are feeding on the living. After the white fog and the Earth shook, dozens of people returned to the city. But the Ammit have ripped out their hearts and consumed their souls. Now there are not so many people left in the city."

Rachel pulled her neck gaiter down under her chin. "Was there a nuclear explosion?"

"There was a gigantic explosion, more like the earthquake of Jericho than a nuclear bomb, and there has been no radiation sickness," the woman said.

Shaun knew about the night of judgment. He had been there, underground in the Tomb of Thoth, returning the Emerald Tablet with the others, sealing the gateway to the negative realms as the tomb imploded, which could have caused tremors, maybe even an earthquake, and could be what the old woman believes to have been an explosion.

"I'm looking for my eema Tamar, and brother David. Maybe you know them?"

"Two months before judgment day, many people saw the star Sirius burning in the night sky. It had never burned so bright. Many believed it was a sign from the gods. They packed their belongings and walked like pilgrims – deluded, believing the ascended masters were calling them home. Ridiculous! Some even claimed to have had dreams, seeing angels telling them they must arrive at the Lion's Gate in Egypt ready for the arrival of the constellation of Leo."

"Where in Egypt did they go?" Shaun asked. The woman ignored him, so Rachel repeated his question.

"Giza. Maybe your mother and your brother were among the pilgrims," the woman said.

"I can imagine them being pilgrims, but not deluded. Why Giza?" Rachel said. "That's over 750 km away. Ten hours' drive. It would take a month to walk."

"Did they have vehicles?" Shaun asked as the woman turned her head away ignoring him.

"If they walked, it would have taken at least a month. How did they get past the military?" Rachel was asking herself as much as asking the woman.

"The military warned them the infected would kill them before they could reach Giza, but they didn't listen. They kept walking like the children of...."

"When did they leave? And how many were there?" Shaun asked.

The woman refused to make eye contact with Shaun.

"Why are you ignoring my friend?" Rachel asked.

"He is a Nephilim. He has the fire of the gods in his hands."

What's a Nephilim? Shaun thought but didn't bother asking because he wanted to get moving. He didn't like the way the kid was looking at him.

"That's ridiculous. Please, when did they leave? And how many were there?"

"Like I said, they left on the eighth day of July, a month before the arrival of the constellation of Leo. Thousands of fools embarked upon the pilgrimage."

Behind a rough barricade of tables and chairs, the young boy kept his rifle pointed at Shaun.

"We need to go," Shaun said. "There's no point in staying. We should make the most of the daylight."

Sunlight streamed through the bullet holes in the iron sheeting onto the tiled floor. Shaun peeked outside. The Ammit were nowhere in sight, but probably hiding close by. Shattered cement pot plants and dead date trees lay in the square.

"You need to come with us," Shaun said. "You might not survive if you stay here."

"We cannot come," the woman said.

"Do you have water," Rachel asked.

The woman said something to the boy who jumped out from behind a couch and went into a back room.

"That's not what I meant," Rachel said.

The boy reappeared with an old-style water bag made from animal skin, shaped like a stomach. It was full of sloshing water and he handed it to Rachel, along with a loaf of bread wrapped in a tea towel. He quickly ducked behind the couch and resumed his position, aiming the rifle at Shaun.

"I meant for you. Do *you* have water? Do you have a car? In case you need to leave," Rachel said.

"We will be fine. Please leave now. Take the water and the bread and go," the woman said, pushing up from the chair. Her joints were old and stiff.

Shaun looked again through the hole in the iron. The wind had picked up again. He could see plenty of abandoned cars. "Come on, Rachel, let's go. I'll get us a car."

The two of them slid out through a gap, and quickly and

quietly Shaun broke into the first vehicle they found, a gray van. He wished it was as easy as in the movies where he would pull down the sun visor and a set of keys would drop into his lap. Who does that? Fortunately, it wasn't a new car, because, of course, there were no keys hidden behind the visor and newer models were mostly harder to hot-wire.

A wooden cross and rosary dangled from the rearview mirror. He pulled it off and shoved it in the console. Shaun found a screwdriver in a toolkit in the boot. Rachel jumped in the front passenger seat, keeping hold of the water and bread. He forced the screwdriver into the ignition, turned it, and the engine burst into life.

He noticed on the control panel, beneath the digital speed display, was the average fuel consumption. And saw that whoever owned this vehicle had gassed it up for a long journey. Maybe it had been a pilgrim and they had decided to walk with everyone else instead.

"We've got a full tank of gas and I think this thing is diesel, so that should get us at least five hundred miles. Which way?" he asked Rachel.

"South toward Eilat. We can find a place to stop for the night then head west to Giza in the morning. We have plenty of time to get there and back to meet Kevin."

3

Out of the city, embankments of red earth lined both sides of the road. The flat barren landscape beyond revealed no signs of life, which made Shaun feel vulnerable. Anyone could be hiding behind the embankments, pointing a rifle in their direction, right now. One shot of a portable anti-tank type missile at the van and they would die in a fireball. The only thing he was always afraid of was losing Rachel. He felt foolish because of the twinge of anxiety he would get whenever he thought of being parted from her. A few times he had told himself he was weak because of her, and should just ditch her.

"Can you stop the car?" Rachel said. "I have to use the bathroom."

"What here, in the middle of nowhere?"

"I will not wait for the next town."

He pulled over, and she went behind the van. Through the rearview mirror, he saw her duck down.

Shaun waited, watching the terrain for snipers. He thought he saw the ground ripple, moving like a wave. He felt the van rise and fall. "What the hell?" The van tilted toward the passenger side as if a tire had blown. Rachel screamed and his blood curdled, his heart raced. He sprang into action, jumping from the van and running to the back. Rachel was pointing toward a growing mound that went from four foot to fifty foot in seconds. It kept rising higher into the air. "Come on, it's another earthquake. Get in the van!"

Rachel just stood, watching the earth rise into a small mountain. It was like the ground was hemorrhaging, ready to explode, as it continued to rise. It blocked out the sun, casting a shadow over the van.

Rachel shivered. "This is not good."

"Get in the car, Rachel!" Shaun said, jumping into the van and starting it up.

"I want to know what happens," she yelled over her shoulder.

"Dammit it, Rachel!"

He stood on the running board and hung onto the door as the earth exploded. A giant creature erupted from the red mountain. Its arms were human-like, its skin reptilian, and its hands were claws. The head was in the shape of a squid with a beard of tentacles that moved like snakes. Dirt slid off its muscular torso and legs. The creature raised its head up to the sky and bellowed, announcing its presence to the world.

"Get in the car, Rachel," Shaun said, jumping out of the

idling van. He pulled her around to the side of the car. She stumbled, walking backward, trying to watch the creature. Before she could protest Shaun had scooped her up, opened the front passenger door and dumped her onto the seat. He ran around the front, dropping his sunglasses on the ground in his hurry. He didn't stop to pick them up.

The creature's tentacles grew and draped themselves around its shoulders. A tentacle stretched out like an arm as the creature stepped forward; its humongous foot dropped, the Earth shook, and the van bounced inches off the ground, stalling as it landed. Shaun turned the screwdriver, and the motor labored for a few seconds before starting. The creature took another step, and the van shook as the seismic wave traveled through the ground. Yards in front, the road cracked open. It raised the van up on a wave of tar and then back down.

The wheels hit the ground spinning, screeching when Shaun accelerated and released the handbrake. As the creature stepped on to the roadway, the whole terrain shook: it would have reached a magnitude of five on the Richter scale. Suddenly, gunfire rang out from behind the embankments and missiles exploded as they impacted the torso of the creature, but they only made the monster angry. Three army tanks moved out into the open from the shelter of a distant hill. It was as if the army had known the monster would show.

Shaun didn't slow down. He looked in the rearview mirror and saw the explosions getting smaller as the distance grew between the van and the monster. However, something big was hurtling through the air in their direction. Shaun squinted and looked closer into the rearview mirror, trying to identify the object.

His eyes widened. "It's a tank!"

Rachel turned in her seat. "What?"

Shaun slammed on the brakes and the van began to skid. The tank crashed on the road and exploded. A fireball of debris was now dead ahead. The brakes had locked, the van now sliding sideways toward the burning tank. Pieces of metal smacked against the windscreen and Rachel protectively crossed her arms in front of her face. The glass cracked, the fractures mapping their way toward the driver's side. Shaun took his foot off the brake, sped up, and swung the van off the road, away from the inferno. His heart in his mouth, he looked in the rearview mirror at the carnage that clouded the landscape in dusty smoke and glowing fireballs.

"Stop! Stop the van! Shaun, stop! We have to help them."

"Rachel, they're dead. The tank exploded. The force of the blast would've left nothing of them."

"Maybe they're still alive inside." Rachel pulled at the steering wheel.

"Stop it, Rachel. You'll kill us both," Shaun said, regaining control of the van. "They couldn't have survived the impact or the explosion. They can't be alive. It would be impossible for us to get past the flames even if we were to try. We can't save them, Rachel."

Rachel thumped her fists into the dashboard. "Dammit, Shaun!" Her tightly-drawn eyebrows slowly relaxed, her anger simmered to anguish. Her expression showed her torment.

"I'm sorry we're not able to help them." Shaun glanced sideways at her.

Her eyes softened. She turned and faced the front, staring straight ahead through the damaged windshield, unable to see anything.

Rachel used her side mirror to look back at the destruction. "What was that creature? Did you see how big it was, did you feel those tremors?"

"Crazy. We now know what caused the earthquakes. Those soldiers were lying in wait, they knew it was coming."

"Shaun, why do you think my eema would believe she was a chosen one? Why would anyone believe something so preposterous? Do you think someone infected them before we returned the Emerald Tablet?"

"Maybe," Shaun said concentrating on the straight road ahead, occasionally scanning the barren landscape.

"The media, before it stopped broadcasting, showed countless mass suicides. Long before the devil's virus – that's what we called it over here – people would go to Giza in droves in the month of August, during the constellation of Leo, because the pyramids and Sphinx align with the stars on Orion's Belt. Some people believed the Sphinx gazed to the east, to the heavens, because it is a portal to our creator. Every two thousand five hundred years the creator returns to Earth. You don't think my eema gave up and joined a pilgrimage to a mass suicide?" Rachel asked Shaun, running her fingers through her hair as if combing out her confused thoughts.

"It all sounds ridiculous." Not having any genuine answers, he mostly kept quiet and let Rachel try to answer her own questions. He focused on the landscape, alert for unexpected happenings.

"It's a mess," she said.

"I heard about cults recruiting followers for a transition from this life, and they all committed an online mass suicide before the Internet shut down," Shaun said.

"My family doesn't believe in that stuff. You should never have to take your own life or the life of somebody else to return to a place of love."

"Many people, before the apocalypse, would have disagreed with you. People were constantly creating separation. We lived in a world of hypocrisy," Shaun replied.

They fell silent, caught up in their own thoughts.

4

They had been driving for a few hours and had traveled over three hundred miles. They still should have had plenty of fuel, but the fuel gauge flickered past empty and the warning light came on. A piece of debris from the exploding army vehicle must have punctured the gas tank, or the fuel line. He felt relieved that they were now entering a town, and prayed they would find a gas station. Rachel pulled her body through her open window and sat on the edge, her booted feet resting on the leather seat. She was silent as he drove around mounds of rubble. Some buildings were still standing, although they had collapsed roofs. It looked like a war zone. If they didn't find fuel soon, they would have to walk, and that meant they would eventually be the Ammit's dinner.

"There!" Rachel said, tapping on the outside of the cracked windshield and pointing. She wiggled back inside the van. He could see it now, coming up on his left. He crossed the street and maneuvered the van into the station, pulling up next to the first bowser. It was incredible the pumps were still standing. A car embedded in the shop's front wall blocked the entrance. Its driver's door was wide open. Shaun imagined the driver of the vehicle might have meant for the car to explode upon impact.

"Do you know where we are?"

Rachel jumped out of the van and headed to the store. She clambered over the crashed car's black bonnet to enter the store. "I'll get a map."

"Be careful in there!" Shaun shouted. "Why don't you wait for me?"

She turned and gave him a dirty look. "I'm capable of taking care of myself. I'm no spoiled American girl afraid to break her nails."

"That's not what I meant, and you know it. There could be a bomb in that car and you don't know what movements could set it off." Shaun kept pumping the gas into the van. He knew she wouldn't listen; sometimes she was reckless. He was just going to make sure he was ready to catch her. Something he would be happy to do for the rest of his life.

He noticed his muscles were tense. He expected a scream, or something sudden to happen. He got on his knees and looked under the car. The fuel line had a slow leak. They should find a new vehicle, and soon. He stood and grasped the fuel nozzle handle.

It was too easy to imagine the whole place blowing up in seconds and it was freaking him out. He shook his head to clear the destructive image. He had an urgent sense to find a restroom and get out. The fuel was rushing up the pipe about to overflow, so he let go of the trigger. He jammed the nozzle back into its holder and tightened the lid of the fuel tank. He paused and used his peripheral vision to spot anything creeping up on him. He had the jitters.

He had to take a leak. He leaned over the black bonnet and peered into the shop. "Are you okay?"

"Perfect," she yelled.

He clenched and unclenched his hands, busting for the bathroom. He wasn't comfortable picking a spot out front, but the chances of finding a working lavatory were slim. He raced around the side of the building. As he turned the corner, there was the familiar sign, a picture of a man, and a woman. Shaun pushed open the door, the stench hitting his nostrils. A sewer pipe had ruptured. He held his breath while he relieved himself. Washing his hands, he heard clicking. He turned the corroded tap off and listened. Someone or something with sharp nails was tapping on the wall of the building. Slowly, hoping to avoid making a noise, he turned the door handle: it squeaked. Shaun peeked outside. Across the road, about fifty meters away, two Ammit climbed over the rocks and cars, sniffing the debris for bodies, their food. Suddenly he was grateful for the burst sewerage pipe. Fingers crossed it would mask his scent. He slinked out of the bathroom, keeping close to the wall. He rounded the corner in slow motion, trying not to make any sudden moves. There would be no time to find a new car, the van would have to do for now.

The Ammit were still twenty feet away. He touched the gemstones in his pocket, hoping they would activate as they had at the pizza shop. Shaun had carried them with him for twelve years, and he still didn't know what had activated them in Jerusalem, why they had started to glow and channel lightning bolts of energy. The most likely answer would be because the stones had come in contact with the Emerald Tablet and its cosmic power ... but that was over six months ago.

He quickly clambered over the black car and entered the shop. The shelves and vending machines were still upright, but not for long, Rachel, cursing, kicked a vending machine to try and access a few of the packets of crisps and snacks inside. Her packet was stuck. The shelves had a lot of choices, so why was she so adamant on those? Shaun quickly ran over and grabbed her before she could subject the machine to another blow with her boot. He should have known better than to come up from behind and startle her. She shook him off and pushed him hard against the shelves. Her knife was drawn, her arm and elbow were wedged against his throat, and her body pressed up against his. Her blade was inches from his left eye. He absolutely loved her strength, but he worried she would get herself killed one day.

"The Ammit is outside," he whispered because her elbow was restricting his ability to speak. She was a powerful woman. It didn't intimidate him, it just made him want her even more.

She stepped back, apologizing, and looked out of the shop for the Ammit.

"We have to run for the van," Shaun said.

Rachel went back to the vending machine, stuck her arm in the bottom and reached up to get her packet of crisps, which she added to the bag of items she had set down beside her while trying to get the crisps. She picked the bag up and looked at him.

Shaun nodded, and together they ran to the car. He jumped into the front seat, pleading with it to start. He saw the Ammit look up, and pushed his foot down on the accelerator. The car stalled. He grabbed the screwdriver. Rachel drew her knife out.

"Damn it! The fuel must be contaminated. Shit!" Shaun said.

The car sputtered into life on the second try and they drove off. The Ammit were in pursuit, but the van built up acceleration.

"They're gaining on us. Faster! We need guns," Rachel said, looking over the back seat and out the window.

In the rearview mirror they were getting smaller and smaller as the van reached ninety miles per hour. He let out his breath.

Rachel was still holding onto her knife, looking in her side mirror now, excited the Ammit were receding into the distance. "Yes!" she grabbed his face and pulled him toward her. She kissed him while he hung on to the steering wheel. Her blade, again, was inches from his face.

"Can you put that thing away!" Shaun said.

They cleared the town, and there was nothing behind them but dust. It was pushing late afternoon. Shaun thought there was no chance of reaching Giza by nightfall, they hadn't even traveled halfway. They could travel through the night, but it wasn't a good idea. He should find a place for them to spend the night, but first they needed to change cars.

"What was so important about the crisps?"

"My brother's favorite," she said, going through the grocery bag. She pulled the items out and put them on the console between them. Digging to the bottom, she pulled out a packet of mint gum and offered him one.

He accepted, and she unwrapped it for him. He was on fire as she leaned up against him to put it in his mouth. She moved back slowly, then pulled out a baseball cap and sunglasses from the bag. She put the cap on his head and pushed the sunglasses over his eyes and behind his ears.

"Hot stuff!" she said, taking another cap and sunglasses from the bag and putting them on. She then put the rest of the things back in the bag and popped a can of soda.

"What's with the comic?"

"It's for me. Comics help me relax when I'm stressed. I love Wonder Woman. Sophia is like Wonder Woman, don't you think?"

"I know little about comics, but Sophia is awesome. Can Wonder Woman astral travel and magically create protective energy shields and blast energy from her hands blowing up everything and anything in sight."

Rachel playfully slapped him on the leg.

"What's that for? You can't be jealous?" He waited for an answer, but she ignored him and read her comic.

"You pretend you don't like her, but I think you do. I think you like all of them. You're just a big softy, Mr. Shaun Grady," Rachel said, not taking her eyes off the comic book.

He ignored her comment. She did not understand who he was without her, and he hopes she never finds out.

Her knee-high brown leather boots lay on the floor and

Rachel put her bare feet up on the dash, rolled the bottom of her jeans up and continued to read her comic.

Out of the corner of his eye, Shaun spotted her head drop a few times. She quickly regained her composure before it dropped again until she slumped her head sideways against the passenger's window and slept. It reminded him of better days riding the trains, something he had loved to do when he was a kid that now seemed like it was part of a different life.

5

He needed a break. His eyes were tired and his neck was stiff. His neck cracked as he stretched it out. Suddenly, he leaned forward over the steering wheel, seeing a glint up ahead, possibly a reflection off headlights. He slowed the vehicle to a crawl, and stopped at the edge of the road, waiting for the other vehicle to come closer.

Rachel must have sensed something was wrong when he stopped the van. She stirred. "What is it?" she said, putting her feet down and pulling on her boots.

He pushed his sunglasses up on the rim of his cap to peer through the splattered bugs and dirt on the windshield. "I'm not sure. I thought I saw a car ahead." He pulled his glasses down and shifted into drive. Slowly, he pulled back on to the road. A mile or so up, he saw a parked car off to one side of the road. Its doors were closed. Shaun brought the van to a crawl as he came up alongside the car. He rolled down his window and tried to peer through the car's tinted windows. The side one, covered with a baby's sunshield, prevented anyone from seeing in, but he clearly heard a baby crying. Rachel jumped from the van before Shaun stopped. She pulled at the back door handle of the white sedan, but it wouldn't swing open.

She knocked on the window. "Hello!"

She climbed onto the hood of the car and peered in the front window. "I can't tell if there's anyone else inside."

"Where are the parents? A baby locked in a car can only survive for a short time in this heat. The temperature inside the vehicle must be like an oven."

The baby screamed. Shaun looked over his shoulder and saw a mirage-like image. In the mirage was an all too real pack of Ammit racing down the highway. He opened the van's side door and searched under the seats for a crowbar, or anything to smash a window. He left the door open and opened the back hatch. The baby's cries were getting weaker. He found a tire lever under a black rubber mat. He pulled Rachel away from the car and swung at the front passenger side window, away from the baby. Rachel reached through the car window and pushed a button in the middle of the dash twice, unlocking all the doors.

Rachel opened the back door and reached in for the baby. Shaun ran around to the other side of the car and found a woman lying on her back. She was faceless, her heart had been violently removed, and her intestines lay beside her. Shaun suspected it was the baby's mom, mauled by wild dogs, or Ammit. He looked around for the father.

He felt a tingling up his spine. His gemstones had activated:

the blue light was shining through the pocket of his jeans. Three Ammit were racing toward them, and they were getting closer. Stretching to the driver's side, he found the lever to pop open the boot, while Rachel began to remove the baby and its capsule from the cradle.

"Stop. We should take this car!" Shaun said, checking the dead woman's pockets. "The Ammit. We've got a few minutes before they're upon us." He found the keys and pushed the remote control and the car locked and unlocked.

"Get your things from the van. We'll take the car." Rachel cleared the glass off the front seat and set down the baby in its capsule before racing back to the van to grab her shoes and the plastic bag of goods from the gas station.

Over the roof of the sedan, Shaun saw the group of Ammit traveling at least forty miles per hour and heading straight for them. He checked the boot for a gun. He didn't want to use his knife as he didn't want to get that close to them. He found travel bags packed with clothes sitting next to a box of twelve cans of baby formula.

"Two more Ammit coming your way." He pointed away from the car. Rachel's eyes widened. Carrying her things, she rushed back from the van. Heading for the sedan she dropped a boot halfway across the road and had to stop to pick it up. She chucked her things in the back of the car and collected the baby's travel bag, which had outside mesh pockets holding two baby bottles. Shaun slammed the boot closed and jumped in the driver's seat. Rachel had the baby in the capsule on her lap. It was crying, and it was loud. The bag was on the floor between her feet.

"What are you doing? The baby should be in the back."

The first group of three Ammit stormed the van. One leaped into the van's open side door. Another was trying to force its bulky frame into the front passenger seat, while the last one climbed in the back.

Secure in the sedan Shaun put the key in the ignition. *What if they stopped because they had engine trouble?*

"Oh, god." He pushed the ignition button as the second group reached the car. An Ammit reached its elongated snout through Rachel's smashed window, just missing her face, while the other one crashed into the side of the car, skewing it sideways, further away from the road. Shaun forced the car into drive and pressed his foot on the accelerator before he had even released the handbrake. The car's back wheels spun. Dirt filled the air as he immediately released the brake.

Shaun had the pedal flat to the floor and the distance between them and the Ammit grew.

"Can you stop it from crying?"

"How about I drive and you look after the baby?"

Rachel skillfully stripped the chubby curly-haired baby with very red cheeks and put him back in the capsule. "I need to cool him down. He's only about eight months old, and he's getting sleepy, which I don't think is a good sign." Rachel poured the cold water from the goat's bladder over the baby's sweaty black hair making sure it didn't go over its face, but it poured into the capsule wetting the sheets.

"Do you want me to pull over for a minute or two?"

"I can manage. It's best we keep moving," Rachel said, holding the bag with her feet.

She pulled out one bottle from the side pocket that had a layer of dry formula at the bottom, while balancing the capsule on her lap. She removed the rubber top and filled the baby's bottle with fresh bottled water she stole from the gas station.

Rachel handed the baby's bottle to Shaun and said, "Shake this." Next she lifted the baby out of the capsule and wrapped it in the wet sheet.

Shaun stuck the baby's bottle between his legs then eased the baby capsule off Rachel's lap and, without taking his eyes off the road, he placed it on the back seat. Rachel was soothing the baby in her arms and it stopped crying.

"Is he okay?" Shaun handed her the bottle after giving it a good shake.

She gently rubbed the milky teat over the baby's lips, trying to entice the baby to open its mouth. Rachel blew on the baby's head to keep it cool, as the baby drank slowly. Each time it stopped sucking, Rachel ran the teat over its mouth again.

"The little angel is exhausted," Rachel said. The baby fell asleep in her arms.

Things were getting complicated. It was meant to be a quick dash to Israel to pick up her family, not a border crossing into Egypt to get to Giza ... with a baby. He shook his head, wondering why he had thought it would be easy. *Nothing in my life has ever been easy!*

"What are we going to do with the baby, Rachel?"

"What do you mean? We'll care for the little guy, of course. We must try to find his family. There really isn't anything else we can do."

Shaun knew she was right, but he hoped the baby wouldn't

become a liability. "What if the child cries and attracts unwanted attention?"

"We have to find his family."

AS THEY MOVED CLOSER TO EGYPT, SHAUN FOCUSED ON THE road, waiting for the next town, the next place where he could get gas and a place to stop for the night. He kept a watch on the terrain; any one of the mounds could turn into a giant beast. All the hills and mounds looked like sleeping giants to him. He saw the creature in his mind: it had bulging muscles like a weightlifter and its skin was reptilian; a beard of tentacles that wiggled like snakes; possibly an individual and a collective mind. The creature could have easily caused the earthquakes.

"We have to pull over," Rachel said. "I need to put a nappy on him."

Shaun slowed and stopped. He looked at her – life is very strange, he thought. He felt like he had just woken up and found himself in the middle of nowhere with a beautiful girl, and then there was a baby. The past year has been the strangest. The girl was Rachel: the woman of his nightmares, his first love.

He stretched his legs. It was so quiet. No birds, no trucks coming down the highway. There had been many people praying at the tomb of the patriarchs when they returned the Emerald Tablet. Surely some of them had survived. There should be thousands of people in the area. Surely the Ammit couldn't have eaten them all. He stood outside keeping guard, while Rachel dressed the baby in a fresh singlet, with the pacifier pocket on the front, and a disposable nappy. She was speaking in soft tones to the baby while fastening the capsule in the middle of the back seat. She tucked a blue, fine cotton sheet loosely around the baby, now secure in the capsule. She wound down the back window, closed the door and came to stand by Shaun.

They stood in silence. Shaun put his arm around her and she wrapped her arm around his waist. For three minutes, they said nothing, watching the sun go down. Their breathing synchronized. It felt like they knew what the other was feeling and thinking. He squeezed her waist a little tighter, and she squeezed back. He held her close and gently kissed her.

"We'd better go. We've been driving for hours, so we're nearly halfway. It shouldn't be too long until we come up to the Gulf of Aqaba and the town of ..." He took the map from the red leather side pocket on the door and opened it up: "Eilat,"

"It will be dark soon," Rachel said. She walked around to the front passenger's side door and climbed in.

PALM TREES LINED THE ROAD. A BLUE TRAFFIC SIGN SHOWED A roundabout, restrooms, fuel, and coffee were up ahead. He followed the procession of street lights. The next sign showed an arrow to turn right for Eilat.

The town was just like the rest, abandoned. He missed seeing and watching people. He'd never thought he would miss people and the hustle and bustle of human activity. "Which way? Should I follow the signs to Eilat?"

"Yeah, go right at the roundabout," Rachel said, sitting up straight in her seat.

"Let me know if you spot a gas station. I'm hungry, we'll need more supplies," he said.

"We should go into one of the motel rooms." Rachel leaned over and checked the fuel gauge. She calmly sat back in her seat, as a road blockade of green buses forced them to take a left. Shaun noticed how the date palm trees gave the town a seaside vibe. They passed an airfield, which reminded him of Kevin and how he had crashed the plane in the front yard of Casey's estate. He smiled. Coming up on the right, there were buildings with car logos. He went around a roundabout, and spotted a shopping area. The colorful buildings stood out against the earthy tones of the desert. He slowed at a pedestrian crossing from habit. There was water in the bay off to his left. Motels loomed up ahead, damaged, but still standing. There was less destruction here and the town was in a reasonable condition.

"Why don't we stay in the motel over there?" Shaun said, and then he slammed the brakes. Two military men with guns were standing in front of two black four-wheel drives blocking the road. Shaun stared into Rachel's eyes. They didn't need to be telepathic to know what the other was thinking.

"Maybe they can help us with the baby?" Shaun said.

"We have to talk to them," Rachel said. "I might know them, and they might know where my brother and eema are." She kissed Shaun on the cheek and said, "Let me do the talking. And the baby is ours."

"What? How would you know them? And shouldn't we be

giving the baby over to them?" Shaun said. "I can't pull off being the kid's dad."

"You trust me, right? I know what I'm doing. We're married, and we are looking for our family. Don't mention the portal, don't mention the Emerald Tablet, and maybe don't speak. Just let me do the talking." She unrolled her sleeves and pulled her neck gaiter up and wore it like a hood covering her hair. "Ready?"

Shaun released the handbrake and drove closer to the soldiers. He stopped a few feet away, because he wanted to limit the soldiers' view into the car. Shaun put the car in park, but left the engine running. He pulled her close and kissed her. "Ready, Mrs. Grady," he said.

"Grady's not an Israeli name. Maybe we use my name, Rosenberg."

"All right, Mrs. Rosenberg, what's our baby's name?" Shaun said.

"His name is ..."

While Rachel decided on what the baby's name would be, Shaun monitored the men and their guns. The soldiers started getting nervous, aiming their weapons at them. Shaun and Rachel opened their doors ready to get out of the van.

"Maybe we should name the baby after my father, what do you think?"

"What was your father's name?" He felt ashamed. He had never asked her what her father's name was. Shaun carried the guilt of his death without even knowing his name. Her father had always been his dad's boss, the head archaeologist, and Rachel's dad.

The advancing soldiers were yelling and waving their guns.

"His name was Ari," Rachel said.

"Then Ari it is."

She pulled his face around to hers and kissed him on the lips – for a second, Shaun forgot about the soldiers. Her lips were soft. There was nothing that he didn't love about her. She didn't fear the soldiers.

"Kill the lights," she said, and exited the car. She pulled the back door of the car open and reached inside for the baby. The soldiers took aim and yelled at her.

"What are you doing? You're making them jumpy," Shaun said.

In Hebrew, Rachel started shouting at Shaun as if they were arguing. What was she doing? The baby started crying, and the men looked at each other. Rachel kept yelling at Shaun. He didn't understand a word she was saying, but by the look on the men's faces, he could imagine it wasn't good. She brought the baby into view and stepped closer to the soldiers.

Whatever she was saying was disarming: the guns tipped downward. She looked back at the car and waved for Shaun to join them. Shaun quickly stuffed his gems inside his sock and down the side of his boot, just in case they searched him. He rubbed his sweaty palms on his pants and cut the engine.

He hesitantly climbed out of the car and stood beside Rachel.

What caught Shaun's eye was the gunmetal necklaces the soldiers wore, quite out of place with their uniforms. Their pendants were nearly identical and sat at chest height, sporting a pulsating red stone held in place by snakelike tentacles. The stones looked as if they were hearts beating at the same rate. They were slightly different shades of red. The soldier with a bushy mustache had a dark cherry-red stone, but the older soldier's stone was more sunburn-red.

The two men raised their eyebrows at Shaun. They didn't seem threatened by his presence and seemed to pity him. The soldier with the mustache smoothed it down as he spoke to Rachel. He pointed behind the black army SUVs, down the street toward the motel. The other soldier nodded to Shaun and slapped him on the back and chuckled. Shaun smiled and made a mental note to ask Rachel what had been said.

Rachel touched his hand and turned back to the car. She kept the baby in her arms and climbed in. "There is a refuge, an underground bunker the size of a city. The soldiers said if my family is alive, they will be there, in the underground city. They said we should take the baby and get checked by the doctor. They are Israeli soldiers and mean us no harm."

"Did you see those pendants?" Shaun asked.

"Yes, did you see them moving?" she asked.

"God, yes. I thought my eyes were playing tricks on me."

"It was like it was a heart encased by metal snakes," she said.

"Have you ever seen anything like it before?"

"No way. Shh... here we go," Rachel said.

The soldier with the bushy mustache moved one SUV while the other soldier waved them through and Shaun proceeded down the side street. It was a dead end.

A roller door on their right slowly opened upward and Shaun steered the car under it and into a one-car space.

6

They sat in the idling car while a female soldier, with a mirror on a retractable stick, searched the undercarriage of the car. Ahead of them was a soldier in his early thirties, holding his gun at chest height, standing next to another metal roller door. The female soldier moved methodically, seemingly without emotion. The two soldiers both wore the same gunmetal pendants, with the dark cherry-red stone held in place by what Shaun saw as tentacles. The female soldier gave the all-clear and the second roller door rose to reveal a downward ramp. Shaun fumbled to turn on the headlights before realizing they came on automatically.

The cement ramp, like a giant corkscrew, penetrated four floors. They emerged into a military zone. Bright floodlights illuminated a compound the size of at least six football fields. They drove between red witches' hats to a yellow and black boom gate and stopped.

A quiet hub of methodical military activity spread out before them. Above-ground, close by, had been a coastline of holiday resorts in various levels of destruction. This underground facility was undamaged, well organized, and clean. He wondered if being close to the ocean allowed them to use the sea. It would only be a few miles from here. They could easily channel in water to the compound for purification and drinking. Shaun had always had a fascination for bunkers. He'll have to ask Kevin to open a portal to check the military compound the US government owns in Colorado, the one built into Cheyenne Mountain there must be survivors there.

Shaun watched soldiers organizing supplies with forklifts, and moving heavy machinery into rows. The latter looked like generators as well as building equipment. This place was solid! Large wooden crates stacked up to the ceiling were locked behind cyclone fencing. There were rows of civilian vehicles, trucks, off-road vehicles, light aircraft, plus an assortment of other military vehicles filling the back of the hangar, with room to move. He wondered how they would get the helicopters and planes out of here: there must be an elevator up to a flight deck, something like aircraft carrier ships he'd read about.

Off to Shaun's left, behind cyclone fencing, he noticed dozens of soldiers seated in front of computers and electronic equipment. It appeared to be a communications or control center, and one man casually turned and looked in Shaun's direction. He was only twenty feet away. Shaun held the steering wheel and leaned forward. He saw the soldier's cherry-red pendant blink, which gave him the chills. It was even creepier how the soldiers at the consoles wore headphones with microphones, but no one was speaking or typing. Surveillance drones circled the compound and one dropped from above the car, faced Shaun and hovered in place.

A soldier stepped forward, opened the car doors, and waited for them to exit the vehicle so he could search it. Shaun glanced at Rachel before he left the car and they gave each other a reassuring nod. Two other military men, with mirrors attached to retractable sticks, checked the car's undercarriage, no doubt searching for bombs. Their pendants were deep dark red. Shaun grabbed the baby's bag. A female soldier snatched it from his hands and looked inside it. Satisfied, she dropped it at his feet then patted him down. The woman took his bowie knife from around his hips. He dropped his arms, relieved she didn't make him take off his shoes. The officer frisked Rachel, then Ari. She even removed Ari's diaper, checked it then stuck it back together again. Shaun picked up Ari's bag and flung it over his shoulder.

A woman, her hair tightly pulled back in a bun, waited a few feet away, smartly dressed in a gray business pantsuit and holding a clipboard. She was wearing the same pendant as the soldiers', but her stone was amber. She looked like a robot waiting for activation.

Meanwhile, the soldier searching the car was now lifting the lid off each tin of baby formula with a knife and then stirred the formula with the blade, searching. When satisfied the tins contained nothing suspect he secured the lids. He searched the baby's capsule before removing the sheets and lining.

The woman stepped forward and handed Rachel the clipboard. Before Rachel took the clipboard, she said, "Can you refasten the lining, Shaun." Everyone waited.

Shaun secured the lining in the capsule and Rachel gently placed Ari down, tucking him in with the sheet. She took the clipboard. "Shaun, can you get the light blanket from Ari's bag, please, and tuck it around him?"

The administrator scanned through the documents and stamped some forms. The woman spoke in Hebrew. Rachel asked her to repeat her words in English.

"Now the security checks are complete, let me introduce myself," she said in a matter-of-fact tone, adding unnatural inflections at the end of the sentences. "I am an administrator assigned to your induction. Welcome to the refuge, the genesis of the New World."

What New World, Shaun wondered? So far, it was a military bunker. He positioned the capsule holding the baby at his feet. Ari was staring up at him. He was so small and vulnerable. Shaun reached down and grabbed the handles of the capsule and lifted it up. Ari smiled at him.

"I'll show you to the medical unit. The doctor and the Supreme Master must examine all new arrivals. Follow me."

"Supreme Master?" Shaun whispered to Rachel.

Rachel carried Ari in his capsule and followed the administrator. Shaun was close behind with the baby bag. She marched them past rows of cyclone cages stacked with supplies. Some cages contained boxes stamped with symbols showing packaged and tin food. Some pallets were clear shrink-wrapped plastic water bottles. There was enough food and water to feed a small town. The facility had probably been stocked years before the disaster. They moved into an arched, rendered-concrete corridor. Shaun figured they were heading even further underground.

"This isn't a makeshift refuge," he said to Rachel. "This facility would withstand a nuclear blast."

"Yes, it would," the administrator said. "And any other natural or unnatural disaster you can imagine. This is a very safe facility. It will withstand a nuclear or biochemical strike, and it has the comforts of a five-star resort."

They turned into another concrete wing that went westward. He was making an effort not to lose his sense of direction. They turned another corner and proceeded past half a dozen closed unwelcoming metal doors, and yet not one door was marked as a stairwell exit. Shaun tapped the side of his leg, agitated. The administrator entered an alcove and stopped in front of an elevator, although there were no buttons to push. Instead, there was a black square he assumed was a sensor. The administrator reached to her pendant and held the amber stone out toward them as if it were a scanner.

"Did that just blink?" Rachel asked, as the administrator waved the pendant close to Rachel's face. "Did you just take my photo? Was that a shutter opening and closing?"

"Keep still. There's no need to stress. Unless there's something you're hiding?" The administrator turned her head slightly to the side, as if listening for a command through an earpiece. "We're good to proceed." The woman let the pendant drop, and pulled from her jacket pocket a lanyard with a plastic security card. She held it in front of the elevator sensor and the doors opened, illuminating the dim alcove with a yellow glow that made Shaun uncomfortable. Hesitantly, he stepped inside with Ari and Rachel. The administrator turned her back to them and held her card over an internal sensor. There were two rows of buttons broken into zones. She pushed four buttons: seventy-two, seventy-three, and seventy-four, and seventy-five. The elevator car went down, moving deeper underground.

Shaun leaned over to the administrator. "Is this the only elevator back to the surface?"

Her lack of emotion was spooky. "You have entered a remarkable underground city, which, technically, is an extremely elaborate bunker originally built for the wealthy. The city stretches across seven and a half hectares and we are two miles underground. They designed the city around two towers: A and B. Each tower is self-sustaining and has eighty-eight floors broken into seven zones. Zone one: Ground floor, Entry and Exit to and from the city. We dedicate forty floors to our security. So, to answer your question, yes, it is the only way for you to get back to the surface," she said, looking at Shaun as if he was part of a tour group.

"Zone one looked more like a military operation," Shaun said.

"Sir, you need not bother yourself with any of the zones except four, five and six." The administrator turned away from Shaun and continued to speak while facing the doors. "Zone two has fifteen floors dedicated to production, power, and air. We have state-of-the-art nuclear, biological and chemical air filtration systems, water purification systems and desalination plants, and generators. Zone three has fifteen floors dedicated to a water reservoir and vertical farming. If you know anything about horticulture, they may appoint you to jobs in this zone," she said watching the numbers light up as they passed floor fifty-six. "Zone four has four floors dedicated to general administration, hospital, labs, pharmaceutical, and general civilian medical needs. Zone five comprises seven floors dedicated to civilian residential apartments; each tower can accommodate two thousand people spread over seven floors each. Zone six has five floors of education facilities, shops, entertainment, and leisure. We have a Botanical Garden, parks and walking tracks stretching between the two towers. Zone seven has one floor dedicated to waste recycling, and another water purification system and desalination plant."

Rachel shifting the baby capsule to her other hand, away from the administrator. "What's your name?"

The administrator frowned, confused, as if Rachel had asked a strange question. She looked at the camera in the elevator's corner as if for guidance or permission. The amber stone in her pendant darkened and then lightened again. The administrator blinked rapidly as the color faded from the stone. She seemed to be released from a spell...

"Helen."

"Helen, we don't want to stay," Rachel said, looking up at the camera. "I'm here to find my family. If they're not here, we'll be leaving."

Shaun thought he saw a glimpse of emotion in Helen's face when Rachel said family.

"No one leaves," Administrator Helen said matter-of-factly. Whatever emotion Shaun thought he had seen was gone.

The elevator stopped at the seventy-first floor, but the doors remained closed. Helen was a tad unsure of herself for two seconds. Then her pendant turned a deep, burned-orange. She moved her clipboard to her other side as if she was carrying a heavy load and mumbled something.

"What?" Shaun said.

"They will take care of you," the administrator said loudly, waving her security tag over the sensor, trying to get the elevator to move again.

Rachel's arms were covered in goosebumps. The fine dark hairs on her arm were standing on end. She reminded him of a cat that was sensing danger.

Administrator Helen turned to face them. "Turn around, please," she said in a monotone.

They turned as they arrived at Zone four, the seventy-second floor. Helen pushed a button and the wall retracted in two parts like doors, but revealing a transparent wall. The elevator continued down, but this time it was at a much slower pace.

The administrator, like a department store guide, continued with the information. "We'll be disembarking in a moment on the seventy-fifth floor, Zone four."

Shaun glimpsed people on the seventy-second floor. "Do you have any penthouse suites? This place has got everything else." People on the administration floor wore the generic gray pantsuit, giving the appearance of regular businessmen and businesswomen, and they wore the amber necklaces like Helen's.

"Does everyone wear the pendants?" Rachel asked.

"Yes."

Everyone seemed solemn, emotionless. Shaun didn't know how he or Rachel could fit in.

"To answer your question, sir, no, we do not have a penthouse, but we have an equivalent which we call the Primus. It crowns the civilian apartments and has two floors. It also has its own elevator to access the medical facilities."

"Well then, Helen, take us to the Primus suite," Shaun said.

Rachel nudged him in the side and gave him a cross look before she stepped closer to the transparent wall.

"The Supreme Master is in the Primus."

Shaun faced Helen. "Who is the Supreme Master?"

"This is the seventy-third floor, research labs and science, right?" Rachel said.

"Yes," Helen said.

This was the first time that Shaun saw a mix of colored pendants. Workers wearing lab coats had pendants of different shades of blue, vapors drifted from the pendants like they were all connected. *I wonder if Rachel can see the trails of energy.* Others wearing everyday clothing, appeared to be in a daze. Their necklaces were the color of baby-shit brown, mustardy. A color he was now becoming acquainted with courtesy of Ari. Shaun had never thought of having children; he had never thought he would ever fall in love. In his mind, Shaun had always expected to die young because of his own reckless behavior.

The elevator stopped, and the doors opened on the seventy-fifth floor.

"Turn around, please. This is where you will have a medical assessment and be sorted. Follow me," Helen said, with another fake smile. *Why does she bother?*

"The residential Zone is below us. Hurry this way."

7

They walked into the annex and through hydraulic bulkhead doors that swung outward as they approached. Instantly, it was like walking outside in the sunshine. Shaun and Rachel stepped onto a connecting walkway and looked up at a glass ceiling four floors above radiating artificial light to the zones below. He leaned over the railing of the waist-high transparent wall and looked down past the residential zone into a stunning scenic rainforest atrium. He tapped the polycarbonate blast-proof wall while looking over the atrium landscape. There are probably no birds and the trees are probably plastic, he thought. In the canopy of two trees were speakers. He wondered what sounds emanated from those speakers. He looked around him and wondered how he would get them out of this humongous bunker, the underground city.

"Whoa!" Rachel exclaimed.

"Each floor has bulkhead doors that will lock and isolate each floor in an emergency."

Rachel put the capsule down next to Shaun and pressed herself against the side and reached out to touch one of a few trees that rose high enough to meet them. "They're real!"

Zone six was spectacular.

Rachel feasted her eyes on the hive of activity below. "How is this all possible?"

There were joggers on a track that circled the gardens and passed a tropical waterfall. Children rode bicycles, played on swings, and climbed on play equipment. There was over two acres of greenery and leisure space, surrounded by boutique stores. People were leaning against balconies talking while overlooking the gardens as if it was a general pastime. They truly could've been at any five-star resort.

"This is incredible," Shaun said.

"Below we have shops, theaters, gyms, two worship halls, restaurants, an artifact room, museum, child-minding, learning centers, a library, bars, swimming pool."

"It really is an underground city," Rachel mused.

"This way," she said, leaving the comforting light of the glass ceiling and walking down a sterile dark corridor. Shaun scanned the new section and noted all the doors were made of metal.

"Is this quarantined?" Rachel asked.

"It's more like a solitary cell block," Shaun mumbled.

"This is the processing area. We will test you for any contagions; we will review your general physical and mental health. If you're fit and healthy, then we will decide how you can best serve the Supreme Master's greater cause." Administrator Helen walked on. Shaun studied floor, doors and walls: they all looked like steel. The doors were odd, and the walls too.

"It's a lot to take in, I know," Administrator Helen said, "but it won't take long until you settle down."

"You mean to settle in?" Rachel said.

"No, I mean to settle down, your emotional reactions will settle down."

"Docile," Shaun said.

"We will not have any trouble from you, will we?" Administrator Helen said, and her stone darkened to a blood red.

"No. No trouble from me." Shaun hoped that Rachel's eema, Tamar, and brother, David, were here, so they could get out quickly and return to Casey's estate. This place looked great, but there was one hell of a weird vibe.

"What do you mean about serving the greater cause?" Rachel asked.

"The growth and maintenance of the alternate world. First, you need to go through your medical and take an aptitude test. Then you'll go to the Supreme Master for sorting. There's nothing to worry about. Everyone who comes to the refuge goes through the medical center and goes before the Supreme Master. Now, I hope you have exhausted all your questions, because we must move on."

"Presented?" Shaun said.

"Yes, you will meet him in his private rooms."

"The Primus suite?" Rachel asked.

"Yes."

"What if we don't pass the test?" Shaun said.

"We will terminate your stay," Administrator Helen said.

"How many people did you say were here?" Rachel said, cutting Shaun off from asking his next question.

"I didn't. I said how many people could be accommodated, comfortably, in the civilian residential areas of Tower A and Tower B. Any more questions before we head into the processing center."

"How can I find my family?" Rachel asked.

"When your data is in the system, including your DNA, we will link you with your family. Everyone's details, on entry, are recorded and sorted."

"What's the deal with the pendants? What are they for? When will we get one?" Shaun asked.

"At the end of your medical processing, the results will determine if you're worthy of a colored eldritch pendant representing your assigned task, or Zone." Helen opened the metal door by pressing her pendant onto a metal console, which had the same shape as the pendant. The pendant seemed to be a key of sorts. She paused, turned, and looked at them again. Her eyes were glazed over. "Have we met somewhere before?" she said in a strange, deep gargling masculine voice.

Rachel looked at Shaun wide-eyed, dumbfounded. "No, No, I don't think so," she said hesitantly.

The door clicked open, and the woman snapped out of her trance. "No what?" Helen said as if unaware of what had just happened.

"You asked if we had met before," Shaun said.

"Did I?" She pushed open a heavy metal door and held it

open for them to step inside to the medical reception waiting area.

At first glance, it was like any public medical center. It had that antiseptic smell he hated that reminded him of his mother's painful, slow death. To the left, underneath a picture of a tropical island, were four rows of joined, blue plastic chairs, facing two receptionists. Next to the plastic chairs was a cushioned play and reading area for children. Beyond that, through an opened partition, was an additional, not so comfortable, overflow waiting area. It was uncarpeted and looked sterile. Shaun felt something was amiss in the way they grouped people. They divided the room into sections. Although no sign said, elderly sit here, or families here, that was how it was. All parents with children sat next to the padded play area in the corner. In the overflow area, everyone seemed old, sick, or were parents cuddling sick, crying children. Young people, ranging from ages eleven to twenty-five, were sitting along the wall under the picture of the tropical island, and people over twenty-five to around forty, were sitting opposite them.

Through the partition, in the overflow room, nearly out of sight, was a large group of elderly people being ushered by soldiers through a narrow metal door. The old people looked worried. Their shoes squeaked on the checkered vinyl floor. The overflow room looked bigger than he initially thought. There must have been at least another half a dozen elderly and some twenty odd sick people waiting.

Nobody wore eldritch pendants except the staff. The necklace chains were visible around their necks, but the countertop hid the pendants.

"You wait here in the queue and the receptionist will take care of you. Don't worry about anything, you're safe here," Helen said, removing their forms from the clipboard and placing them in the tray on the reception desk.

She left without saying goodbye. Not that Shaun cared; it was just odd behavior.

You're safe here didn't sound right, it made him nervous. He tried to catch Rachel's eye, but she was busy making sure the baby stayed peaceful. *How often did he need to eat?* Shaun sensed they were being watched and thought the baby sensed it too. Ari's eyes were wide open, and he sucked vigorously on his little fist while eyeballing Shaun. So far he was an excellent baby. He worried Ari would scream and attract attention, and when everyone stared, they would know he did not know how to soothe the baby. When Ari would drink a bottle of formula, in the car, he would make little fuss unless Rachel woke him suddenly, as she did when she took him from the car to greet the soldier with the mustache, which seemed like hours ago, but was probably only about thirty minutes.

In the queue in front of him, waiting to speak to a receptionist, was an old man, a girl about twelve, and a rounded elderly man with his plump wife.

As they got closer to the desk, Shaun noticed the two receptionists behind the counter wore amber eldritch necklaces. He wondered what color they would give him and Rachel ... and did the baby get one too? Shaun tried to recall if the children playing, on the floor below, had worn them. He didn't think so.

Shaun leaned forward and whispered to the elderly man, hoping he spoke English. He had a long white beard and a black cap on the top of his balding head. "Do you know what's going on?"

In English, with a thick Israeli accent, the man said, "They will assess our health. If we are healthy and found to be useful, they will allow us to stay. They will tell us which part of the refuge we will belong to. I'm a Rabbi, I'm sure there will be a place for me. What is your skill?"

"I don't have any skills per se," Shaun said.

"I'm sure you do. God put you on this planet for a purpose, son. Have a little faith in yourself."

It was taking too long and he was feeling agitated; he needed something to distract him, but Rachel was busy with the baby. Finally, the twelve-year-old finished, and she sat down under the picture of the tropical island. A commotion broke out in the overflow room and one of the receptionists left the safety of the reception area to go and sort it out. She quickly solved the problem and returned to process the plump woman.

Three soldiers entered the overflow room from the side door that Shaun had seen the elderly group take earlier. One guard stood at the door, while another walked over and stopped just before the threshold of the two rooms. The third soldier handed out eldritch necklaces the color of baby-shit yellow to the next group of waiting elderly and sick people.

Shaun watched as they were instructed on how to put on the necklaces, and when. It reminded Shaun of a flight attendant explaining how to put on a life jacket in the event of an emergency. He didn't think the necklaces would have the same lifesaving impact. Maybe he was just being cynical. The patients were muttering sounds of concern and protesting mildly. One woman didn't follow the instructions and put the necklace on her sick teenage daughter before she was allowed. The teenager collapsed. The girl's mom was hysterical. A soldier roughly picked up the girl, and the mom gave chase, begging him not to take her daughter. The soldier exited through the back metal door and the mother disappeared with them. Shaun tried to see through the doorway. The soldier was back in seconds.

The people waiting under the tropical picture were oblivious to what was happening in the back room. Shaun kept watch as the third soldier showed it was time to put on the necklaces by placing another necklace over his own neck. As soon as they did, the protests and muttering ceased. Parents placed the necklaces over their sick child's head. The room hushed. A nurse pushing a trolley entered the room. Without swabbing with antiseptic, she administered an injection to the sick toddlers. They didn't get a necklace with a pendant. The children went limp in their parents' arms.

Shaun looked at Rachel and whispers, "What the hell!"

The Rabbi was reading the posters on the wall behind the receptionist, and the couple being processed focused on the receptionist. It seemed to be best, for now, for Shaun to keep his thoughts to himself. The parents, with their children in their arms, lined up with the elderly ready to proceed through the door to who knows where.

Shit! An elderly couple had refused to wear the necklaces. They both put their necklace on the seat they had been sitting on, and the elderly man took his wife by the arm. They shuffled their way toward Shaun, making for the entrance, choosing to leave. The soldier standing at the back drew his gun as the frail couple reached the opening between the two rooms. The old woman held Shaun's gaze. She was very pale and distressed. A metal door violently dropped from the ceiling, cutting off her mortified stare. The patients in the main waiting room started in shock. The overflow section was sealed off by the heavy door. Shaun could have sworn the old woman had tried to say something to him, or to the Rabbi.

Three minutes later, the metal door retracted into the ceiling. The back room was empty, and a cleaner was pushing a mop and bucket out of the silent room. He quickly counted the chairs, six rows of eight: forty-eight chairs. It was the Rabbi's turn, and the receptionist sent him into the overflow room beyond the partition.

"*B'hatzlacha*," the Rabbi said as he passed.

"What did he say?" Shaun asked Rachel before he stepped up to the window where the receptionist was retrieving their forms from the tray.

"He wishes us success," Rachel said, stepping forward with a smile for the receptionist.

Shaun watched the Rabbi take a seat in the middle of the room and rock back and forth – praying.

Rachel looked at Shaun as if he'd done something wrong. He looked at her questioningly. She jiggled the baby up and down anxiously. "They want the baby's passport."

"Buried under rubble," Shaun said to the receptionist. "I'm grateful my wife and baby are safe." He kissed Ari on the head, and Ari smiled with his eyes. The young woman smiled condescendingly. This entire process was creeping him out more and more.

He was never good at taking orders from authority and this place would test his patience. The receptionist directed him to the seating area for families. Two more people came into the room.

"Where did they come from? We didn't run into anybody in any of the towns, but people keep coming," Shaun said to Rachel.

"Shh..." a scared man seated next to Shaun said.

8

Every fifteen minutes for the past hour a nurse had entered the room via a door next to the reception area and called in the next patient. Shaun's gaze drifted over every door and he noticed that none of them had handles.

He estimated they might be next in line for the nurse, so he inconspicuously removed his gems from his sock and boot to hide them under the lining of the baby capsule. Before he could secure them there, he saw a spark of blue coming from the pouch. He clenched his fist tight to hide the light, and the energy disappeared. He shoved his hand down the side of the capsule, hiding his gems under the lining, then returned his hand to his pocket.

The nurse came out again. "Shaun and Rachel Rosenberg?"

They stood up and followed the nurse. She was approximately thirty years old and had a genuinely warm smile. She wore no makeup, and looked as if she hadn't slept in days. She seemed to be trying to keep herself busy, to forget about what was really troubling her. Her eldritch pendant was a soft, pale-green glow that he thought might suit her personality.

"Where are we going?" Rachel said to the woman. The nurse didn't answer, so she said it again in Hebrew as they walked through a doorway.

The nurse sized up Shaun and spoke in English for him. "You will see the physician." A door whooshed open and she ushered them into the examining room.

"But we don't want to stay. We are on our way to Giza to find my family, Tamar and David Rosenberg. I need to find out if they are here or not. If they are not, we must leave."

The woman looked at Rachel and then Ari. She looked like she wanted to say something, but couldn't get the words out. Her eyes glazed over. "The doctor is waiting. We mustn't keep the doctor waiting."

The nurse's necklace glowed a deeper shade of green. The slight emotion in her voice and the warm smile disappeared.

Shaun scanned the medical room. He tried to shake the chill coursing through his body. Rachel frowned. "You okay?"

"Yeah, sure, it's just a little chilly in here," Shaun said.

"I'll check your temperature, blood pressure, and glucose levels before the doctor comes in," the nurse said.

METHODICALLY, THE NURSE PERFORMED EACH STEP AND BEGAN typing the results into the computer. Before she finished the door opened, and the nurse, in mid-sentence, stopped typing, stood up and faced the door. A soldier walked into the room, followed by a doctor. He smiled at Rachel, shook Shaun's hand and tickled Ari under the chin. He casually sat in the chair the nurse had occupied. The nurse left the room with the soldier.

"Thank you, Esther," the doctor said to the nurse as the door was closing.

"Now then, what do we have here?" he said, reading over the nurse's incomplete notes. "You both understand this is a refuge, and everyone needs to pitch in to make it work. We all have skills, and we need to put those skills to work." His pendant was green, with gold and green flakes that appeared to be sparkling.

Shaun had been quiet for too long. "What's with the pendants? And why is yours twinkling?"

"It's a trick of the light, an optical illusion. Neat, hey?" the doctor said.

What sort of language is that for a doctor? Shaun thought.

"They're like the stripes on the soldiers' arms. They tell us which Zone and section we belong to. I'm a professor of medicine, and I specialize in gynecology. The gold represents a specialty, and the green represents medicine, healing. The soldiers have red, which is action because that's what they do, they take action. The thinkers and scientists are blue, and the administrators are amber or orange."

"What's the mustard yellow?" Shaun said, reaching out to touch the pendant.

"Don't touch it." The doctor cupped the pendant in his palms. "You can get a closer look at one of these beauties after we have presented you to the Supreme Master for sorting and have identified which Zone you will belong to. At the moment, your future is in my hands. I need to determine if you are both ideal for the breeding program."

The pendant pulsed when he said breeding, Shaun was sure of it. The doctor tucked it under his shirt.

"We're just here to find my family," Rachel said. "We're not here to populate the alternate world."

"Ask the administrators. Most of the time, by the end of the examinations, families are connected on the computer," he said clicking his pen and latching it to his top pocket.

"We don't want to be examined, we want to find Rachel's family!" Shaun said.

The doctor spoke as if he was reading cue cards, in a monotone voice. "The Supreme Master is very particular with families. He likes to keep the genes together. Best-case scenario, they will notify your family you have arrived, and they will arrange a meeting in the common area later this evening after prayers with the Supreme Master. So, let's get on with it. Let's start with the baby, and check out the quality of your breeding, shall we? What did you say your baby's name was?" he said, taking out a plastic tube with a stick in it.

Shaun knew he hadn't mentioned the baby's name, and he knew Rachel hadn't either. Rachel gave him a sideways glance. He would play along with whatever crazy idea Rachel was about to come up with.

"His name is Ari, after my father. My father was the archaeologist, Ari Rosenberg."

"Ari Rosenberg? The name rings a bell. Maybe he's on the science floor or works at the artifact museum."

The doctor's pupils shrunk suddenly, and a look of recognition crossed his face. "He's not one of the archaeologists who found the...?" The professor's eyes widened in horror, the pendant glowed, and the color darkened before his pupils dilated and glazed over. The emotion drained from his voice. "I'm sure we'll all find out who your family is soon enough." He took the baby from Rachel and laid him on the scale's curved platform. "It appears to be healthy, a good chance of survival without biological parents."

"What do you mean, without biological parents?" Shaun said. *We're busted*, he thought.

"Well, if anything happened to you or your wife, the baby will survive if cared for by another. Are you still breastfeeding?"

"No," Rachel said without hesitation.

"Overall, the boy's health is good considering how long since the..." His eyes fogged over and lost all color.

"We had a well-equipped, safe room given the importance of my father. We had what we needed to survive. But my family went missing, when ... well, you know. Shaun and I had the baby to care for, so we waited until the whiteout cleared, and the baby was a little older, before we could search for the rest of our family."

The doctor wrapped the baby up like a burrito and took a swab from inside the baby's mouth. He gave Ari to Shaun and pointed to Rachel: "You're next."

Shaun smiled at Ari and tried to look relaxed holding him.

The doctor pulled the modesty curtain across and began examining Rachel.

Shaun didn't know what to do with Ari. Should he just keep

holding him until Rachel took him again, or should he try to put him back in the capsule before he dropped him?

Shaun listened to the doctor asking Rachel questions.

"Did you have any problems during the pregnancy?"

"No," Rachel said.

"Any complications after birth?"

"No, none. It's been textbook."

Shaun thought she was reflecting on the birth of Amy's twins at Casey's estate. During the whiteout, and before it was safe to venture beyond the protecting psychic shield that Sophia had created daily, Amy gave birth to twins, a boy and a girl. Everyone held the twins, except Shaun. He wished they were back at the estate – this place was suspicious.

"When was the baby born?"

Rachel was slow to answer. Shaun worried they would get caught. *Why did they have to pretend it was their kid, anyway?*

"It was during the first month of the whiteout, October last year. The baby was born in our apartment," she said.

"In your safe room?"

Rachel hesitated. "Yes," she said, sounding nervous.

"Who did the circumcision?"

There were too many questions. Too many lies to remember. As soon as the DNA results were available, the doctor would find out they have been lying.

"My husband," she said.

Oh, great! Now I circumcised the baby. I hope he doesn't ask me how I did it.

"Relax." Rachel winced in pain. "When was the last time you had sex?"

Shaun was ready to pull back the blue paper curtain and hit the guy in the face. But Ari reached out and touched the stubble on his chin. It was like he was trying to hold him back with his little hand. Shaun let go of the curtain.

"A week ago," Rachel said.

"You can get dressed."

The doctor drew back the curtain as Rachel was doing up her jeans. She was furious. Shaun could tell from the way she pulled on her boots and zipped them up that she was liable to explode if they didn't get out of here soon. But she maintained her cool.

"One more question: what skills do you have? Besides the obvious."

What did he mean, "besides the obvious"? If this examination didn't end soon, Shaun was sure Rachel would end up thumping the doctor, and if she didn't, he would. It was all in his tone, or more like in the lack of emotion.

"After I served my compulsory year in the military, I went to London. While there, I studied computer programming. That's where I met Shaun. He was my coding tutor. We graduated, got married in Israel, and we have worked here ever since," Rachel explained, tucking her shirt into her jeans and buckling up her belt.

The doctor just asked what skills she had, she didn't have to give him a life history, Shaun thought. He tried to remember the story Rachel was fabricating. Coding ... the only coding Shaun had done was at school, and most of the time, he hadn't been paying attention.

"Okay, Shaun. Let's make this quick, shall we?" He checked Shaun's pulse. "Your heart's racing."

"I've never liked examinations," Shaun said.

"Where did you meet?"

"London," Shaun said.

"What college?"

Shaun didn't know any colleges in Australia, but he remembered his dad attended Oxford. "Oxford in the United Kingdom."

"Well, I'm sure you too will go into the breeding sector. So relax and give me a cough."

9

The soldier entered the room without knocking or being summoned. He had a no-nonsense air about him. The nurse walked in behind him. *How did they know the examination had been completed?* Shaun scanned the ceiling for cameras: nothing.

"What's wrong?" Rachel whispered.

Shaun shook his head slightly.

"Nurse Esther, excellent! Just the person I was thinking of. Mr. and Mrs. Rosenberg are perfect candidates for the breeding program; they are also good with computers, programming, and coding. I think they can proceed to the sorting room. I'm sure the Supreme Master will approve." The doctor printed out a label and attached it to the DNA specimen containers.

Shaun watched the nurse's pendant glow a different shade of green as the doctor spoke. It was like the necklace was listening.

"Come with me, please," Nurse Esther said.

Shaun bent down and picked up Ari in his capsule. Rachel grabbed the baby's bag.

Exiting the surgery and entering a new section of Zone four, Shaun became aware this hallway, like the corridor they used from the walkway, was of the same metal as the pendants. It didn't seem to belong to the construction of the towers. At the end was a fifteen-foot high bolted gunmetal door. In the center of the door was a giant inverted ammonite framed just as the eldritch pendants were with curved claw-like tentacles. It looked foreign, like the door to an alien spaceship.

Standing in front of the door was an army officer. He looked small in comparison. People without pendants sat restlessly on a metal bench while waiting to pass through the alien doorway. One guy had his legs crossed and was jiggling his foot; the woman next to him was twirling her hair. They were at the end of the row and would be next to go in. Two guys were holding hands anxiously.

Shaun and Rachel joined the queue and sat down on the cold hard bench. Shaun placed Ari in between them and tucked in the sides of the blanket, checking to see if his gemstones were still there. No artwork hung on these walls, no colored carpet anywhere, no fire extinguishers ... the walls felt alien. He wanted to touch them. Shaun wished Casey was here to use his powers of psychometry to tell him what he felt and saw. Shaun sensed they had somehow moved beyond the underground city towers to an adjacent group of rooms.

Shaun pretended to wipe his nose with his index finger to

whisper: "When they run our DNA, they will know he is not ours, and they will know we lied."

"While the doctor examined you, I hacked the computer," Rachel said.

"You can do that shit!"

She gave him a cheeky half-smile. "You'd be surprised at some things I can do. It was easy. I found the administration files. There were a few families with my surname, but there was no Tamar or David. There are thousands of files, and someone organized them by pendant color. Families are not together like the doctor said. I'm sure they changed the program to sort by color. I didn't have enough time to go through the entire system." She moved as if uncomfortable in her seat. "Shaun, some files had the status: extermination."

"Maybe Administrator Helen wasn't joking when she said people who don't qualify are terminated," Shaun said.

"No talking!" the soldier guarding the door said. His voice amplified and echoed in the empty hallway.

Rachel looked up at the soldier and unobtrusively leaned forward to study his face better. "I think I know him. We served together."

"When? You're only twenty. I thought you made all that stuff up," Shaun said.

"Military service is mandatory when you turn eighteen. I wanted to join. I wanted to learn all I could so I could find the man who had the Emerald Tablet, which I did," she said with a smile. "I wanted to reveal it to the world and claim it as my father's discovery."

"Why didn't you tell me?" Shaun said, leaning his cheek

against her head. "No wonder you're good with a gun and a knife."

"I wonder if he will recognize me," she said.

"How could any warm-blooded male forget you?" Shaun said.

Rachel nudged him hard in the ribs. "During hand-to-hand combat practice, I broke his nose."

"You two. Silence! The Supreme Master will not look favorably upon you if I alert him to your inability to comply with an officer's order of silence." He took a step toward them.

"Reis. Sergeant Reis Levin?" Rachel pushed the bag under her seat and stood up.

"What are you doing," Shaun said, reaching for the back pocket of her jeans to pull her back down.

"Watch Ari. I'll be back in a minute." He grabbed her arm. "Shouldn't we be trying to find Ari's family?"

"Shh, someone might hear you."

Rachel walked up to the soldier. "Ma'am, please sit down until I call your name."

"Sergeant Levin. My name is Rachel..."

"Rosenberg. You're Mr. and Mrs. Rosenberg." He gave her a slight smile. "I remember you."

"We served together, before I went to Oxford where I met my husband," she said.

"Oxford, well done. I hope you still don't carry a grudge about that hand-to-hand combat," he said, holding himself rigid and not looking her in the eye.

"Me, hold a grudge? Never," she said.

Shaun watched. The soldier refused to look at Rachel. He

kept looking past her and down the hallway. His pendant was a light shade of red. He appeared to be suppressing his emotions on purpose, not like the others wearing the necklaces who were emotionless through some external action working on them.

It occurred to Shaun that the tentacles on the door were like the monster they had seen on the road that erupted from the ground and attacked the army. He thought he saw them move over the door.

"You will be appointed to the military."

"My husband and I," she said, turning around and looking at Shaun, "are apparently good for the breeding program."

He now turned and looked at her, holding his lips tight. His jaw flexed. He wanted to say something, but was restraining himself. "It has been nice chatting with you, but you need to sit down. Perhaps when you have been processed, we can chat again in our free time." He looked past her and down the corridor.

"Have you seen my brother David or my eema?"

"Please sit down, or I'll have you removed," Reis said.

Rachel finally let Sergeant Levin off the hook and walked back to her seat next to Shaun.

The tentacles moved, and the door opened. A man in his thirties walked out and the tentacles shifted back into the first position of the closed door. They had given the man a necklace pendant of deep blue. His friend stood as if to ask him a question. The man kept walking, his eyes foggy and glazed over. His friend grabbed his arms, and the pendant darkened to an almost black. The friend removed his hand as if he had touched fire.

Sergeant Reis Levin called the next name on his list. The man's friend turned and looked at the sergeant. "That's me!" he said.

In an uncertain voice, he said to his friend, "I'll catch up with you later," and approached the door. The tentacles moved, and he disappeared into the room behind the door.

SHAUN ASSUMED THEY WOULD BE NEXT ON THE LIST. THE GROUP was dwindling. But not everyone who went in came out, and not everyone going in was in there for the same amount of time.

The door opened and believing they were next, Shaun and Rachel stood together and walked to the door.

"Rachel Rosenberg," Sergeant Reis Levin said, putting up his hand to halt Shaun. "Only one at a time."

Rachel was holding the baby capsule.

"Leave the baby with the father," Reis said.

Rachel handed the capsule to Shaun and gave him a quick kiss on the lips to silence him from protesting. He watched in horror as the tentacles moved and the door opened. As she walked past Reis, he whispered something into her ear. She entered and the tentacles soundlessly moved, locking the door behind her.

Shaun wanted to ask Reis what he said to Rachel, but instead he sat down on the bench next to a woman. He placed Ari between them, and tried to stay emotionless, holding his urge to flee. He scanned the hallway again for something to break down the door. There was no emergency button, no fire hose or axe on any of the strange walls. He touched the wall and felt a zap. His hands were sweaty. Ari cried and Shaun rubbed his temples. The door was thick as a bank vault.

"How old is your baby?" the woman next to him said. He was glad she spoke English. Ari wouldn't stop crying. Shaun calmed himself then picked up the baby to soothe him. *This had better work.*

"First baby? Maybe rub his back, he might have a bit of wind. I had two children, but I lost them to the virus."

"I'm sorry." Shaun jiggled and rubbed Ari on the back. Ari burped and vomited a bit of milk on his shoulder. *Gross.* Ari stopped crying and smiled. Shaun wiped his shoulder with Ari's sheet. Shaun wondered who was comforting who as he relaxed after Ari settled. "It will be all right. She'll come back," he said to Ari. He sat with Ari in his arms and waited for Rachel to return.

It was the longest two minutes of his life. The tentacles moved. Shaun held his breath then breathed a sigh of relief as Rachel came out wearing a pale pink pendant. Her eyes didn't look as glazed as much as some of the others, but she was looking straight ahead down the corridor. She walked over and took Ari into her arms.

"Mr. Rosenberg," Sergeant Levin called. Shaun hesitated for a second and Levin called out again: "Mr. Shaun Rosenberg."

Rachel put the baby in the capsule. She paused and leaned into Shaun. "Close your eyes as soon as you enter. Keep them closed until you exit. Stay close to the door."

She then walked away without looking back.

10

The gunmetal tentacles came to life as he approached. He wondered if they moved in different combinations. The door opened just enough for him to enter. There was nothing but darkness. He could hear heavy panting animalistic breathing: it sounded like a snorting bull. Quickly, he closed his eyes.

Puffs of wet, hot air covered his face and body. An animal not of this world was snorting, inches away. Whatever it was, it was big. It smelled of rotting fish and garbage. Shaun held back a dry retch, flinching as something like a giant slug or slippery eel touched his face and neck and images of the tentacles on the door, and pendants, came into his mind. He cringed, clenching his teeth. It was hideous. There were at least half a dozen giant slimy tentacles touching his body. One thick slimy slug-like tentacle wrapped around his neck, tightening like a boa constrictor. Shaun's imagination was going wild. He pictured an attack by an army of leeches that would suck his insides out, stars filled his vision, he felt he would pass out; if he had his bowie knife, he would have cut this slimy creature into pieces.

Pressure was building up just under his ribs. It was like someone was pushing its way through his skin into his stomach. He felt sick. The pressure around his neck eased as all the slimy tentacles roaming over his body slipped away.

An alien sensation of power erupted inside his stomach, which was warm and rushed under his skin. He felt the sensation to urinate. Suddenly, he felt a presence; something had entered his mind. He heard a gurgling beast say, "Leave."

Shaun, disoriented, shocked by the awareness of a presence inside of him, nearly fell over as he turned with his eyes closed, and left the room.

When he saw light penetrate his eyelids, he opened them and blinked. The sergeant looked him up and down, and quickly turned away. Shaun felt a weight around his neck and something heavy against his chest. He was wearing one of the gunmetal necklaces with a pink stone, the same as Rachel's. He, too, had passed the weird test and had been sorted for the breeding program.

Shaun had watched several people go in and out of the room, and those that came out had a glazed look, even Rachel, so he did the same and fixed his eyes on the end of the long hallway. When Shaun reached the end, a gunmetal door whooshed open, and silently closed behind him. He found himself in an ordinary, carpeted elevator annex.

Rachel was standing in a line with others who had passed the sorting. Everyone had lined up in order of their pendant color. Ari was crying and Rachel acted as if she couldn't hear him, and so did all the other people. He didn't recognize most of the people. *How long have they been waiting?*

No one acknowledged Shaun's presence except Ari, who cried even harder. He thought he saw Rachel's shoulders drop as he stood next to her, close enough for their arms to touch. The warmth from her upper arm flowed into his. He said nothing. It was good just to be near her. Usually she smelled like flowers or soap, but right now she smelled like a fish market. He joined the others, ignoring Ari's cries, and stared at the empty wall. *Why was she not comforting Ari, maybe he should?* He tried not to look down at him in his capsule.

The pendant around his neck made him lethargic. It felt as if every movement he made was monitored, even his breathing. He tried to shut out Ari's crying and focus on the wall. The length of the chain dropped the pendant below his ribs, just where he had felt the strange energy enter his body. He needed to take off the pendant, because it was freaking him out. He was slipping into a strange, waking sleep. He would lose himself if he kept the necklace on. Shaun recalled the slug-like tentacles moving over his body, seeping into his internal being, he could still feel the evil supernatural energy roaming inside him. It was easier to believe the hideous appendages were slugs, but he knew it was a lot worse than he could yet imagine. Shaun cursed himself for not peeking and getting a glimpse of the creature when he had entered the Supreme Master's sorting room.

His pendant darkened with black ink. A hundred tiny threads of energy from the pendant continued to enter his stomach. Vines of an unseen force were winding from his stomach to his chest, into his neck, and blanketing his brain. It paralyzed Shaun. He could do nothing to stop the creature from roaming freely through his body and mind.

He felt the tentacles receding into the darkness from where they had come. An echo of sinister energy remained: a thin tapeworm coiled itself in his stomach and kept a light connection. His pendant became lighter and the soft pink returned. Ari was sound asleep. *How long was he gone for?*

Shaun let out a breath. He was sweating. He wiped his face with the back of his trembling hand. *What the hell!* He tried not to look shaken as he moved his legs. *This is what the pendants were for: control!* The Supreme Master and its slimy creatures controlled everyone in the underground city through the stones in the pendants.

It was paramount they get out of here.

Administrator Helen and two other administrators turned into the hallway and marched toward them.

"Everyone, follow in an orderly fashion," Administrator Helen said.

They did as they were told.

11

S haun stepped into the elevator behind Rachel. They went down one floor to the seventy-sixth, Zone five, and stopped at the first level of the residential area overlooking the atrium. Shaun stepped from the elevator and looked up at the clear dome ceiling above. Nobody else reacted to the light so he quickly looked forward, eyes on the back of Rachel's head.

Every person on this level, except the children, wore pink pendants and a white cotton pantsuit, caftan style. If they had to wear those clothes, at least he could hide his gemstones in the pockets. Otherwise, he would have to strap them to his body. The tunics were long sleeved and had three buttons near the neck. He peered over the rail, down at the trees and people. They all wore the same garments, but in different colors. Except for the few soldiers. He could see there were a lot of mixed-color necklaces on people in the gardens and parks. The administrator saw Shaun leaning over the edge.

"That's where you can visit your friends and family who have been allocated other colors and tasks. After tonight's assembly and prayers, we will allow you to mingle in the common areas," Administrator Helen said.

"I thought you brought together families, and they lived in the same quarters," Rachel said apprehensively, as if she was unsure if it was all right to speak.

The administrator spun around and held Rachel's gaze. Rachel didn't blink, her face was relaxed. The woman's pendant was deep amber. She continued to study Rachel's eyes, as a vein in Rachel's neck pulsed. No one else was bothered. Finally, Helen turned away and indicated for Rachel and Shaun to follow her. She led them to their room, where she waved a security tag over an infrared lock, similar to the ones in the elevators. The door was like any other motel apartment door. It was white and had a gold number attached to the door: TA512.

Rachel stopped at the threshold. "Has my family been located?" she said without emotion while looking forward at the door.

"We will contact you when they are. Now then, your room is equipped with everything that you need for breeding." Administrator Helen handed them both a pink lanyard with a plastic swipe card.

What does that mean? Shaun wondered, taking the tag. He felt a sharp pain in his temples, as if zapped.

"You must wash and change into the clothing provided. Harvest will be on the Friday of the new moon."

"Harvest?" Rachel asked.

"In twenty minutes, an administrator assigned to the

breeding program will come and escort you to the induction, and they will give you the gritty details," she said, giving a fake smile. "You're fortunate to be in the breeding program. I would've been honored if the Supreme Master had selected me."

They went into the apartment, which was similar to a motel suite. There was a small black dining table for four, a white kitchenette with a bar refrigerator, a microwave, a kettle, and a sink. Closed, heavy fawn drapes gave the illusion of a window, allowing the imagination to believe the outside world would be visible once they were opened. There was a plush cream carpet. Shaun felt he was noticing the oddest things. It was like he was responding to someone else's suggestions.

Administrator Helen walked across the lounge area, past the dining table and beyond the kitchenette.

"This is where you'll find the bathroom and bedrooms," she said opening the door wide so Shaun and Rachel could look inside. "While you are in the breeding program, you have the use of this luxury apartment."

"I'm sure we will be comfortable," Rachel said.

"There is a main restaurant on Zone six for family dining. There is a general store if you would like to make purchases, just swipe your room card. You earn credits and access to the facilities when you contribute to the whole. Being in breeding, you're automatically awarded ten thousand credit points each, and you can move freely between Zone five and six. Your card will not allow you to access the elevator for Tower B. After the induction, follow the herd to the service then on to the main restaurant. The next mealtime is an hour after prayers. Questions?"

Rachel looked at Shaun, and he could tell she had a million questions, as did he, but they both shook their heads. "No, no questions."

Administrator Helen stood at attention with her clipboard under her arm. She about-faced to leave the apartment. The door clicked shut, leaving Shaun, Rachel, and Ari alone.

"Herd? Feeding schedule, what the hell! Are we cattle the Supreme Master is trying to fatten up?" Shaun said. "What is that smell?"

Rachel put the baby capsule on the table. Rachel hugged him and whispered in his ear. "Reis told me not to open my eyes. Did you open your eyes?"

"No," Shaun said, taking off his pendant and putting it on the kitchen bench.

"I think that is why we differ from everyone else. The pendants are controlling the others more than us," Rachel said.

"When we exited the elevator, I felt the Supreme Master watching. I felt him looking at you through me. I felt him moving around in my head and my body. It's only a matter of time until he takes over. If we don't take off the necklaces, we will become a puppet-like everyone else. This place is hell."

There was an urgent knock at the door and the sound of security-tapping on the infrared panel. The apartment door clicked and unlocked. Helen stepped into the room. "Under no circumstances are you to remove your necklaces. It is what identifies you and permits you to be here. If we find you without it, we will shoot you." She didn't wait for a response.

She took Shaun's necklace from the bench and forced it over his neck.

"Shot! Isn't that a bit drastic?" Rachel slurred her words as if she was falling asleep. Her pendant darkened slightly.

"Sorry, it felt like it was burning through my shirt," he said, hoping to turn Administrator Helen's, and her hosts', attention away from Rachel.

"You will get used to it," she said, leaving the room and scanning Rachel up and down before closing the door firmly behind her.

Rachel's pendant calmed to a soft, pale pink.

12

Shaun took the gemstones from under the capsule's lining and put them back in his pocket. He instantly felt no longer alone. He thought it might be how Sophia feels when she wears her medallion or holds her old Bible. He raised a hand to the side of his head, then blinked rapidly as if trying to clear something from his eyes. He shook his head from side to side and widened his mouth to unblock his ears. The fogginess was lifting and he wasn't as drowsy. The strength of the pendant had slightly weakened.

Ari started crying. Rachel rocked the capsule soothingly. His crying became louder, so she checked his diaper.

"What's wrong with him?" Shaun said, not sure if it was the pendant or not, but she seemed too calm. "It's like you've done this before," Shaun said.

"When I snuck into the sheikh's palace, where the Russian who had the Emerald Tablet stayed, I had to become a concubine, and a few of the women had babies. We were all together – a harem, I suppose. Because I was one of the youngest, the older women ordered me to help care for the babies. Here, take him while I get his bag, will you?"

"What happened while you were a concubine?"

"You came just before anything happened."

Shaun wanted to ask her more questions, but he needed a shower. He could not stand the smell of himself or the baby. "I'm not comfortable holding him. When was the last time you changed his diaper or fed him?"

"On the side of the road, before we ran into the soldiers. It has to be hours ago."

"The diaper is heavy, it's soaked," Shaun said.

Rachel unzipped the baby's bag for a fresh diaper. "You don't smell so good yourself. Poor little fellow, he must be very uncomfortable."

Shaun laid Ari on the carpet.

"You change him," Rachel said, handing Shaun the clean diaper.

"No, I don't think so," Shaun said, standing. "I'll go for the first shower."

Rachel changed the diaper and put the dirty one in a bag. Ari settled down and Rachel held the dirty diaper up for Shaun to take. "Before you go …"

Even though it was in a bag, it still stank of stale urine. Shaun went into the kitchen and beside the wall was a metal bin marked Disposables. He dropped the diaper in, which instantly combusted and vaporized the nappy.

"Oh my god, that's crazy! What if we accidentally drop

something in there? It would vaporize in an instant." He touched the outside of the cylinder bin but it was cool to the touch, and rising heat vapors were still visible. He waved his hand over the opening, and it was warm.

Rachel looked down into the disposable machine and said: "Well, let's not drop anything in there that we want."

"Maybe we could drop the pendants in there," he said.

Shaun took off his pendant and dropped it into the Disposable. It combusted into white and blue flames. There was a high-pitched squeal like a rat might make. Together they looked in; the pendant was still there. The process was over, but it was still there. Shaun went to activate it again for a second time when he thought he saw the tentacle squirm. He reached in, but he couldn't get past the residual heat. There was an abrupt knock at the door.

"They know you've taken it off again." Rachel quickly got a bottle of water from the refrigerator and doused the necklace.

Shaun wrapped a towel around his hand, not waiting for the rising steam to dissipate. The knock was impatient and aggressive. Hearing the faint tap and the door clicking open, Shaun picked up the necklace and put it on. The hot metal burned the skin of his neck. He could smell his skin and shirt burning. He shoved the hand towel down his shirt to protect his chest. But no matter what he did, his neck would blister.

Nursing Ari, Rachel opened the door.

It was Administrator Helen.

"Sorry, it won't happen again," Shaun said, stepping in front of Rachel. "I was just changing the baby. It hit Ari in the head, so I took it off. It was just a few seconds."

The administrator looked at Ari's blotchy face red from crying. She looked back at Shaun. Her glazed eyes and the pendant turned into swirling black energy. She penetrated his eyes, digging into his psyche. She searched him as if reading a book. Her head tilted from side to side like a curious puppy.

Both their pendants darkened. He felt the drowsy fog creeping up. Shaun put his fingers to his temple, as Administrator Helen flicked through his mind. He visualized Ari's little scrunched up tear-streaked face and the dangling pendant accidentally hitting him in the head. He hoped he would be undetected as he stalked the insidious energy trolling in his mind. It was dark magic. It searched for his memories, like Kevin did, but this was frightening, menacing: he felt hunted. It never felt threatening when it was Kevin doing it. Shaun hadn't felt fear like this since his father had died. His father had been one of the infected, he accepted that now. His dad gotten infected the moment he had stolen the Emerald Tablet and sold it to the Russian. The gemstones had protected Shaun at the peak of the virus and were protecting him now from this new dark force. He immersed himself in the serenity of the gemstones: he controlled himself and refrained from lashing out at Helen and breaking the connection.

"You'd better not," Helen said in a voice like his father. Satisfied, she turned on her heels and left the apartment. It was as if she was trying to use the memory of his father to instill fear.

She will have to try a lot harder than that. Shaun kept quiet while his pendant returned to a pale placid pink. He closed the door behind her and pressed his back against it. He lowered his head. The plush cream carpet loops filled his mind, then he raised his head and put his fingers to his lips for Rachel to be silent. He stepped away from the door and began searching the apartment for any security surveillance equipment. Rachel laid Ari in the capsule and joined Shaun in checking the apartment for hidden cameras and microphones. There had to be some way they found out when one of them took off their necklace.

They searched behind the curtains, the analog clock on the wall, in the cupboards, under the furniture, in the lights, smoke detectors and sprinklers. Everywhere they could think of where cameras or microphones could be concealed.

"It's clean," Rachel said as they stood back to back in the middle of the living room.

She stepped back, and pressed against him. She fit neatly within his frame.

"I think they communicate through the pendants," she said. "Did you see the way the eldritch stone changed, and Helen's eyes? It's like the days of the infected all over again."

Shaun glanced at the curtains that covered the wall as he mulled it over. "This differs from the days of the virus and the infected. I think you're right about the pendants, but how?"

"I think the eldritch necklace is connected to an entity, the Supreme Master. He is calling the shots. He plugs in through the necklace," Rachel said.

"Have you felt its presence?" Shaun said. "I have. It's sinister."

"Yeah, I get a strange sensation in my stomach. I put my hands over my tummy when I do and it settles down slightly," Rachel said. "Don't laugh, but I think I saw a reptilian eye blink from within the pendant when it turned black, when Helen scanned me at the elevator."

"It's not funny. I thought I saw a blink too, when the pendant darkens. I still feel the same energy, but I didn't think to try to physically block it like you did. The energy searched through my mind and body. It's evil," Shaun said. "When I took my gemstones back from Ari, I felt a lot better."

"Better how?"

"Clearheaded, not so distant from myself. I felt like I was riding the horse, rather than being the horse, if that makes sense. The feeling of lurking evil energy disappeared."

Rachel put her hand over her mouth, then pulled it away to speak. "The bogeyman has a looking glass? I'm drifting further away from myself, foggy. Maybe I'm just being paranoid?" Rachel turned and looked at him. "I'm not sure. But maybe this place won't be so bad. Especially now we have a baby." Her pendant was taking on a darker shade. Her eyes glazed over.

Shaun thought about it while staring hypnotically at the pink wall behind Rachel. Considering the state of the world, next to Casey's place, this wasn't a bad setup. They had everything they could want and more. "Our job is to breed. Our job is to make love, make babies, and live happily ever after," he said. "Maybe it's not so bad. But what do you think they meant by harvest?"

"I don't know," she said, blinking, trying to clear her eyes. "The obvious is they have hydroponic crops with accelerated growth, so they can harvest monthly."

"Now *you* sound like the nerd," Shaun said. His head was still clouded and not right.

Rachel lightly backhanded him in the arm. "Don't call Jade that! It is the new moon in three days. This coming Friday. Maybe we should just relax and be part of this breeding program that will populate the alternate world," she said, making air quotation marks.

Shaun watched all traces of emotion fall from Rachel's face as her muscles went lax.

"As much as I would like to agree with you, it's not like you to give up so easily. You're not thinking straight." He rubbed her arms as if she was cold. She looked down at his hand as if she could see the gesture, but couldn't feel it. "Rachel!" he said in a raised voice. She just stared at him like the administrator had. He pulled her pendant away from her body and placed his hands over her solar plexus.

She blinked several times and yawned. "What was I saying?

"I don't know. It's like being trapped in a daze. A few times I get a sense of slipping away into a trance. There's something about these pendants..." He frowned. "What was I saying?"

"You said you would have a shower," Rachel said.

"Really?" It was like a vivid dream that dissolves on awakening. He could feel the essence of it through a haze. He felt as if he had been on the verge of figuring out something important, but couldn't recall it. "No, it was something else," Shaun said with a muddled expression.

"I'm not sure. We should have our showers. Administrator Helen said we needed to wash and get dressed in our new clothes."

"What shower? Ari's hungry," Shaun said.

Rachel looked at Ari. "Why do you think he is hungry?"

"Because he is crying." Shaun couldn't believe she hadn't heard the baby. He couldn't remember when he noticed the crying. He picked up Ari and his fogginess lifted. "Jesus! What the hell is happening to us?" Shaun said agitated.

Rachel rubbed Ari on the back. "Maybe he just wanted cuddles from his daddy."

"Rachel, we're here to find your family, not his father. We should leave him with the administrator and let them find his family," Shaun said.

"Ari's our son," Rachel said, looking at Shaun in horror.

"I think we should leave this place," Shaun said. He looked down at the eldritch necklace. His neck was sore as he moved it. Suddenly he remembered trying to vaporize it in the disposable bin. He took Ari with him into the bathroom and checked the back of his neck in the mirror. It was red, and the skin was pinched and burned. He tried not to rest his eyes on the pendant. He turned it around, so the stone was facing his chest. The gemstones in his pocket glowed, and Ari wobbled around in his arms as if happy. "Okay, little man, let's get you a bottle."

Rachel was crying. "Why did you say that?"

"Say what? Why are you crying?" Shaun said.

"That he is not your son. What are you implying?"

"What the hell has gotten into you?" He didn't know where this was going, but it wasn't right. She was delusional, lost in her own story. Her eldritch stone was changing to a murky black pink. He hadn't noticed it changing; he had to get the necklace away from her if he could.

"I'm sorry. I don't know what came over me." He put Ari back in the capsule and held Rachel. He fumbled around the front of her shirt. She relaxed against him. Shaun lifted the necklace over her head and placed it straight over his. He was woozy, instantly he felt drugged, he stumbled. He couldn't remember what he had been doing or saying. Shaun rubbed his eye and let his finger trail down his face to his chest. He flipped his pendant over and allowed hers to nestle on top. "I'm going to have a shower," he said, leaving the room.

"Wait, Shaun. You took my necklace," Rachel said following him to the bathroom.

"Can you feed our little man, I need to freshen up and rest a bit for the induction," Shaun said.

"You're taking this happy little family act pretty seriously," she said, smiling. "Shaun, give me back my necklace, two is making you act weird."

"Maybe we should just start the breeding program now? Shall we try for a girl?"

"How about I feed the one we have, so he stops crying." She kissed him lightly on the cheek, took her necklace back and picked up Ari. Shaun walked into the bathroom and stripped off his shirt.

Through the bathroom vanity mirror Shaun watched Rachel make herself comfortable in the chair with the baby and begin feeding him.

Shaun stepped into the warm water. The white tiles were smooth under his outstretched hands. Shaun faced the shower nozzle and let the water trail over the back of his head and neck. The pressure stung against his burns. There was nothing good about where they were.

There was so much about Rachel's life that he didn't know.

13

There was a knock at the door.

Standing naked in the bathroom, Shaun couldn't recall getting out of the shower. His hair was wet and he no longer smelled like a fish market.

Bang bang bang. There was someone at the door. He turned toward the door and listened, thinking he was mistaken. Someone was definitely knocking on the apartment door. He didn't remember taking off his clothes. The last thing he recalled was taking Rachel's necklace and putting it over his head. It was gone.

Shaun put on his jeans, confused and frustrated, thinking it was the administrator again, because he had taken Rachel's necklace off. He left the bathroom and checked Rachel's neck for the gunmetal chain. It was there. She must have taken it off him. She was wearing the new clothes and smelled fresh.

Rachel had fallen asleep in the chair and the baby's bottle, empty, rested on the side table, and Ari was missing.

He rubbed his wet hair, confused and started yelling at the door. "I didn't touch it. I swear. Your radar is out of whack," he said, tapping his pendant before opening the door.

Sergeant Reis Levin was standing at the threshold. He put his finger to his lips. He reached down to touch Shaun's chest. Shaun grabbed his wrist. "What do you think you're doing?"

With his other hand, Sergeant Levin quickly turned the pendant over, so the eldritch stone was facing Shaun's chest. He nodded to an awake Rachel, implying she should do the same.

Rachel flipped over her pendant. "Where's the baby?" she said, checking the bedrooms.

Shaun shut the door behind him and followed Rachel. Ari was asleep in the crib in the nursery. "I don't remember putting him down," she said.

The soldier had his pendant tucked into his uniform as if it were a tie. He approached Rachel, and kissed her cheek, quickly removing her necklace and putting it on Ari.

"Now you," Reis said to Shaun.

Shaun quickly pulled his pendant over his head and gently put it on Ari, nearly getting it caught in the baby's little black curls.

Reis took off his pendant and put it over Ari's head, too. Ari stirred but went back to sleep.

In a calm, assured quiet voice, Reis said, "You can remove your necklaces to take back control of your mind, if you're willing to let the baby wear them."

"What? Why?" Rachel said.

"It won't hurt him. The eldritch pendant has no power over any child under the age of four. It will not harm your baby. You're blessed to have a child," said Reis raking his hair back.

"Is he all right?" Rachel asked.

"He appears to be okay, just sleeping. Let's go into the lounge room."

Shaun looked questioningly at Rachel. "When did you have a shower?"

She looked down at herself and noticed she was wearing a white jumpsuit. "I don't know."

"Sorry I couldn't talk before," Reis said. "The Supreme Master watches us closely, especially when it's sorting through the new arrivals. We think the pendants communicate like one super consciousness in tune with the Supreme Master. He, it, has left the compound, the city, for now. We call the bunker, the City of Ascension, or Olivet. The Supreme Master comes and goes underground and can return at any moment. Its power reduces when it's offsite, but not so much that we could take over the facility. The Supreme Master is always back for worship and harvest." The tone in Reis's voice changed, and he raised his eyebrows. "You both need to be concerned. How are you? Have you been losing time, forgetting what you were doing?"

"Yeah, we have. How close were you two?" Shaun asked with a hint of jealousy.

Rachel dismissed Shaun's question and asked, "Who is the Supreme Master?"

"First things first, you are one of the lucky ones because you have a baby. Every two hours, take off your necklaces and place them on the baby. That will give you time to each clear your head and reorient yourself."

"How the hell do we get out of here?" Rachel said, sounding like her old self again.

"You can't. Everyone who's tried has died. I know because my brother tried."

"Joseph's gone?"

"His wife too, I saw them disintegrated," Reis said.

"There has to be a way out."

"There is a group that has been trying to find a way out for months. There isn't much left outside of this elaborate bunker. Olivet is as big as an aboveground small town and extremely well equipped. A takeover is in the cards, and we will kill the Supreme Master. We have shortwave radio contact with soldiers on the outside, who are trying to kill a beast that prevents them from attacking the compound. Follow the system until they do," Reis said.

"I want on that team," Rachel said.

"You can't, you have a baby now. You can't go off half-cocked like before. You will get us all killed," the sergeant said.

Shaun could tell by the way her eyes wandered over to Ari that she was contemplating telling Reis that Ari was not her baby and, perhaps, that he was not her husband, but she didn't.

"When you're outside your room, wear your pendants at all times. Show no emotions and restrict your questions. Be submissive, Rachel!" Reis said.

"What or who is the Supreme Master," Shaun asked.

"I have never seen it in its true form. Two months ago, two soldiers were the only survivors of a team of a hundred men.

They said a monster walked from the Red Sea, near the Gulf of Aqaba, when the fog lifted. It killed all the men in their outfit and destroyed their equipment with its serpent-like beard." Reis paused, catching his breath. "Its beard moved like powerful snakes at the command of the beast. They said it was worse than the legends of Medusa. The brigade of men went mad and shot themselves. The two who witnessed the madness died mysteriously in their sleep after returning to base camp. They called it the Leviathan, meaning monster from the sea. The story has mutated and there are different versions and more stories being told by the soldiers. Some say it is an alien, and that the sorting room door is actually the door to an alien spaceship buried thousands of years ago, and unearthed during the construction of Olivet. There is a lot of speculation. Others say it's a madman with powerful mind-altering abilities, hiding behind an army. Some say the breeding program is to feed its insatiable appetite for human flesh. A child is a delicacy. There is dark black magic here, which allows this Supreme Master to rule over us, but a monster a hundred feet tall from the Red Sea, or an alien from outer space, I don't think so," Reis said. "It sounds too fantastical for me." Reis went into the kitchenette and opened the small refrigerator and took out a bottle of water.

"We've seen it," Shaun said. "A hundred feet high is an understatement."

"*What?* When?" Reis said.

"On the road, ten minutes before the junction on Highway 224. It rose from beneath the ground. Soldiers were waiting for it, but it was a slaughter," Rachel said.

"It swatted the surface-to-air missiles as if they were mosquitoes," Shaun said.

"That's near the base. I have to tell the others." Reis put the bottle on the bench top. "You will feel a tremor when the Supreme Master returns to Olivet. If you do, put on your necklaces. It will check on you because you are new. It may search for you and try to connect to know how well you're conforming to the control of the pendant and your new state," Reis said.

"To check our state, why?" Rachel said sitting on the arm of the lounge chair.

"Those who don't adapt, their stay is terminated," Reis said.

"What do you mean? Can we leave?" Shaun said.

"No. The people vanish. The soldiers on the outside, not under the influence of the eldritch necklaces, have seen no one leave," Reis said.

"Are you sure?" Rachel said. "What about the bodies?"

"Waste combustion."

Shaun looked at the garbage disposal and recalled the heat and how quickly Ari's diaper vaporized.

"Reis, who are *the others* you mentioned?"

"The Resistance, and the army on the outside. If you're interested, I will ask if you can join the movement," Reis said.

"Hell, yeah," Rachel said.

"We're in," Shaun said, rubbing his face. He stopped leaning against the back of the sofa and shoved his hands in his pocket.

"Considering you witnessed the Supreme Master in its true form, it should be easy to get you both in, and being ex-military is good. Having a baby is valuable. I'll see what I can do. I'll contact you after prayers." Reis made to leave, but first went back into the nursery and took his necklace off Ari.

"How will we know if the Resistance accepts us?" Shaun said.

"When you go to your induction for the breeding program, you will meet my wife."

"You married Maria?" Rachel said.

Reis smiled.

"That's wonderful. I can't wait," Rachel said.

"You must keep your emotions in check at all times," Reis said. "Yes, Maria and I married a few months after you left."

"Can you check the records for my eema and David?"

"I will do what I can. But I don't remember them being presented to the sorting room. If they showed up here and didn't make it to the sorting room, I'm sorry, because it means they are dead. It gets rid of anybody who arrives if they're over the age of forty or have an injury or illness. I'm sorry, Rachel. Let's just hope they never made it here. Tonight I will let you know if the Resistance will allow you access. I have to go. I have been here way too long. It'll arouse suspicion if I'm here much longer. It's good to see you, Rachel," Reis said. "Real good."

Reis took Shaun's hand and shook it. "You're her knight in shining armor," he said with a smirk. "It's crazy that you two ended up meeting again. Destiny, I suppose. We all thought she was crazy!"

Shaun got the sense Reis wanted to hold Rachel in his arms. Maybe Maria wasn't Reis' first choice? He wondered what had happened to her while she was undercover as a concubine, or as a soldier. Had she killed people? Maybe they were as bad as each other: he had been cruel, for sure, but he had never taken a life. He was slightly jealous of Reis and Rachel's history. "If your wife conducts the induction, does that mean she is in the breeding program?"

"Yes, she is."

"Then why don't you have a pink eldritch necklace?" Shaun asked.

"I'm no longer fertile. I apparently don't have good genes. After the sorting room, it sterilized me. I was reassigned as a soldier only because my wife is fertile and was chosen for the breeding program. Otherwise, my destination was extermination. As a matter of course, the Supreme Master sterilizes all the soldiers wearing eldritch pendants." He clenched his teeth and swallowed. "I've said enough." He looked embarrassed and let himself out the door, gently closing it behind him.

14

Walking to the elevator, he felt tense, like an Englishman going to play a game of cricket against Australia. He had shoved his pouch of gemstones into his pocket. He checked for any sign of a bulge. Confident they were concealed, he took Rachel's hand.

Rachel's hair was naturally wavy and dropped to the side of her chin, framing her beautiful face. She walked beside him as they followed the administrator taking them to the induction.

"Good afternoon, Mr. and Mrs. Rosenberg." A woman wearing a yellow-stone eldritch necklace stepped from the elevator and stopped them from getting in. "My name is Hagar. I will care for your baby while the administrator takes you through to the induction."

The administrator held the elevator doors open for Shaun and Rachel. Hagar went straight for Ari and tried to take him.

"No, that's unnecessary. I'll keep him with me," Rachel said forcefully.

The administrator frowned. "The child cannot come. We do not allow children at the induction."

Shaun whispered in Rachel's ear as he took Ari out of her arms and reluctantly handed him to the Hagar. "No emotions."

"Well, isn't he cute," Hagar said in a monotone.

"Hagar will meet you after the induction, before you enter the worship hall for prayers," the administrator said.

Shaun knew that wearing the pendants for the next two hours would be a challenge without Ari's help. He just hoped he remembered who Ari was, later. They needed him just as much as he needed them. Ari cried and reached out his arms to Rachel as they walked into the elevator.

They went up two floors to the seventy-fourth: hospital and laboratories. The hallway and corridors were more like a private hospital, not like the medical assessment level. It was warm and homely, with pictures of autumn fields and sunsets. They could see down into the atrium. It was the centerpiece between the two towers.

"My sister is in the breeding program. She might choose you," the administrator said, sizing Shaun up.

"What?" Shaun said.

"The Supreme Master gives the right of choice to women. My sister might choose you."

Rachel cleared her throat. "He is spoken for."

"Wait until after your induction and then let me know what you think," the administrator said, winking at Shaun. "Relax," she said as they arrived at the research facility. "When the

Supreme Master is away, we all become a little drunk with freedom."

A smoked glass sliding door opened into a room painted in shades of white. Clean and sterile. There were other couples waiting for the induction to begin.

A man and a woman stood behind a white Formica countertop. They wore salmon pink caftan top and pants, with pink eldritch pendants. The woman's auburn ringlets tumbled over her shoulders. She stepped out from behind the counter.

"Ladies and gentlemen, I am Maria and this is Samson. We are glad that you could join us today. The Supreme Master has deemed you worthy of the breeding program: consider it an honor. This Friday will be your first harvest, and I hope it is pleasant for you," Maria said with a humble, but false, smile, looking directly at Shaun. "The Supreme Master will mate with one of you lucky women," she said, without the smile. "We will now break into two groups. Men on my right and women to my left, please."

Rachel let go of Shaun's hand, not looking at him.

"You will meet your partners at the end of the induction."

The administrator waited while the room divided into two groups.

"We will show you a short film on reproduction and the way the gametes – your female ovum, or eggs, and male sperm – unite, and how we will store your zygotes for future selection. We will explain what happens to the low-quality zygotes and how the Supreme Master uses them for regeneration. The stem cells are a significant source of protein. If a woman's egg does not fertilize during the coupling, which will occur down one on the seventy-fifth floor, then you will come up here and your eggs will still be harvested."

Shaun glanced over at Rachel. *This is ridiculous, we're not cattle.*

"Men who are not selected by a female on the day of harvest, will have to provide a sperm specimen. If a man's sperm does not impregnate an egg by the end of the third month, we sterilize the male, removing their pink pendant and replacing it with a red one," Maria said, shifting on her feet.

"Questions?" Samson said, stepping forward.

Shaun had questions, but they didn't matter because he wasn't sticking around.

"Okay, then. As I said, my name is Maria. If questions do occur to you, please see me after we reconvene in the main lounge room of the breeding center, down one floor, before we head off to the atrium for supper," Maria said, bringing her hands together in front of her chest in a prayerful, thank you gesture.

He watched Rachel leave with the group of women. Without her boots and sassy attitude, she looked vulnerable. She loved those boots; she had picked them up on a supply run back at Casey's estate before Christmas, and had worn them every day since. He gave her a half smile and warily she smiled back.

"You men will love being part of the breeding program," Samson said after the women had left. They moved further away from the smoked glass entrance to a room in the middle of the breeding center where they'd watched a brief video.

Samson led them from the room and began the tour. "The

most important thing to remember is to relax. No one wants to cut your nuts off. But if you don't perform, the Supreme Master can be ruthless. He has an insatiable appetite."

What does that even mean, he has an insatiable appetite. Appetite for what? Shaun wondered. He tuned out Samson. He would not stay, no matter how inviting they made it. Shaun felt the strength of his necklace, and he could easily understand how the men around him were controlled, and simply agreed to everything no matter how strong or powerful they might be.

During the tour through the center Shaun, lost in his own thoughts soon after viewing the first couple of laboratories, drifted to the rear of the group. He kept his hand in his pocket and held on to the pouch of gemstones. He was sure they were helping him, and he needed to find time out to study them further. Shaun wanted to recreate the beams of energy he had manifested, and the photon blasts that had knocked the Ammit off their oversized paws back at the pizza shop in Jerusalem; it had been like Sophia's powerful magical energy rays, but only a fraction of her power. He had to learn how to create the photon blasts, with no one knowing, and fast. He fiddled with the icosahedron sapphire.

The temperature dropped suddenly as they entered the gamete room, knocking Shaun out of his train of thought. Hundreds of thousands of cold metal cylinders containing frozen life surrounded him. During the whole induction, he never saw a single baby.

"This program is the future." Samson said. "Together, we will produce the next leaders. You, me, together we will father the alternate world."

These guys are tripping. What planet do they think they are from? Shaun nodded in all the right places and kept quiet. He followed the group of men out the back of the Laboratories and Research Center into a main lobby and through a set of doors to an annex. Nestled in an alcove was a separate one-door elevator. Samson swiped his access card. The silent doors promptly opened. Shaun sensed the pendant was messing with his sense of direction and he was woozy and a little lightheaded.

The elevator was a tight squeeze. "This isn't the elevator we arrived in, is it?" Shaun said, knowing it wasn't.

"This is the Supreme Master's private elevator to the Primus suite, where he has taken up residence. It's good if he needs a midnight snack."

"But the restaurants and stores are on the eighty-seventh floor. Do they go straight down, too?" Shaun asked.

"The Primus suite is like a two-story apartment, and there is a floor dedicated to the breeding program. The Primus has an internal studio apartment, in which he lives," Samson said, swiping his card on the inside of the elevator and watching the door close, stepping back to make sure it didn't nip his belly.

Everyone stared at the head in front of them until the journey was over.

"Follow me, please, and keep up. We'll head to the main lounge and the atrium where you will meet your partners and exit the coupling area." They passed lounge rooms, bedrooms, a games room and a kitchen before entering a plush narrow hallway that had a charismatic scent.

Samson didn't stop talking. Shaun got the drift that Samson

believed it would be a man's paradise. Shaun wanted out; he was afraid he would give in to physical desire, the charismatic smell was so hypnotic. They had four days to find Rachel's family and get back to the portal. If they are still around on harvest day, Rachel will have to choose him before anyone else.

"On harvest day, your wife or partner cannot choose you," Samson announced as if he had read Shaun's mind.

Oh, no. Shaun noticed his pendant was a fraction darker.

"She can choose you every other day, but not on harvest day. On harvest day, the Supreme Master will select one woman for himself. It should be considered an honor."

The pendant was burning against Shaun's lower chest. *Why aren't any of the men protesting? There has to be a way out.* He didn't want Rachel subjected to the breeding program. Shaun wanted to get Rachel and Ari and run, and keep running back to the portal. He looked into the common lounge, the informal sitting rooms, and the coupling areas as instructed. Shaun was trying not to show his anxiety, which was increasing by the minute as they passed the men's single rooms.

"You have been blessed by the grace of the Supreme Master to be here, remember that," Samson said, glaring at Shaun. He turned away and led the group of men back into the main foyer and living room area.

"When will we meet up with our families in the common area, the atrium," Shaun asked.

Samson's pendant turned to a darker shade of pink.

"What if we leave?" Shaun asked.

The group leaders looked as if they had never been questioned before.

"Well, I don't think anybody leaves," Samson said, as the color of his pendant continued to intensify. Within seconds, the women's induction ended, and they joined the men.

"My husband is trying to make a joke," Rachel said, with little emotion. "This is a wonderful facility, and we're grateful to be part of it. I pray I am selected by the Supreme Master on my first day of harvest."

"Praise the Supreme Master!" Maria said.

Everyone repeated. "Praise the Supreme Master!"

SHAUN'S PENDANT WAS GROWING IN STRENGTH. HE WAS detaching from his emotions and his head was light. He'd been wearing the pendant for a little over an hour, and he felt he was slipping into a void. The others in the group were like robots, already lost in that void. They believed the bullshit. It was eerie watching them. They were acting as if they were pre-programmed, their responses without free will. He was so pleased to see Rachel and tried to catch her eye. He noticed the women in her group were eyeing him. He felt like the last piece of fresh meat. Rachel met his eyes and headed toward him. She kissed him on the cheek as a show of affection. He hoped they accepted their display of affection, since nobody else was greeting their partners warmly. Shaun didn't care. He hugged her.

"You're a sight for sore eyes," he whispered in her ear.

Rachel kept her arms around his neck and whispered, "Maria said we're in."

"Did she say anything else?"

"Not about the Resistance, she's very wary of the unseen eyes and ears of the Supreme Master. He is close because the pendants are darkening, so we should not be complacent."

"So why is everyone so excited about this fucked-up program?" Shaun said, breaking away from her embrace. The looks the other women gave Rachel made him uncomfortable.

"Keep your voice down and your emotions tucked away," Rachel said. "The sudden surge of emotion strengthens the connection the eldritch stone has over you. The more emotionless we are, the more psychic distance will be between us and the Supreme Master. The lighter the color of our stone in our pendants, the less control the Supreme Master has over our minds."

They moved a few steps away from the leading group and stood up against the wall. Shaun was next to a green plant that was half his size. At first he thought it was a fake, but he could smell the alluring perfume of the plant, and it was the same smell from in the hallway. It was lovely. He leaned in to breathe in deeply. He touched the leaf. It was silky between his thumb and index finger.

Rachel brushes his cheek with her lips. "What the hell are you doing?"

"Smelling the plant, it smells so nice. It's soothing. What sort of plant do you think it is?"

"Forget about the plant. Everyone is on board with the program because it sedates them during the initial sorting. The wet muck the Supreme Master pasted all over us during the sorting is a pheromone that causes sedation. It seems to enter our bloodstream through the skin. And the longer you wear the pendants, the more tranquil and compliant and emotionless you become," she said, pushing back his hair. "And the plant, well, that's just seductive!"

He smiled at the other women who were watching them closely.

"Now that we have all completed the induction," Maria said, "it's time we celebrate the honor of being in this beautiful place and the opportunity to be part of the breeding program that will populate the ultimate world. Let's all head downstairs to the worship hall in the atrium and celebrate with evening prayers and connections. We shall rejoice in the good fortune the Supreme Master has given."

Shaun whispered into Rachel's ear, "What the hell!"

"Shh, you will get yourself killed," Maria said, as she led the group to the exit.

15

It was like being outside. The trees, from a distance, looked artificial, but they smelled fresh and alive. The lighting had a natural glow. He stepped off the path and walked on the grass. It was spongy and thick. He touched a few leaves, which were soft, and moist as if there had been recent rainfall. He didn't know if it was him just appreciating the plants or if it was the influence of the pendant.

People were waiting at the entrance of the worship hall. The administrator waited to the side of the white doors for the new people to congregate before ushering them in.

"Where's Hagar?" Rachel asked the administrator. "Hagar has my baby."

"Inside," the administrator said.

There were no pews. Shaun scouted the room. Hundreds of people were on their knees, sitting on colorful woven mats neatly lined up in rows. Men were on one side and women and children on the other.

Shaun spotted Ari with the carer, who was walking toward them. She handed Ari to Rachel. Ari took Rachel's pendant and started sucking it. *Gross.* Rachel followed the other women without turning back, which bothered him so he waited and watched Rachel and the other women with small children. He saw that Rachel was copying their movements and behaviors.

She took a rolled-up mat from a pile arranged in the shape of a pyramid, and another for Ari. She sat beside a woman in her late thirties, who, sadly, had a deformed baby, its head being slightly too big. It had two legs, but no fingers or hands on its six arms. Rachel neatly put the mat for Ari next to the child and lay him down. Rachel smiled at the woman and spoke to her baby. The woman wrapped the child in the cheese-cloth to hide its arms. Shaun smiled at Rachel ... she was feisty, but kind and had a good heart. He missed her already.

REIS AND SIX OTHER SOLDIERS WERE ON GUARD. TWO BEHIND Shaun at the main entrance, one on either side of the hall and two up front at the side of the pulpit. Shaun tried to find where the exits went, but Reis slightly tilted his head to the side, encouraging him to take his place among the men in front of him. Shaun took the hint. As Shaun passed Reis to join the row of men on mats, Reis said, "Whatever happens, don't react. Keep it together. This could get ugly."

Shaun allowed himself to get comfortable, making sure he

could see Rachel and Ari. The worship hall smelled like the ocean. He closed his eyes and he could've believed he was at a resort by the sea. The parishioners were quiet, reflective. Shaun expected people would talk in hushed tones.

The soldiers on guard stood at attention. Their pendants were darkening. Shaun felt a tremor. A wave of dark, unearthly energy was coming, penetrating the walls and floor, and he could feel it in his soul. All the babies and small children cried. Everyone else bowed.

Shaun slightly bowed his head, and tilted it to one side, to spy on a figure of a man standing at the altar. He was over seven feet tall and bulky. He was clean-cut with chiseled features, handsome and mysterious. He radiated power and authority. He didn't look like a monster, but Shaun felt his dark energy. *A wolf in sheep's clothing*, he thought. The Supreme Master was accompanied on either side by two soul-sucking, heart-eating hungry Ammit.

"You may feast upon my beauty, for it is the gift you have given me with your generosity."

As one, the parishioners raised their heads and in unison cried out, "Praise the Supreme Master."

Two men dressed in black rushed forward to aid the Supreme Master as he walked over and took his position on a regal chair fit for a king.

A cloaked man stepped up from the front pew. He looked like a monk. He raised his arms and said in a loud voice, "Pray with me. Let us pray that each one of you will continue to survive our predecessors' cruelty, which brought on the damnation of the world as we once knew it. May you all continue to be worthy to take part in the Supreme Master's alternate world."

"Praise the Supreme Master!" the room amplified.

Shaun was sitting close to the side exit in front of Sergeant Reis Levin.

"What the hell is this guy on? Who does he think the Supreme Master is? This is bullshit."

The man next to Shaun elbowed him in the ribs. Shaun took the hint and kept quiet.

"Praise the Supreme Master."

While everyone was listening to the sermon, he thought of Casey and spoke to him with his mind. *If you can hear me, pal, see through my eyes, and know where we are, just in case we need help to...*

The words of the sermon were like a spell and Shaun's vision glazed over. He slipped near to the edge of an abyss of darkness, struggling to keep control of his mind. He shuffled on his mat and breathed heavily through his nose.

"Bow your heads and repeat after me, I pledge my allegiance to the Supreme Master, and I give to him my body, my children, and my soul. I am his to use at will. I renounce the light and love of the predecessor, who has abandoned us in our time of need and declares the end of all battles for his name's sake. I beckon the power of the Supreme Master to fill my being, to guide my every move, so I may know how to best serve the Supreme Master and his alternate world."

Shaun moved his mouth, but did not repeat a single word. He knew there was only one God, and he would never doubt God's power or love. His mother, and Casey's mother, are there, in heaven, with Kevin's brother, Alex. The creator of the universe is kind and just. Shaun felt love fill his heart, something he never allowed when his father was alive, but now, it is the same life force that kept him sane. It's the darkness, the ungodly creatures wearing the masks of men and false righteousness that create the battles of religion. The struggle of heaven and hell. And this jerk was undoubtedly a disciple of the latter.

"I don't know who this dude's predecessor was, but it is not mine, or Rachel's," he mumbled. Shaun had been resisting the urge to call out in protest. Silently, he held onto the outside edge of the abyss and prayed – something he hadn't sincerely done for a very long time. *God help me and Rachel to stay strong and not fall into the darkness before us. Protect us with your almighty power from this monster that calls himself the Supreme Master.* With his head still bowed, he saw his pocket glow with a soft blue light. It had to be the sapphire icosahedron. He put his hand over his pocket. The fabric was cotton, white and thin. The radiance from the icosahedron was highly visible to the man on his left. If the man turned his head slightly, he would see the glow. If someone noticed, the gemstones would surely be taken from him. Worried, Shaun covered his pocket to suppress the glow. He needed to learn how to control them, he needed time to practice. After all these years, they finally revealed their hidden power to him, in a place that restricted him, stopped him from exploring, but it was also here where they could be most helpful. He glanced sideways to see if Reis noticed.

The Supreme Master rose from his chair and left the

chancel area. He walked down the center aisle between the first rows of men and women. It was almost like a bridal party leaving a chapel. The Ammit walked close to the heads of the bowed congregation, snapping their elongated snouts above their exposed necks. "There is someone here who defies me. There is a nonbeliever amongst us."

People shuffled on their mats and bowed their heads even lower. The men next to him looked as if they were kissing the floor.

What a jerk! Shaun thought.

The Supreme Master went back up to the chancel and stood next to the altar. He stretched his arms outward as if to embrace the congregation. Shaun tucked his head back down for a second before peeking again. A dark swirling mist reached out from the Supreme Master's chest and expanded outward. Shaun glanced along the row of men. All their eldritch stones darkened and pulsed like swollen hearts. Shaun's necklace was no different. The strength of the darkness pushed Shaun's consciousness aside, and he was sliding over the edge of the abyss into a dark negative infinite space. Shaun felt at one with everyone in the worship hall, and it was a terrifying sensation. He hoped Rachel had the strength of a lion to overcome the darkness, as all sense of hope for him slipped away.

Negative evil energy forced its way into everyone's inner being; people's heads raised involuntarily, and Shaun was mesmerized by streams of black, inky swirls of matter mixing with each eldritch stone. The room was a map of streaming black smoky matter. Shaun's pendant was a murky black pink, and had not turned completely black like the rest. He needed to stop fighting and hand himself over to the Supreme Master. Otherwise, he'll be caught, and jeopardize Rachel and Ari's safety. The necklace burned into his chest. An uncomfortable, furious rush of darkness filled his being. He was in darkness; the beast was in him.

"You!" the Supreme Being said, standing at the pulpit pointing in Shaun's direction.

Shaun couldn't move or protest, it was like he was miles away from his body watching everything on a distant screen.

The black energy turned to misty vapors and vanished, releasing everyone from its hold.

Shaun fell back into his body through the screen in his mind. It was the freakiest sensation of vanishing and reappearing. He blinked rapidly. He looked at his hands and touched his face before glancing sideways at the man on his left, who was staring at him. The man lowered his head and Shaun copied, nearly touching his head to his knees.

The soldier standing up front of the hall, closest to the Supreme Master, began walking in Shaun's direction. His heart was racing; he clenched his fist ready to fight, every muscle flexed, ready to spring up from the chair. The soldier marched up the rows, stepping over men. The soldier was two rows away. Shaun saw Reis change his stance. The soldier stepped into the next row and moved along the row. *This is it*, Shaun thought. The soldier stopped two men away from Shaun, and everyone in that row shuffled away from the marked man, and the soldier who was controlled by the Supreme Master. Dark, insidious vapors surrounded his body, while delight seemed to swell around the soldier's lips as he opened his mouth wider and wider.

Shaun couldn't take his eyes away, he needed to watch. He tilted his head a little further to the side to see. A slug, as thick as a man's arm, wormed out of the soldier's mouth, and slithered over the older man's face. The victim's pendant was empty of color. Released from the hold of the eldritch stone the poor man was frantic. He screamed, confused, and tried to get to his feet, but the slug wormed its way into the man's screaming mouth. The victim choked on the giant slug, and he wrapped both hands around its body and tried to pull it out. Shaun wanted to jump up and slice the slug in half, but he didn't have his knife. It was too late, in any case, as the man stopped struggling. He was dead, his body slumped to the floor. Two soldiers came up from behind and stepped over Shaun. They removed the victim's body from the worship hall. The possessed soldier returned to his position at the front of the hall by the pulpit. The soldier rocked uneasily on his feet as the Supreme Master released him from his control, and his pendant was again toffee apple-red.

We're screwed.

The Supreme Master yelled, his voice amplifying through the hall and the collective mind: "Anyone else dare to defy me? Now, bow your heads and pray to me."

Shaun couldn't lower his head any further; instead he surreptitiously looked up and saw the Supreme Master abandon the pulpit and walk toward the rows of women.

Oh, Rachel, keep still, do nothing to attract attention, please, stay down. The Supreme Master was heading toward the row of women with children. The women he passed by, relaxed. Some men, probably the partners of the women the Supreme Master was walking among, tensed up. It was as if the Supreme Master relaxed his hold just enough to let the husbands' squirm in fear, as its shadow darkened the row of women and children. It is enjoying the anguish, Shaun thought, feeling it through the collective consciousness. The congregation sat motionless, unable to act. The Supreme Master was a few steps from Rachel. Shaun made to move, and the man beside him touched his knee, pushing his leg down, holding Shaun back. The Supreme Master bent down and picked up a baby. Shaun's heart was racing, not knowing if it was Ari or not. The armpits of Shaun's white caftan tunic were soaked, his body totally wired. He could not hold himself back any longer. *Why the hell wasn't anyone doing anything?* Shaun began to stand, but Reis leaned forward and pushed him back down.

"You will get a chance," the man next to him whispered. "He's a shape shifter; he's not what he seems."

The Supreme Master raised the baby above his head. It wasn't Ari. It was the deformed child. The woman was crying, begging him to return her child.

"Look at this! It is an abomination? What shall we do with something so hideous? Even its own mother covers it with a blanket to avoid looking at it." He pulled the blanket from the child's body. "Look at it!" he said.

Some members of the congregation were reluctant, but they obeyed and gradually everyone raised their heads.

The child's legs, and its extra arms, were wiggling in the air like a squid caught in a fishing net. Dark purple energy emanated from the Supreme Master seconds before he snapped the baby's neck and tossed the child back to the weeping mother. The mother sobbed and rocked the lifeless baby. The Supreme Master touched her head, and she fell silent.

"We can't just sit here," Shaun said. He was afraid the Supreme Master would step on Ari's head.

"Before we part for the evening and close with a prayer, I would like you to choose an offering," he said to the baby's mother. "I want you to prove you're still loyal to me. No one can leave until you have presented an offering to me. On the new moon, if I am inclined, I may breed with you again, and if you produce another abomination, I will snap your neck too."

Shaun realized that the unfortunate woman lost out either way. And what was meant by "an offering"?

"Stand up!" The woman did as she was told. The soldier with the toffee apple-red stone came from the side and took the dead child out of the room by the feet.

"Now, choose!" he said, walking back to his throne on the chancel area.

The woman looked around at the room of people and closed her eyes. She turned around three times and pointed. The soldiers descended on a teenage boy and took him up to the chancel and presented him to the Supreme Master. He held the boy's chin and gave a nod of approval. They took away the sedated boy through a door at the back of the worship hall.

"Praise the Supreme Master! Praise the Supreme Master!" the congregation roared.

It's outrageous! Everyone is crazy. Reis Levin has a gun, why doesn't he just shoot the Supreme Master?

The voices were in perfect harmony. A few minutes into the hymns, he found himself hypnotized by the harmony. The melody was a sedative. When the singing finished, Shaun felt good, and at peace. The pleasant smell of the plants in the breeding clinic filtered through the worship hall. Shaun realized they were pumping a scented gas into the room. He remembered being angry, even outraged, but now he couldn't remember why. He knew something was amiss. The Supreme Master walked down the aisle between the men and the women, and Shaun thought, *What a handsome guy the Supreme Master is; he has everything going for him.*

The soldiers ushered the people out by necklace color. The chapel emptied. As soon as Shaun's eyes meet Rachel's, he recalled seeing a teenager leave before everyone else, he recalls seeing a baby, and images of swirling black mist in the hall flooding his mind. His heart beat faster as he recalled the collective consciousness and the fear for a teenager and the sorrow for the mother of the deformed baby. The baby was murdered. How could anyone eat or celebrate? People mingled in the atrium gardens before going to dinner as if nothing had happened.

Shaun and Rachel mixed with blues, pinks, ambers, yellows, greens, and a few scattered brown. The brown were the men who had been dressed in black in the front row of the worship hall, fussing over the Supreme Master.

Shaun was trying to keep his agitation hidden while people made small talk. Maria and Reis rescued them and showed them to the dining hall. Shaun immediately asked, "Why didn't you just shoot him?"

"Hush, you need to be quiet," Reis said.

Reis and Maria went through the motions of showing them the dining process and the washing of their hands with seawater. The man who had been sitting next to Shaun disappeared into the line-up to wash his hands. He was watching Shaun a lot.

They joined the line to collect their meals then sat down at a table keeping to themselves. Shaun didn't have an appetite. He was contemplating sneaking back into the chapel to find the door behind the pulpit, when Rachel, who was giving Ari a bottle, kicked him under the table and shook her head, slowly and slightly.

16

Reis tapped Shaun on the shoulder and walked into the kitchen. Shaun and Rachel assumed it meant they were to follow. They entered the kitchen and saw Maria pick up a bag of trash and exit the kitchen via a door marked Waste & Recycling. Reis looked at them and indicated they should pick up a bag of trash too, as he followed Maria. They went through the door onto a metal landing. Shaun, in front of Rachel, carried Ari, and proceeded down a set of metal stairs to the waste and recycling area. Maria waited for them at the bottom with Reis. Maria took their trash bags and tossed them into a recycling container.

Reis took the necklaces from Shaun and Rachel and placed them over Ari's head, along with his and Maria's. Maria and Rachel briefly hugged before Reis led them down a dim concrete corridor with train track rails in the middle. The corridor ended and opened up to a garbage recycling plant. Three men had their backs to them. Ari sneezed as a compressing machine paused. The controller turned, scanning the area. He went back to compressing the waste into blocks, then into ice cube-size squares, and the four of them sneaked behind some compost bales and entered a room via a heavy metal submarine-style airtight door.

"What do they use the compost cubes for?" As soon as he asked Reis the question, he knew the answer. "Never mind ... vertical farming."

They headed down a tunnel that had caged lights on the ceiling. It reminded him of large disused storm water pipes that channeled under the city that he used to ride dirt bikes through. He would find homeless people living there sometimes – city moles. Reis spun the wheel in the middle of another metal door and then closed it behind them. Shaun wondered if it really was a submarine, but knew it was a stupid idea, because he could see the walls were concrete. Reis picked up the pace; they turned right. Shaun was losing his sense of direction. God, he missed his cellphone, he was useless without his phone and map app. Ari was fascinated by the lights in the ceiling, and Shaun kept gazing up, trying to find what was so fascinating about them.

The longer Ari wore the necklaces, and the further away from the Supreme Master they got, at some point they instantly felt they were no longer part of the collective consciousness. Shaun's head had cleared.

"How much further?" Rachel asked.

Shaun spotted, up ahead, a guard blocking the next metal door. "We're busted." He put his free arm out to protect Rachel from being seen.

Maria turned around. "It's okay, he's one of us."

The guard swung the wheel in the center of the door, and it opened. Shaun cautiously stepped through after Reis and Maria, and Rachel took Ari from Shaun and followed them. They saw several rows of bunk beds, stacked high. Reis parted a gray felt cloth acting as a curtain that separated off a large kitchen area where several women and children were sitting around a long, old wooden table eating and chatting casually. None of the women wore necklaces, but they dressed in everyday clothes.

"Leave the baby and your necklaces here. He will be safe. These women and children are the families of the Resistance." Reis said, picking up a wrench chained to the side of the kitchen bench and using it to tap out a code on another submarine bulkhead door. There was no wheel in the middle to open it. The door opened and Reis held it open, waiting for Rachel.

Reluctantly, Rachel handed Ari over to an older woman wearing a flowered apron.

Shaun and Rachel entered with Maria and Reis bolted the door shut from the inside.

"If coerced, the women in the kitchen could not open the door because they don't know the code," Maria said to Rachel, rubbing her shoulder. "He'll be okay. He's in excellent hands. Come on, come meet the team."

Shaun wondered how deep underground they were. He

estimated they would be closer to the ocean, maybe even under it. Above him were huge steel pipes that disappeared into the ceiling.

"Where do these pipes go?" Shaun asked.

"They're coming from the ocean and carry seawater to the desalination plants."

Rachel looked over her shoulder. "How much further? We've been walking for over five minutes."

"Just up ahead, one more door," Maria said.

They stepped through the last bulkhead door. Immediately, Shaun and Rachel were forcefully spun around and pushed against the door, their legs and arms were spread, and they were searched. The men turned them around to face an older man seated at a desk in front of an old radio and fiddling with its dials. He wore headphones over an olive-green cap turned backwards, showing a star with a sword inside with a branch wrapped around it ... and Israeli Defense Forces insignia. The man saw Shaun's gaze fixed on the device he was fiddling with.

"You probably don't know what this is. It's a base station, an old shortwave radio." He had a pencil behind his ear. He was happy and excited. "I'm Gil Peretz."

"I'm Shaun, and this is Rachel."

"Don't mind him," Gil said, as a heavy-handed pint-sized soldier continued to pat Shaun down. "He's a bit over-enthusiastic. Short man syndrome, I reckon." Gil sniggered slightly.

The soldier wasn't that short, in fact. He was about five-three in height and looked to be about Shaun's age. Shaun held his arms up, allowing the tense soldier to continue to search him. The soldier was also wearing an olive-green cap. He had a gun slung over his shoulder, and Shaun thought how easy it would be to take it from him. Shaun saw into the next room. A group of men and women surrounded a metalwork table with blueprints rolled out on top, while two other men watched on, sitting on a workbench next to a mainframe computer station.

The soldier turned his cap around and emptied Shaun's pockets. He took the pouch of gemstones and Shaun made a grab for them. The man gripped Shaun's crotch, causing Shaun to bend over and the soldier checked Shaun's head, neck, shoulders, and ears. There wasn't a lot to distinguish one man or woman from another. Their clothes were different shades of dirt. They all looked like miners. It was so hot and stuffy Shaun felt like he was in a furnace.

Satisfied he had made a thorough search of Shaun and Rachel, the young soldier walked under the bulkhead to the adjoining room. He tossed Shaun's pouch to a man in his late forties, who had jet-black hair pulled back in a ponytail.

"Hey, watch it!" Shaun said, concerned the pouch would drop and the gemstones damaged or broken. The stones have been around for thousands of years and Shaun didn't want to be the one responsible for their destruction.

Whoever the ponytail guy was, it was clear he was the man in charge. He held up Shaun's leather pouch of gemstones and looked inside. "What the hell are these? Where did you get them?"

Two more men were sitting on a countertop against the concrete walls eating bread rolls. They were watching four women and two men who were working at a large metal table. He wondered what ponytail guy, who now had his gemstones, would do. No one moved. The men and women dripped sweat over a set of blueprints, waiting for Shaun to answer and their discussions to reconvene.

"What are these?" the man said again. He pushed away from the table with the blueprints, knocking a metal stool over behind him. It fell with a bang. He got up into Shaun's face. "You a tough guy?"

Shaun was waiting for the man to get a fraction closer, so he could head-butt the guy and snatch back his pouch.

"Quit it, Abba," one of the younger women said. She was wearing a gray singlet that once must have been white. In fact, everyone seemed to be wearing the same. She had been sitting with her knees tucked beneath her chin. She leaned down and picked up the fallen stool, turning it the right way up.

"These would be worth a fortune," Abraham said, peering into the pouch.

"A gift from my dying mother," Shaun said, looking at the attractive woman. "They're just a bunch of gemstones, nothing more."

"Well, she must have loved you to trust you with these precious babies," Abraham said.

"I'll vouch for him, give them back, Abraham," Reis said.

Abraham kept his eyes on Shaun, pulled the drawstring tight on the pouch and tossed it back to Shaun.

"How long have you been down here?" Rachel asked.

There were maps and blueprints scattered across the table. A man with a sandy-strawberry colored beard, who was taller than the rest, quickly rolled them up. Shaun recognized him from the worship hall. He was the one sitting next to Shaun, who held Shaun's knee down when he went to attack the Supreme Master and told him he would get his chance. Shaun assumed the plans were of the underground city of Ascension, and they obviously preferred he didn't see them. It was a bit obvious to call it the city of Ascension, because being miles underground they had no choice but to ascend, to go up. Olivet, as Reis called it, was a better name.

"We'll ask the questions," Abraham said to Rachel.

"This is Rachel and her husband, Shaun. She finished her two years' service in the IDF nearly twelve months ago. They want to help, Abraham, although they are on their way to Giza. And they have seen the monster in its natural form," Reis said.

"Supreme asshole," said the young woman on his left side. Shaun assumed, given the likeness, that she was Abraham's daughter.

"It rose from the ground on Highway 224," Rachel said. "It slaughtered the soldiers lying in wait."

Everybody was paying attention now, as Rachel described the carnage.

"Maybe that's why there has been radio silence all day," Abraham's daughter said.

Abraham glanced at the radio controller, Gil Peretz.

"Their story has just been confirmed," Gil said.

Olivet resembled an underground resort, except the Resistance headquarters actually looked like a no-frills bunker. Shaun noticed there was dirt on everyone's boots. Beyond the headquarters meeting room was another room that was dimly lit, shrouded in darkness; he couldn't see where it went. Shaun put two-and-two together. In this room, everyone was covered in dirt, except for the ginger-bearded fellow. "Is that how you plan to escape?" Shaun said, nodding toward the next room.

"Ever since the whiteout cleared and the Supreme asshole arrived, we've been digging a series of connecting tunnels to the surface," Abraham said, looking at his daughter, who was smiling. "We're not planning to escape, we are planning to free Olivet, and the people. We'll bring in the army from above and take down the Supreme asshole and destroy its mind-controlling eldritch pendants."

"We will take back the City of Ascension," the big guy with the ginger beard said.

"What's the plan? Troopers storm in and start shooting?" Shaun asked.

"I can tell you've never been in the military, son. Not sure what good you will be," Abraham said, snickering.

"We can dig," Rachel said.

"I suppose if you can use a shovel, you'll do." Abraham didn't wait for Shaun to reply. He picked up a bottle of water. "We don't want to kill anyone. We want peace and freedom. That monster controls everyone here. We need to destroy the eldritch pendants and the Leviathan without hurting the hair on anyone's head. This is a good place, with good people."

"What is a Leviathan," Shaun said.

"A monster of the sea; a biblical beast that cannot be destroyed," said Mia.

A woman in her late forties, with a slight frame and

muscular arms covered in sweat and dirt, stepped out from the darkness of the next room. She wore a miner's hat.

Shaun's clothes were clinging to him from excessive perspiration and he now understood why everyone was wearing singlets and shorts. He wiped his brow. The woman picked up a rag and cleaned her hands and took some bread from the guys on the countertop.

Everyone was silent. She exuded more power than Abraham. One guy jumped down and fetched a bottle of water from an overhead cupboard for her.

"Maybe only a mile to go," she said, and everyone slapped each other on the back excitedly.

"Send the message and make sure the encryption is good," Abraham said to Gil.

The woman looked Rachel and Shaun over.

"We can use her," the woman said to Abraham.

"Good work," the woman said, looking at Reis. "She is perfect."

"But eema! I want to be the one," said Abraham's daughter. "I want to do this!"

"Quiet, Mia," Abraham said.

"And who are you?" Rachel said, exuding her own inner power. "What do you think I am perfect for?" she said, looking at Reis and Maria as if they had betrayed her.

"I am Delilah Chadad. That is my daughter, Mia, my husband, Abraham. The two men on the bench are Doron and Cowan. Doron is my son. You know Reis and Maria, and around the table, next to my daughter, are the rest of the team. Our plan," she said, sweeping her arm out to include everyone in the room, "is to sedate the Leviathan with passion and then poison him, on the next day of harvest."

"How do you think you'll do that?" Shaun asked.

"The army from above will enter from the tunnels we have labored over the past six months. Together we will tactically remove the eldritch pendants from the soldiers under the control of the Leviathan and replace them with fake ones made of pewter and gemstones. Starting with the soldiers, we will take back the control of Olivet!"

"Wait a minute, Delilah. Harvest day? This harvest day?" Abraham said. "It's too soon. How will we finish the tunnel in three days? We have to be patient."

"It must be this harvest. She is the one I've been waiting for," Delilah said.

"What do you mean you've been waiting for her?" Shaun said.

"I saw her, and you, in a dream," she said, pointing at Shaun.

She stepped around Shaun and said, "You have secrets, powerful secrets. You will work in the tunnel. Once you leave here, think nothing of our meeting, and tomorrow one of us will come for you to dig."

"But you haven't said what you need from me?" Rachel said, matching Delilah's stance.

"He will choose you this coming harvest," Delilah said. "You radiate feminine power."

"Who will choose her?" Shaun said, getting frustrated. "What are you talking about?"

"We saw the army launch ground to air missiles at the

Leviathan, and nothing made it flinch. How do you think a woman and a bottle of poison can kill it?" Rachel said.

"Wait! Hang on a minute. She's going nowhere near the Supreme Master, The Leviathan, whatever you call it. Rachel is not doing this!" Shaun said. "Look, just wait a minute. Why don't we just steal one of the access cards, go to the top, hide in a truck, and get out of here?"

"My brother-in-law and sister tried that. It killed them," Maria said.

"You would run and leave everyone else behind to suffer." Abraham glared at Shaun.

"Yes, in a heartbeat! I have to keep Rachel and Ari safe," Shaun said.

Rachel took his hand. "No matter where we go, it won't be safe if the Leviathan rules over everyone. We have to help if we can." She ignored everyone in the room and took both his hands. "We can do this," she whispered. "We have four days to get to Giza and find the Lion's Gate and my family."

"Stop whispering!" Abraham said, pushing himself off the edge of the table he was leaning against and pulled Shaun away from Rachel. "You're a coward!" He pushed Shaun in the chest. "No Israeli woman should be married to a coward." He shoved Shaun into the short soldier with the olive green cap. Shaun lashed out and punched the soldier in the face. The soldier grabbed Shaun from behind. Everyone was up on their feet.

"Stop this! We need him," Delilah said.

"We don't need a coward." A well-built man in his thirties stood up from the metal table, no longer interested in the blueprints. He clenched his fists. The young men on the countertop jumped off the bench, and every male was ready to pulverize Shaun.

"Everyone calm down!" Delilah said.

"We need to get to Giza to find my eema and brother," Rachel said. "We will do what you want, but you need to help me get to Giza afterward. Let him go!" Rachel shoved Doron and the soldier holding Shaun's arms behind his back.

"I was at Giza," Delilah said, breaking the tension.

"What did you see? How many survivors are there?" Rachel was now doing the questioning. "My mother's name is Tamar and my brother is David Rosenberg. Maybe you met them. Tell me what you know?"

"No, I don't know them. They are not there anymore, they are all gone," said Delilah.

"What do you mean by 'anymore'?" Rachel said, taking Delilah's bottle of water and offering it to Shaun. "Were you at Giza, too?" Rachel asked, looking at Mia and Abraham.

"No, we accidentally separated," Abraham said. "But we found each other again. Delilah returned to us to fight the Leviathan."

"And what do you mean by returned?" Rachel said.

"Slow down and let me answer your questions," Delilah said, leaning against the bench.

The room became quiet. Those who had stood to get a piece of Shaun now sat back on the stools, or up on the countertop. Gil was the only one that hadn't moved. He was glued to the two-way radio sending out an encrypted message to the soldiers' topside. Reis and Maria sat down and Mia offered

Shaun a seat, which he refused, although he wanted to sit down. His head was light, it was so steamy in the room. He was grateful for the water and sipped slowly. He waited for Delilah to speak. Whatever she was going to say made the others uncomfortable.

"You would not believe me," Delilah said.

"Try me. We won't help unless you tell me what you know, and once I have sedated the Leviathan, I want help to access topside and a vehicle waiting," Rachel said, leaning forward to emphasize her point.

"They are no longer in this world." Delilah said.

"I don't understand? For god's sake, just spit it out."

"They disappeared," Mia said. "She told us. They all disappeared, sucked up by a beam of light."

Shaun tilted his head and raised his eyebrows. "Aliens took them. That's the best you can do? Aliens?"

Rachel touched his hand with her pinkie to silence him. "Let her speak. We've seen stranger things."

Delilah spoke up. "They have gone back to the creator, among the stars, where all life is created. I too entered the light and traveled through the portal to our ancestors amongst the stars. I was separated from the others on arrival and received counsel. I was sent back with the honor of guiding others to the portal, so they too, may go home."

"The Lion's Gate," Rachel said.

"Correct." Delilah walked across to the table for more water. She leaned her backside on the edge of the metal table next to Abraham and drank half a bottle before folding her arms and continuing. "Everyone willingly entered the light of the portal and transported to our ancestors among the stars. Where our creator waits for us in heaven, our home."

"I know it sounds crazy, but it's true," Abraham said. "My wife doesn't lie, and she is no coward."

"Help us defeat the Leviathan, and you can join us on the eighth day of Av at the Sphinx, the Lion's Gate, and travel to the stars to reunite with your family."

"That's months away. Nobody left but you?" Rachel said. "Why you?"

"That's enough talk," Abraham said.

Rachel was talking in her mind to Shaun as she stared at him. He knew it even though he heard no words. He knew she wanted to do this, and she was hoping he was all in. He frowned and glared at her, but nodded in agreement.

"We're in," Rachel said to Delilah.

The moment she said it, he knew he feared for her life and regretted agreeing. "Let Mia do it, Rachel, she wants to."

"It's okay, Shaun. I've got this," Rachel said.

"We'll reconvene the night before harvest to go over the details. We have allies scattered through all the Zones, and the laboratory is one of them," Delilah said, looking at Maria. "Our ally is making a potion as we speak that will subdue the Leviathan while Rachel administers the poison."

"Tomorrow after breakfast, we will come for you, Shaun, and you will help us dig," Abraham said, stuffing a filthy handkerchief in his back pocket. "For your sake, you'd better know how to use a shovel!"

What a dick. Shaun didn't bother arguing with any of them, and especially not with Rachel. Once her mind was made up, nothing could stop her from following through with her decision. Shaun would do whatever it took to help, but it didn't mean he had to stop trying to find an alternative way out. He could not let her subject herself to the Leviathan at harvest.

Reis said, "We'd better go."

Shaun ignored Reis and said, "Show me the tunnel."

"It's late. You need to get back to your apartment. You're the newest members. The Leviathan's hold over you, through your pendants, is at its weakest and he will check on you."

"What about all of you? What Zones do you belong to? Won't they miss you, too?" Shaun was irritated and anxious. He moved forward closing the space between them. He wanted to rebel, he was ready for a fight.

"We don't exist. We were here before the Leviathan. As soon as it took control of Olivet, we hid down here," Delilah said.

A wave of energy vibrated under the floor, a slight tremor. Delilah stopped talking and was scanning the walls. Abraham put a finger to his lips, waiting for the tremor to subside. Shaun didn't think it was possible, but the temperature multiplied. He felt like passing out; the room was like an oven. The ground rippled beneath his feet, forcing him to stumble into Abraham. The tremor stopped and they waited with bated breath. Shaun's temperature dropped. Abraham was looking at his wrists, counting the seconds. Abraham, Delilah, everyone waited a whole two minutes before speaking or moving.

"You must go. The Leviathan is on the move, it is restless. He will check on you tonight," Delilah said, wiping her face with a cloth.

"Make sure you're asleep when he does," Mia said, "with your pendants on."

The young short soldier turned the metal wheel slowly and pulled back the metal rod that bolted the door shut. He held it open, peered down the corridor, and whispered to the guard on the other side. They were afraid. The soldier no older than Shaun stepped aside, indicating it was time for them to leave.

17

The old woman sat alone at the long kitchen table. The sounds of men snoring and children coughing in their sleep were coming from behind the felt curtain. Shaun wondered how many people were part of the Resistance. They would need a lot more manpower to take control of the entire facility. He didn't think it was possible.

Ari, still wearing the necklaces, was snuggled up in the old woman's arms, asleep.

"He is a good boy," she said, handing him to Shaun.

"How long have you been down here?" Rachel asked.

"Six months, give or take a week." The old woman brushed invisible crumbs off her wrinkled clothes.

"Have you been to the upper floors?"

"Not since the Leviathan walked out of the sea with his fancy mind-controlling gifts."

"The necklaces," Rachel said.

"Yes. My granddaughter is up there."

"What's her name?" Rachel asked.

"We don't have time for this," Reis said, concerned.

Maria was looking agitated too.

"Leah," the old woman said.

"Soon we will reunite you with her, I promise," Rachel said.

Reis insisted they keep moving.

Shaun was worried about Rachel. *Great, now she is making promises, she never backs out of a promise.* He held the sleeping Ari close to his chest as they quickly made their way through the tunnels and sealed doors.

Shaun slowed down until he and Rachel were a few paces behind Maria and Reis. When he thought he wouldn't be heard, he quietly said, "Do you honestly believe your mom and brother have gone to a place among the stars?" They maintained their pace as they followed the caged overhead lights through the passageways to the last circular submarine door, behind the bales in the waste management area.

"If Delilah insists she saw people willingly enter a portal that took them to another dimension, or the stars," Rachel said, "I have to believe it's true, because that's exactly how we got here: through a portal. I cannot believe one exists and not the other."

Reis went first, making sure the coast was clear, to open the door. Once he gave the signal, Maria, Rachel, then Shaun, stepped through, and Reis turned the wheel in the center of the metal door to lock it. No one was about.

They followed the tracks to the stairs leading to the back entrance of the restaurant.

Briskly Shaun climbed the metal stairs thinking of the old woman and the sleeping children left behind. Before Rachel and Maria could finish climbing the stairs, dust fell from the ceiling. The stairs shook from a slight tremor. Rachel and Maria lost their balance, nearly tumbling over the railing. Reis caught hold of them both.

"Keep moving," Reis called up to Shaun.

On the metal landing outside the kitchen door, Shaun waited for the others to catch up. He held Ari with one hand and to the railing with the other.

"Quickly, take your pendants from Ari, and go as fast as you can back to your apartment," Reis said. "Think of it as the Supreme Master, don't think of it as the Leviathan. He will kill you if he finds out you know he is not human."

Reis rushed them through the kitchen. It surprised Shaun how much dirt and dust covered their clothes. He reeked of stale perspiration.

"Do you remember the way to your apartment?" Maria said to Rachel.

"Yes, but what about the elevator?" Shaun said.

"Your security cards will allow you access. You are on the seventy-sixth floor of Tower A," Reis said.

Shaun glared at Reis. "You never said why you didn't shoot the monster in the worship hall." He felt the gemstones in his pocket warm-up. *What is the deal with the gemstones?*

Maria pushed a finger into Shaun's chest. "Control your emotions!"

"Hey, don't you have a go at him," Rachel said.

Reis steps out of the kitchen. "It's the eldritch pendants. We've tried but he forces the shooter to turn his gun on himself. We have to go. We must separate before we hurt each other."

Shaun handed Ari to Rachel ready for a fight. "Why would you hurt us?"

Rachel grabs his arm with her free hand. "Shaun, no."

"It's the Supreme Master. He is angry, and we are reflecting his emotions. It has happened twice before, and fights have started among the soldiers. They shot civilians. But it hasn't happened for a few weeks. Something has got the Supreme Master on edge," Reis explained, grabbing Maria's arm and hurrying away.

Shaun's gemstones were generating energy and heating his pocket. He didn't know if it was trying to maintain a level of protection against the eldritch necklace, or it was reacting to the anger that Shaun was allowing to run through his veins. His veins bulged in his arms and the veins in his neck were pulsing. As they entered the elevator, Rachel soothed and patted Ari on the back, even though he was sound asleep.

"If I can get the tunnel finished before harvest, are you willing to leave with me?" Shaun asked.

"Hell, no," Rachel said.

"Dammit, Rachel!" Shaun looked away, frustrated, and fixed his eyes on the closing elevator doors. "If you believe your mom and David are no longer at Giza, then we should get out of here and make sure we're on time for Kevin to open the portal back to Casey's estate. Maybe you don't want to go back, maybe you want to stay here with Reis and a kid that's not even yours?"

Rachel stormed into the apartment and ignored him.

Shaun felt another tremor.

Rachel went into the nursery and slammed the door and came out a few minutes later.

"Rachel

She ignored him and went straight for a shower, slamming the door.

Shaun was panting, his jaw hurt. He removed his necklace and put it down with Ari. He took his gemstones out of his pocket and poured them into the palm of his hand. The stones were inactive. "What's happening to us?" Shaun said watching Ari sleep. He poured the stones into the leather pouch and tucked them back in his pocket. He sensed Rachel's disappointment. Shaun wanted to apologize, but confused he waited until he heard her go to bed before leaving Ari's room.

18

He locked the bathroom door before running a bath with cool water. He submerged himself and the water splashed over the edge onto the tiles. The bath water covered his chest and most of his face. Shaun breathed through his nose and thought of Sophia and Casey. They had told him to call out to them with his mind, but he didn't know how and had thought he would never need to know. He had mocked Sophia, the prophet. Mostly when they had first met, so they'd become sort of friends, and it was the same with Casey and Kevin. Now, while Ari was wearing his pendant, Shaun reached out to Casey. This isn't something that he had tried before.

The bathwater was lapping under his nose. He was careful not to snort the water. His arms were floating just under the surface as he tried to meditate. He felt stupid. Instead of being his pigheaded self, he should have asked Sophia to teach him how to connect to her and Casey.

He concentrated on Sophia's face because she was the strongest in astral traveling, and shooting bolts of explosive energy. He'd seen her generate energy from her body and incinerate a ten foot high pile of rubble, which Casey had gathered using his telekinesis. A wave of concentrated white energy, like magic, had flowed through Sophia's entire body and merged into one powerful laser igniting the rubble: a human blowtorch. His mind wandered, he lost focus on the memory of Sophia, and he started wondering about his gemstones and how they had released a powerful force of energy great enough to push the Ammit off its feet, perhaps more.

The blackness behind his eyes turned into the light of dawn. Shaun scanned the infinite space that suddenly appeared and called out Sophia's name. He felt like he was surfing: the wave was coming up behind him and he was ready to paddle and was trying not to take off too soon. He called out to Sophia again. There was no reply, but he had a terrible sense of fear. Something was wrong. He called out to Casey. There was no reply, but as with Sophia, he had a strong emotional surge of fear. They were in trouble. The wave rising into his consciousness had arrived. It was now or never. He now called out to Kevin, and the water in the bath heated quickly, pushing him out of his meditative state. Shaun jumped out of the bath and into the shower, skidding a little along the way. He opened the cold faucet in the shower to cool his inflamed body. *Something was wrong with Kevin, something was wrong with all of them.* The heat of a fever lingered over Shaun. He tilted his head back and let the cold water run over his body until he had goosebumps.

Cold and feeling foolish, he dried himself off. "Get a grip," he said to his reflection. He thought he must have fallen asleep, or imagined the others were in trouble. Casey and Sophia fear nothing; the fear probably, in all honesty, belonged to him, his fear of losing Rachel. He wiped the condensation off the vanity mirror and ran his hand over the day's growth. Rubbing his chin, he decided not to shave it. It would help him fit in; a lot of the soldiers had beards. He removed the pouch from the pocket of his white trousers and held them in his hands, waiting for them to warm up. Nothing. Shaun wrapped a white towel around his waist and sat on the edge of the bath. He selected the icosahedron sapphire, leaving the rest in the bag. He held it up to the light and looked through the facets and concentrated. He turned it around in his fingers, and a glint of blinding blue light made him reactively close his eyes. Shaun let it rest in his palm. He clenched his fists around the stone.

Everything was white in the bathroom, sterile, uninviting, and it was getting on his nerves. The tiles on the wall were white, the floor was white, their clothes were white, even his towel was white. He stood and aimed his fist toward the bath-water, focusing on energy flowing from the icosahedron into and out of his hand. He punched down toward the water. The water rippled. Shaun pulled back in surprise. He had expected nothing to happen. Shaun shifted the stone to his left hand. He wiped his hand on his towel and tossed the stone back into his right hand. He tried it again. He drew on his emotional energy, the fear of losing Rachel and his friends. With his hands clenched simultaneously, he punched his fists toward the water. A bolt of lightning traveled from his hands, displacing the water, forcing it up and over the sides of the bath. Shaun pulled the energy back. He tried it again, and a wave of light circled his fists. It was cool and blue. It felt like something wrapped around his hands with a peppermint cloth. In the pit of his stomach, he felt a ball of energy that fueled his fear and anger. He separated himself from the anger and drew on the invigorating sensation of the power. It surprised Shaun how alike the physical sensation of fear and exhilaration was. He readied his fists and let go of the energy, thrusting down at the water, and solid beams of magical blue energy poured from his fists. Once he let go his whole being filled with the sensation of power. It was a magical, awesome energy beyond this world. It was a life force unto itself. He maintained the flow of energy as the water rocked up the side of the bath like a wild sea. The bath cracked from the force. Quickly, he tried to pull back the energy.

He backed away from the bath. The blue laser beam of energy trailed up the wall, cracking the tiles above the bath. It was like a lightning rod, the energy that blasted the Ammit off their feet. The energy was coming from both hands. The dual laser beams would render any man unconscious. He reined in the energy, like pulling on a rope, until it wrapped around his hands. He turned his fists over and opened his palms. In the mirror, he caught his reflection. His entire upper body glowed: blue light surrounded him. In his palm, the icosahedron sapphire was spinning rapidly, generating energy, which was entering his body through his veins. The sight of the energy mapping his body mesmerized him. He dropped the towel. The force had penetrated his torso and was traveling down his legs. The tiles beneath his feet cracked. The gemstone is a reactor. He needed to get it under control now.

He closed his eyes and imagined the energy reversing. Traveling through his body starting at his feet, moving up his leg, into his torso, down from his head into his shoulders and down his arm, returning to the spinning icosahedron in the palm of his hand, until he felt like the energy was no longer part of him. Exhausted, he opened his eyes. He felt depleted. In the mirror, he saw the blue light vanish and something moved in his peripheral vision. He had locked the door, but now it was open, and he saw the darkness of the living room. Rachel was standing in the hallway a few steps away from the threshold of the bathroom. He went to close his fist around the gemstone to hide it from her. Instead, he held it out to her. It flickered, sparked in his palm as it slowly came to a stop.

She hesitated at the threshold, surveying the room. She stepped forward and gawked at the gemstone in Shaun's hand, then at the walls. "I heard noises, banging, I thought you were being attacked," she said, reaching out to touch the sapphire with the tip of her finger. The gemstone wobbled and tilted to one side.

"What happened in here? Was it the same as with the Ammit?" Rachel asked.

Shaun didn't know what to say or how to explain what had happened. The rest of the light zapped and danced around his fingers as the icosahedron settled.

"I was trying to call out to Sophia and the others."

"Do you think it was her?" Rachel said.

"Well, I don't know. I don't think so," Shaun said opening his eyes wide as if it would help him understand what happened.

Rachel touched him. "You're so hot." She turned on the shower. "You need to cool down."

He was burning up. He thought for a minute. Burning up! "Kevin," Shaun said, placing the sapphire on the edge of the vanity and stepping back into the shower. He wanted to tell her he thought something might be wrong with the others. If anything happens to Kevin, they won't be able to return home.

"How are we going to explain all the cracks?" she said, running her hand over the dents in the walls.

"We could say the tremors caused it," Shaun said.

"This place can withstand a nuclear blast. Those tremors could not have caused this much damage. Maybe if you went berserk with a sledgehammer, but you did all this with that little stone," she said, picking it up off the side of the vanity. "I don't know what we'll say."

"Can you put it back in the pouch?" he said, sounding tired.

She hesitated for a split second, and the gemstone zapped her with a spark of energy.

She turned it over in her fingers. "Incredible." She dropped it into his pouch, and she heard it innocently click against the other gemstones.

"I'm really thirsty," Shaun said, drying himself off. He went to the kitchen and downed two liters of water.

"The power from the gemstone seems to dehydrate you."

He downed another bottle of water and felt marginally refreshed.

"Are you coming to bed?" Rachel said, yawning.

"I'll be there in a few minutes."

Shaun had an idea and took the icosahedron back out of

the pouch and went into the bathroom. He created a mental image of what he would look like if he generated a force field around him. He felt stupid and in his mind heard his father telling him again that he was worthless. It broke his concentration and the connection with the sapphire. He splashed water on his face to wash away the memory and tried again. He has to trust himself. *I can do this.* There was a part of him that desperately wanted to learn the magic of his gemstones, now being offered to him after all this time, and he had to believe he was now worthy.

Shaun took in a few deep breaths, raised his chin, and blew out. He conjured up the mental image of being surrounded by a blue protective shield. Every time something interrupted his focus, he started again, and again, until the mental image anchored in his mind and the blue energy channeled from the sapphire into his body, projecting around him as a hermetic shield. No outside influence or power will penetrate a hermetic shield unless he lets it in. The scintillating orb around him was comforting, peaceful, a safe place. His body tingled with the waves of energy. He could still hear and smell. The hairs on his arms rose. Vibrant, oscillating blue light surrounded him – *impossible!* The shield wavered. *This is really happening. I can do this,* he thought.

The waves of energy constructing the shield retracted slightly. He shut the shield down, drawing the power back into his body by focusing on his love for Rachel. Shaun rebuilt the hermetic shield a second time, quicker and with less intense concentration. He shut down the shield again and recreated it again. He kept going until he could complete the process within seconds. Tomorrow, he would have to test its strength. He practiced expanding it wide enough to touch the bathroom walls. He drew the shield's energy into his body. The outer layer of the orb sparked like lightning, zapping particles of dust now falling like blue stars. If he can see the hermetic orb, then everyone else will see it. "Shit!"

It was late, and he needed to get some sleep. Tomorrow, he will have to make it invisible. But he didn't know if it would be possible. Shaun thought he might be pushing his luck. He was controlling the energy, not creating it. He had to be careful, and hide the energy from the Supreme Master who is bound to connect with him before morning, and Shaun preferred to be asleep when he did.

GENTLY, HE REMOVED HIS ELDRITCH NECKLACE FROM UNDER ARI'S jumpsuit. Ari stirred and opened his eyes. "Maybe other people can't see the blue orb. Shall we try?" He drew on the energy of the icosahedron in its pouch and erected the hermetic orb in front of Ari. The gentle waves of energy sparkled magically. Ari reached out, touching the sparkles and the orb's membrane. He giggled playfully. Shaun drew the energy back, absorbing it into his body and channeling it back to the icosahedron sapphire.

"So you can see it and touch it. It didn't hurt you, did it? It doesn't look like it will be much protection if you can shove your little chubby hand into it. That's not a good sign, Ari. But maybe that was because I *let* you touch it. You didn't actually get inside the orb. You need to go back to sleep. Shh." Carefully, he tucked Ari's arms under the blanket and left the room. Tomorrow he will test the energy while in the tunnels.

Rachel was sleeping soundly. Shaun's body ached and he shivered for a while. He was having trouble sleeping, even though he felt exhausted. The gemstones were now secure in the pocket of his cleaned old jeans. He sensed what happened in the bathroom becoming distant, the longer he wore the necklace.

Shaun rubbed his head and tried to remember how to activate the icosahedron gemstone. He fell asleep and dreamed he was a caterpillar trapped inside a cocoon and covered in slime. His arms were held tight against his sides by silk threads wound around his body. He wriggled his torso to free himself, but the more he struggled, the tighter the silk held him. In Shaun's dream, he tried calling for help. He cried out for Rachel to wake him up. He couldn't move his sleeping body at all. He called out for Casey, Sophia, and Kevin. Shaun saw Kevin being attacked by bats, Sophia possessed by a demon, and Casey stuck in a time loop. No one would be coming to help Shaun. Trapped, he called out one more time, and this time he called to God, the creator of the light, and the bindings disappeared. He woke, gasping for air.

He opened his eyes. Rachel's eyes were fixed on his face. She was standing at the side of the bed, hovering over him.

"Bad dreams?" she asked.

He pulled her into bed with him. The warmth of her skin against his was comforting. He was awake, and she was real. "You could say that."

They lay on their sides facing each other. She was so beautiful. He didn't deserve her love.

"Do you remember last night?" she asked.

He noticed she wasn't wearing her eldritch pendant.

"Do you think you can recreate and control it? It would be a hell of an asset."

He didn't know what she was talking about. He kissed her, and as he did, she slipped his necklace over his head and around her neck before jumping off the bed. Ari was rolling around on the floor wearing Rachel's necklace, and she put his on Ari too. Shaun didn't enjoy seeing Ari wearing them. Rachel tucked the necklaces into the pacifier pocket of the baby's fresh singlet. Shaun had noticed that each singlet's pocket had a different cartoon character. Rachel must have risen earlier, dressed, and changed Ari's diaper, because he looked clean and happy.

"We must wash them when we put them back on, or we are going to reek," Rachel said. "I'm sure he urinates on them." She jumped over Shaun back into bed.

"What's the time," Shaun said.

"Just after seven."

His bladder was pushing against his prostate, and it was aching. He shuffled down the hall into the bathroom. With one hand on the toilet to help him balance, he relieved the pressure and sighed. He looked up and saw someone had punched some tiles in. Suddenly, he remembered what happened last night. He peered over his shoulder at the bathtub. "Shit!"

"Where is my pouch?" he said to Rachel, rushing through the living room into the bedroom.

She jumped out of bed to help him look. "I'll check Ari's bag and capsule," she said, walking into Ari's room.

"Found them!" he said with a sigh of relief.

"Where were they? With Ari's blanket or in his capsule."

"Where they always are, in the pocket of my jeans," Shaun said.

"Then why did you freak out?"

"Because when I woke I had forgotten all about them, until I went into the bathroom." Shaun thought of the eldritch pendant. "I'm glad I get to dig today. I don't think I could wear that thing for too long – it messes with my head. I might just forget everything: you, the gemstones, Kevin, Sophia, Casey, everyone. That necklace is poison."

"Do you think you can control your gemstones?" Rachel said.

"Last night's mayhem was from only one, the sapphire icosahedron," Shaun said, pulling on his jeans.

"You can't wear your jeans," Rachel said.

Shaun kicked them off and went to the cupboard and pretended he was having a hard time choosing which pair of white pants to wear. "How am I going to keep these clean while digging?"

"You'll probably dig in your underwear, or they'll give you some work clothes. They were all wearing singlets and shorts. It probably gets as hot as hell in the shafts."

"I'm worried about you," he said, cupping her face. "What are you going to remember after wearing the eldritch necklace all day?"

"I'll be fine. I wish I could dig too," she said pulling away from Shaun to pick up Ari. "I'll try to stay in the room as much as possible. Ari and I can take turns wearing the eldritch pendant. You know, he is a miracle. It was a blessing to have found him, and he has been nothing but an angel. Do you sometimes feel that we are part of a universal conspiracy?"

"Lately, yeah," he said, thinking and trying to put actions and reactions together. *My frustration and emotions ignite the energy, and love balances it.* "I will try to use the energy to blast out the tunnel to the surface. As soon as it's finished, I'll demand they let us use it so we can leave. We need to get back on track to find your mom and brother."

"I think you will need a lot more power from the sapphire then what you generated last night. You must punch out a hole a mile long back up to the surface. Even if you could, we can't leave, Shaun. We have to stay and fight."

He shook his head and scratched his temple. He wanted to tell her no matter what she thought they were leaving tonight, but he knew it would make her angry. "Dammit, Rachel!"

"Be careful in the shafts. If there are any tremors, get out. That area has no protection like the city," she said.

Rachel held Ari out toward Shaun.

Shaun took back his necklace. "Thanks, Ari." Shaun walked into the kitchenette and turned on the tap. He dipped his head down to rinse the pendant off ... it smelled a little funky. "Would you like to meet Penny and .... um, Rachel, what did Amy and Terry name their twins?"

"Penny and Wyatt," she said.

"That's it."

"How about it, Ari? When we get out of here, do you want to come live with our family?"

Ari suddenly jerked backward as if he was told the funniest joke.

"I'll take that as a yes," Shaun said.

19

The small elevator lobby was a buzz of silent activity. A dozen people were waiting to head downstairs. Shaun had to sidestep people having made it his mission to be in the best position to enter the elevator as soon as the doors opened, but it was near impossible. Rachel was having trouble keeping up as he wove through the crowd. He stopped for her to reach him. The waiting people were either famished and wanting breakfast, or required to report to work.

Shaun tried to take in his surroundings and the general demeanor of the people. He was one of the famished, but he wanted to gauge what level of emotion people were displaying. High or low energy levels were all he could determine, nothing in between. He looked over the rail to the people below. Some were idle and slow, others were methodical, and then there were high intensity people rushing around.

When Rachel had asked him in the apartment if he could

control the energy of the gemstones, he had said yes, but he really he didn't know for sure. He has to control his emotional energy first. Today he would have to find out if he can blast a hole through the remaining layers of dirt that were preventing them from breaking out of this elaborate ant farm. He also had to test the hermetic orb, whether the shield would be strong enough to protect him. He wished he had discovered the gemstones' magic before he left Casey's estate. Maybe Sophia could have helped him, just like the psychic dome of protection she had placed over the estate. Everything inside her protective shield was invisible to the world outside it. Come to think of it, he didn't really need to be invisible. He wanted the power of the hermetic shield for protection, not invisibility.

Rachel kissed his lips. "Stop thinking so hard, your brow is wrinkling."

Shaun returned her kiss. "We have to stop displaying affection."

Before pulling away Rachel whispered against his lips, "The pendants will soon put a stop to it. I know it inside me."

Shaun focused on the gemstones in his pocket and allowed the sea of people to move him toward the elevators. He and Rachel got squeezed into the back of the car. Rachel was standing in front of him, holding Ari in her arms. Ari's chin rested on Rachel's shoulder. He smiled at Shaun. Shaun smiled back and tucked his hands into the pockets of his white baggy pants. Nervously, he fiddled with the icosahedron sapphire, touching its smooth surfaces with his fingertips. He imagined his breath was blue, like frost. He wondered about the stone's potential, recalling the sensation of the energy mapping its way through his body.

The elevator stopped at the seventy-fifth floor and forced Shaun to squash up against the elevator back wall even more. Ari was reaching out for Shaun's face, making it difficult for Rachel to hold him still and to stop him from climbing over her shoulder to Shaun. She glared at Shaun, then her eyes widened and her look became one of concern.

Sweeping her eyes quickly down to his pocket and back up, she hissed, "Whatever you're doing, you need to stop."

Shaun followed her glance. Blue sparks were radiating from his pocket. He removed his hand. His fingertips trailed blue vapor. *Shit!* He almost panicked, but the energy receded as he imagined reeling it in. The elevator doors opened to allow the waiting people on the next floor in. A man with a ginger beard and a prominent brow looked him square in the face. The pendant made him forget what he was thinking. There really wasn't any room left in the elevator, but the man forced his way in. Shaun recognized him from somewhere. The man dropped his eyes and turned around to face the door. Everyone took one more step back and Ari could now play with Shaun's face. Not another person could fit inside the elevator. He glanced at his hands balled into fists – the energy had dissipated.

THE MAIN RESTAURANT WAS BUSY WITH HUNGRY PEOPLE, AND THE food smelled good. Shaun picked up a plate and joined the queue at the buffet line. He stacked his plate with scrambled eggs, bread, tomatoes, spinach, and then filled a bowl with fresh fruit. He found Rachel and took Ari while she got some food. Shaun ate with one hand and held Ari on his knee. Ari grabbed at the egg and squished it in his hands.

He was halfway through his meal when Rachel returned with her food and juice. He paused for a sip of juice when the man with the ginger beard tapped him on the shoulder.

"Come with me," he said.

Shaun glanced at Rachel, handed over Ari, and kissed her before he left with Ginger.

They went through into the kitchen. Before opening the door marked Waste Recycling, Ginger looked over his shoulder checking they weren't being watched or followed.

Without saying a word, they went through the door and down the metal stairs. They set to work collecting garbage for recycling and piled them, with a portable handheld jack, on a cart sitting on the rail tracks. Ginger pushed it through to the recycling area, where the compressor and stored bales were, then they grabbed the portable jack and went behind the bales. They stopped to make sure no one was watching before they disappeared through the submarine door. They moved quickly until they arrived at the resistance living quarters where Shaun had seen the children sleeping the night before.

The short young soldier stood guard, but this time he totally ignored Shaun and opened the door, swinging the big wheel around with considerable strength. They heard the bolts sliding across, unsealing the door. The guard soldier let them in and immediately Mia was there to take their necklaces and put them on a three-year-old boy riding a plastic tricycle in between the rows of bunk beds. Happily, the toddler followed them into the kitchen and rode his trike around the long kitchen table. Just like Ari, the boy didn't appear to be uncomfortable wearing the eldritch pendant.

Mia handed him a bag of clothes. "Change into these, then put your clothes in this bag, and in that pigeonhole against the wall over there."

"Sure thing."

"What's your name?" Shaun said to Ginger, the elevator man.

Shaun could hardly tell if the man's mouth was moving under the beard, but he heard him say, "You need not know my name."

Shaun thought about provoking the man into hitting him so Shaun could test the hermetic shield. "You're American?"

"You're a fool," the man said.

Shaun changed into the work shorts, and the smelly boots that were half a size too small, and put his clothes into a plastic bag as Mia had requested. "What about a shirt or singlet?" he said, looking at the curls of ginger hair on the big guy's chest. He ignored Shaun and walked off. Shaun followed Ginger to the final metal door and tapped out a code with the wrench. They entered the radio room and the Resistance headquarters.

They walked beyond the radio room under the bulkhead into the Resistance's planning room. The metal bench where the two men had sat, was now littered with split wires and copper coils, and a pegboard was hung above the bench holding screwdrivers – including many Phillips-head ones – Allen keys, wrenches of different sizes, pliers, wire cutters, hammers and mallets, a soldering-iron head, plus there was a clear plastic case with different sizes of tiny screwdrivers for intricate work. There were different sized drill heads lined up along the wall. The room looked well equipped, something he hadn't noticed last night. The energy in the room was also different, too, compared to last night, and the air was lighter, not as thick and stuffy. It was easier to breathe, and not so hot. Besides the tool benches, there was a black metal server cabinet with a glass face, which had a key sticking out of the rear door and three mainframes blinking inside it. Gil was working away, plugging in cables at the back of the unit. It was on wheels, and Gil had turned it side-on for easy access.

Patch panels and routers, blue, yellow, and white wires were clearly visible to Shaun. Lights were flashing on and off, showing transmission and receiving. Next to it was a console with three inbuilt keyboards, surrounded by buttons and switches. Above the console on the wall were three seventy-five inch transparent screens side by side. At the end was pigeon-hole shelving holding manuals and books. Underneath the shelving, sticking out of a wooden box, were scrolls he imag-ined to be the plans and schematic drawings. The metal table without the plans and scrolls stretched out across it, looked bigger and sterile.

Shaun shivered at the thought of the metal scraping against the cement floor if the table was moved: that grating sound. Touching velvet had the same effect on him. Gil popped out from the back of the mainframe and locked the cabinet door. He pushed it back into place against the wall. He was heading back to the radio room when he spotted Shaun out of the corner of his eye.

"Morning Geoff, Shaun," Gil said.

"Morning, Gil," Geoff said.

"Gil," Shaun said, "I thought there wasn't internet."

"That's right. Just before the whiteout there was an explosion at Hebron that took out most of Israel. We thought it was a nuclear explosion, but there's no radioactive fallout. All cellular and satellite communications were lost, so we shifted to thinking it was an electromagnetic pulse. Then we hoped it was just the whiteout blocking the signals, but that cleared up months ago, and we *still* have no cellular or satellite. That's why I'm using the old shortwave radio to connect with the guys on the surface. These computers are monitoring upstairs, the internal systems. I've connected with their servers to spy on them. As soon as we pick up a signal, I'm on to it."

"Aren't you worried about getting caught?" Shaun said.

"No. I designed the computer security system. Those computers up there are my babies," Gil said.

Geoff walked on beyond the planning room and Shaun followed. Geoff proceeded through another sealed door. Shaun realized that each section had the same airtight doors. He nearly tripped stepping over the iron doorframe into a weapons room. This was the room Delilah had been in last night before joining the meeting. It surprised him how many weapons they housed in the small space. All makes and models of guns, blades, grenades, rocket launchers, you name it, it seemed to be there. It was more than enough to fuel a takeover, but it wasn't the people that were the problem – it was the Supreme Master and the eldritch necklaces. Shaun had seen how ineffective ground-to-air missiles had been on the Leviathan, and he doubted that any of these weapons would do anything more than piss it off.

This was a suicide mission. First, they had to remove the eldritch pendants from around everyone's necks, then sedate the beast while in the form of a man, and finally kill it with some magic potion. It sounded foolish. The escape tunnels seemed the most practical solution; they should all leave and get as far away as possible from this place before the Leviathan finds out they're doing.

Geoff sealed the watertight door behind them before walking up to the back of the armory, and into a hardware and general storage area. It was like a Home Depot store. It had everything you could imagine.

"How many series of tunnels are there?" Shaun asked.

"It's really just one, with sealed sections," Geoff said.

A scruffy eight-year-old boy, with black curly hair down to his shoulders and skinny arms, came out of an aisle. He shuffled ahead carrying two large plastic water containers.

They walked down the aisles to the back of the warehouse, following the boy.

"Why is this all down here?" Shaun said.

"It was for stage two of the city that never happened," Geoff said.

20

The area expanded to the size of half a football field. Doron and Cowan were drop-kicking a football to each other in front of a bulkhead entrance that was wide enough for a small truck to enter the tunnels. He wondered if these two did anything but fool around. Geoff stopped next to the last pallet rack and pulled down a box of oxygen masks and gave Shaun one. Geoff grabbed some gloves and handed a pair to Shaun. He stuck them in his back pocket.

"Shouldn't we at least take a pick or shovel?" Shaun asked.

"Everything we need is already up there," said Geoff.

"Morning, Geoff," Doron said.

"Morning," Geoff said.

They left Doron and Cowan to their game and entered the tunnels, which slanted upward. It tapered in width and was about eight feet high in the center, just enough room for a small utility vehicle, but there was no way they could get a larger vehicle down into this area of the tunnel.

A few feet into the tunnel was a supply table against the wall. A young girl was filling half-gallon water bottles from the four-gallon containers that the young boy with the skinny arms and black curly hair had delivered. She put the full half-gallon bottles in individual harnesses and sat them on a table next to miners' helmets and oxygen tanks. It put him in mind of kids he'd seen setting up lemonade stands outside their homes, but here there was no sun and very limited light. The boy took the larger empty containers away to refill.

Geoff scooped up a harness and slung it around his waist before picking up a small oxygen cylinder and attached a mask to it. Shaun copied everything Geoff did, and took his own helmet, water bottle harness and oxygen cylinder.

Lights dangled from electrical cables that were strung along the dirt walls. There was no reinforced concrete down here. It was warmer than Shaun expected. He assumed that was because of the lights. He had expected it to be cool considering how far underground they were. Geoff had to bend his neck forward to avoid hitting his head on two large pipes. Shaun wondered if these pipes met up with the ones he saw earlier, which channeled ocean water for desalination. The pipes disappeared into the ceiling and came from a side tunnel. He felt a drop of water. He looked up.

"Condensation," Geoff said.

"What's down that way?" Shaun asked.

"A cave. The men tunneling out this section, during the

second stage of the city's construction, found the cave. Calcite shone like diamonds, they said, and after their shift, they chiseled some out for their families. Further into the cave, they found ancient drawings showing giants, apparently with mystical healing powers. The drawings showed them treating humans as slaves to carry baskets of calcite. The next day a man collecting calcite went missing," Geoff told them.

Shaun studied Geoff's face. "You're bullshitting, aren't you?"

"No bullshit. You can ask the others."

"Then what happened? Why was it sealed?"

"Men constantly went missing and rescue teams tried to find the missing men. They found a luminescent pool and discovered that the cave continued underwater and probably went out to sea. They needed diving equipment. Three men, without permission, returned with their own diving equipment after the last shift surfaced. The three divers went into the cave and into the pool. Only one returned and he blew up the entrance to the cave, sealing it. The explosion knocked him out. The next shift found him unconscious. He came to, babbling about finding an underwater city and a mound of human bones. They searched the city, but something was watching. Suddenly, one diver vanished and they heard him screaming through their headsets. The other two swam back up into the luminescent pool. As they were climbing out of the water, something snatched his friend from the edge and dragged him under. The sole survivor ditched his gear and ran from the cave and blew it up. He was lucky to escape. From then on, everyone feared what was beyond that wall."

Shaun shivered and looked back over his shoulder to the junction. "How far away are we from the girl with the oxygen stand?"

"About two hundred yards."

"How far to the end of this tunnel?"

"About three hundred yards. Then we climb fifteen hundred yards up the shafts."

They continued walking in silence. The tunnel had a continuous slight inclination toward the surface. The further they went, the narrower it became. Toward the end, men were intently reinforcing the walls with wooden beams.

"You guys did this in six months. Impressive," Shaun said.

"The section we just covered was constructed a few years ago. They left it uncompleted."

"Why?" Shaun said.

"I don't know ... superstitions, fear, maybe they just ran out of money, who knows. But if you watch the men when they head back, pass the junction, you'll notice their stiff muscles will relax and they'll breathe a sigh of relief."

Geoff flung his oxygen tank over his shoulders and fastened it across his chest before he climbed up a row of wooden rungs bolted to the rock face. The simple ladder disappeared up a hole just wide enough for a large man.

He looked at the men working on the support beams. Then up at the hole Geoff had disappeared into. *You've got to kidding me.* He adjusted the tank on his bareback and stepped up on the ladder. It was claustrophobic and dark. Ever since he was seven, he preferred to avoid caves, and this place was creeping him out big-time. He saw light streaming down around Geoff's body. *Dammit!* Shaun paused and fumbled for the light switch on his helmet. His foot slipped, the rungs were too narrow. He held on and followed Geoff's light until Geoff stepped off the ladder and disappeared. Shaun, alone, started coughing in the shaft. He looked up. Geoff stuck his head into the shaft, his headlamp blinding Shaun. He was wearing his oxygen mask and looked like an insect. Shaun doesn't know how to use an oxygen mask. Geoff could have at least told him before they started climbing to put on his oxygen mask. He'd never been scuba diving either, but he'd watched firefighters using their masks, although he never really paid attention to them. His focus had been on the fire.

"Put on your mask, fool," Geoff said. "We have five flights, a hundred yards each to go."

Shaun, out of breath, scaled up onto the landing and Geoff showed him how to put on his mask and turn on the oxygen before climbing up the next ladder to the second platform. Shaun filled his mind with as many memories of Rachel as he could to suppress the unfamiliar rising panic. He focused on her face, her smile, her laughter; her stubbornness, her determination, and the sound of her breathing while she slept.

To get up onto the next landing, there was a handrail screwed into the wall, but it was a stretch to reach. His calf muscles were aching already. He barely had the tip of his toes on the rungs as he lunged up. Grabbing the rail, he climbed up to the landing. He lay down, and the oxygen tank pressed against his spine, causing him to arch his back. He got to his knees, panting. Three more levels to go. He is so exhausted and dehydrated. Shaun couldn't imagine how he would blast his way through the bedrock, or create a shield, with such depleted energy.

He pulled himself up onto to the third landing. Another rung loomed above him. He reached out with his hand and slipped. Falling, he hit his chin on a rung before catching himself from sliding further into the darkness below. White knuckled, he clawed the rung tight. Geoff was watching him from above. Shaun focused on the next rung. He made his way back as quickly as possible. He hoisted himself up onto the fourth landing. Shaun considered himself fit, but the climb inside the stuffy shaft was draining.

He was standing on the fourth landing, catching his breath with Geoff before they tackled the final shaft. Shaun was dripping in perspiration.

What he had set out to do, now seemed ridiculous: he needed space to practice using the power of the icosahedron sapphire. He was using all his concentration on the climb to the fifth and final landing. He feared slipping. His hands and body dripped in perspiration. He finally stepped up and across to the fifth landing.

The landing was ten times bigger. The area was about half the size of a basketball court. There was a faint light glowing in another parallel vertical shaft that he hadn't noticed on the previous landings. Two men were using a pulley to lower buckets down the parallel shaft to the bottom. Shaun looked over the edge. "Why don't we use this shaft to climb up?" Shaun asked.

Geoff, short of breath, said, "It stops here. It doesn't go any higher. There are no reinforcements. The shaft could collapse. It's just to get the dirt out, and supplies up to the landings, or to transport an injured or dead man."

Six men were pounding the rock face, digging into the earth. They looked tired, picking up the shovels and picks as if they weighed a hundred pounds. They lined bottles of water and oxygen cylinders up against the wall. Two men saw Geoff and Shaun; the tension in their body fell away, and they looked relieved as they tipped their face up to the ceiling of the cave in thanks. They ceased work, propped their tools against the wall, and made their way to the ladder, slapping Geoff and Shaun on their backs in passing. The men looked too knackered to climb down, but nothing would stop them. The hard hat's light was primitive, but valuable in the shaft's darkness. He wondered how hard it would be to haul the equipment up and down the supply shaft continually. *I could generate enough energy from the icosahedron sapphire to light up this entire section, if I just had some privacy and energy. The climb was just so damn brutal.*

"We must be near the surface. How close are we to breaking through?" Shaun asked.

"We think there is less than a mile to go," Geoff said. "We're digging around the clock, and we hope to finish in the next two days."

"Just before the next harvest then." Shaun grabbed the handle of a pick – it was warm and smooth from previous use.

"Yeah, that's right," Geoff said, wrapping his hands around a pick. "Use the gloves you've got sticking out your back pocket."

Shaun felt like an idiot for not using his gloves while

climbing the shafts. He wished he had at least a shirtsleeve to wipe his brow. The waistband on his pants was soaking wet. He wiped his hands on his pants before putting on his gloves and clutching a pick. He swung the pick at the wall. The shock of the blow vibrated through the handle, hurting his hands and forearms.

"There is a knack to it. Watch and learn, fool," Geoff said.

Shaun watched as Geoff swung the pick. He couldn't see any difference. He should just activate the icosahedron sapphire and let the blue laser beam blast a hole through the bedrock to the surface. Reluctantly, he lifted the pick again and slammed it down into the rock. He dropped the pick and shook his hands.

"Let the pick drop. Don't force it. Don't drive it into the ground," Geoff said.

The next blow was a little less painful. Why couldn't it have been dirt? *You're weak, like your mother. You're good for nothing.* He knew the drunken slur in his head. Every blow of the pick Geoff delivered, Shaun matched blow for blow, no matter how painful, because it was less traumatic than the memory of his father.

Geoff stopped for a breather. They weren't getting very far. The edges of the oxygen mask irritated Shaun's face. He lifted the mask and took a drink.

"You look a bit tired, old man," Shaun said to Geoff quietly, so the other men couldn't hear. Geoff would have been about fifteen years older than Shaun, not exactly an old man.

"Like I said before, you're a fool," Geoff said.

"What part of America are you from?" Shaun asked. "I have a friend from the United States."

"Stop yakking. You're wasting oxygen."

Shaun repositioned the mask and sealed the edges by sucking in the air and pulling the elastic tight. He kept quiet for the next ten minutes and focused on digging. It was impossible – it fatigued him. How the hell was he going to continue digging for an hour without collapsing? Geoff said they would take a two-minute break every ten minutes and check their oxygen levels. After forty-five minutes, change oxygen tanks, and then continue digging for another hour. They would repeat until the oxygen cylinders available on the landing, two per man, were empty. They would head down for an hour's lunch break, then climb back up and pound into the bedrock for another two hours. Shaun looked over his shoulder. Two men were securing the structure, a third shoveled dirt, while another worked the ropes, pulling the oxygen cylinders up from below.

Shaun could feel the weight of the gemstones in his pocket. He imagined an energy trickling from the sapphire up his thigh to his torso, through to his arms, emanating a fraction of the potential energy, then through to his hands and pick. The tip of the pick sparked as it connected with the ground. He did it again, and each blow penetrated the rock deeper, and chunks fell away. The result was ten times that of Geoff's. If only he could cast aside the pick and create a solid beam of energy to burn a hole deep into the wall. The tunnel would be finished ahead of schedule. He watched the men behind him, who had been securing the new section of the tunnel, leave for a shift change. *Now was as good a time as any*, he thought.

He turned back to Geoff, who had ceased working and was staring at Shaun in frustration. Shaun hadn't noticed Geoff had stopped – the man was probably pissed off at being teamed up with Shaun.

"Can I trust you?" Shaun said.

"You're wasting oxygen," Geoff said.

Shaun took off his mask and got up into Geoff's face. He smelled of stale coffee. "Maybe you should put me back in my place?" Shaun said, egging him on. "You know you want to."

"What the hell! You're a loon," Geoff said.

Shaun reached out to Geoff's shoulder and poked him with his index finger. "You're all talk."

"Put your pick down," said Geoff, removing his oxygen mask.

"No worries," Shaun said, laying the pick against the rock. "Big man wants to fight? Or do you just like to touch young men? I bet you're the kind that plays contact sports just so you can touch up the guys." Shaun quickly channeled the power from the icosahedron sapphire to create a hermetic shield between him and Geoff.

Geoff took a swing. Shaun unintentionally raised his arms to block the blow, pushing his arms up and away from his face. When Geoff connected with Shaun's forearms, Shaun felt the energy from his gemstone surge through his body to the point of impact and explode outward. The power launched Geoff backward, knocking the air out of the man's lungs as he hit the solid wall. Gasping for air, Geoff lunged at Shaun again. A tingling sensation streamed through Shaun as the hermetic shield took form. It was up and glowing just as Geoff's heavy clenched fist was about to make contact. Shaun closed his eyes, waiting for the impact to crush his nose and possibly his cheek too. He felt nothing. He opened one eye. A solid blue wall of energy shimmered between them.

"What the hell are you?" Geoff said. "You work for the Supreme Master, you bastard!" Geoff took a few steps back. His hand reached out for the pick.

"Can I trust you?" Shaun said, withdrawing the energy until it diminished to a faint blue light that vibrated around his entire body.

"I'm Canadian, you can trust me."

"I'm not sure why you being Canadian means I can trust you, but I just showed you something I haven't even shared with my closest friends," Shaun said. "Do you want to finish this tunnel today?"

"How?"

"I can direct the power you just saw into a solid beam of energy, and hopefully, it will blast through the bedrock up to the surface," Shaun said. "But there is a catch."

"What?" Geoff said.

"I don't want the others to know," Shaun said.

"There's no way we will be able to hide this. They already know," said Geoff.

Shaun pivoted around and saw the men had stopped working. They stood with picks and shovels raised, ready to strike Shaun.

"And the next shift is here, too," Geoff said, nodding toward the ladder. A man climbed up onto the platform.

Shaun watched the fresh men arrive.

"If you do this, everyone will know," Geoff said.

"But if I don't, we'll be stuck in here." Shaun didn't know how it was possible to finish the tunnel before the day of harvest any other way. He and Rachel have three days to find the Lion's Gate, and Rachel's family, before meeting Kevin at the portal for extraction.

Geoff was signaling to the men to put down the picks and shovels. "Show me what you can do. And we'll soon find out how they respond."

The men lowered their picks, and the new arrivals stood by their side, whispering, wanting to know what was happening.

"Stand behind me," he said to Geoff. "I'm still learning how to use this power."

Shaun stepped his right foot forward and planted his left leg back as if he was about to push a boulder. He clenched his hands into fists, raised his arms to chest height, brought his fists together and faced the wall. He felt like a tool, but he didn't want to get knocked off his feet and slammed into Geoff and the wall, or thrust down into the supply shaft, and he didn't want the energy to go haywire and cause a cave-in. Shaun focused on the icosahedron in his pocket. The energy increased, and the power surged through his body, and laser beams of energy exploded from his fists. He slid backward.

"A photon blast. Are you kidding me? What the heck are you? No way!" Geoff said.

Shaun joined his fists, and the laser beams became one intense blue laser. Shaun wrestled with the magnified power, steadied himself and amped up the energy even more. The shaft was illuminated in a blinding iridescent blue. The energy splayed against the wall, penetrating the bedrock. He maintained the pressure for twenty seconds. He pulled back the power to gauge the results.

Geoff checked the smoldering wall. It was at least ten feet deeper and wider. "Christ, will you look at that. It's burning white-hot." Geoff reached out to shake Shaun's hand, then thought better of it, and retracted his open palm. "Not after that," he said, pointing to the hole. "You're a conduit, a power-house of energy. I'll probably disintegrate, or you'll bore a hole in my hand."

"What's a photon blast?" Shaun asked.

Geoff didn't have time to answer. The other men were motionless, except for one. It was Abraham. He briskly walked over.

"I know what you're thinking, boss," Geoff said. "He left his pendant with the families. He's clean."

Abraham spun Shaun around and checked for an eldritch necklace before he removed his oxygen mask and sized Shaun up. Shaun didn't know why Abraham checked inside his ears for an eldritch necklace.

Everyone was frozen to the spot, waiting for Abraham to respond. *This could get ugly,* Shaun thought.

"Do you have any more where that came from?" Abraham asked, inspecting the opening.

Shaun smiled. "A lot more."

"It doesn't look like it will need reinforcing," Abraham said as he turned to the other men. With his hands on his hips, he looked at Shaun. "Show me," Abraham said, stepping away from the new opening. The other men stepped forward, eager to inspect the new section of the tunnel.

"It's still hot, but it looks smooth and polished, Abba," said one man.

"Show him," said Geoff. "Stand back," he said to Abraham.

Shaun looked from Geoff to Abraham.

Abraham looked at him. "What are you waiting for?"

Shaun stared back at Geoff and others.

"Give the man some room," Abraham said, and the workers stepped back.

Shaun concentrated on the icosahedron and felt it spinning in his pocket. He channeled the power and pushed it from his fists, creating another powerful luminous blue laser beam. This time he was ready for the kickback and held his ground.

"Jesus, Mary and Joseph, he's glowing like a goddam blue angel. Come on, son," said Geoff.

Shaun shouted over the sound of the energy grinding against the bedrock. "I'm too old to be your son. So, I'm not a fool anymore?"

The power was hard to contain in one laser beam. Shaun felt it seeping out through every pore of his body. He stepped forward, keeping the energy focused on extending the size of the hole. The splayed energy was growing with a circumference of about twelve feet.

Shaun stopped and reeled in the energy. He was so thirsty. His feet were burning because the soles of his boots were melting.

Abraham and the men inspected the hole he had extended.

It was twenty feet deep. "Okay, Shaun. Change your trajectory. You need to aim it slightly upward."

Shaun and Abraham stepped into the new section of the tunnel he had created. Heat was radiating off the walls. They looked down at their shoes, and their soles were sticking to the polished stone floor. Shaun swallowed his excitement and pride.

"Get some water up here," Abraham yelled. "We must cool the new section of the tunnel before we can advance."

The man who had been on the bucket pulley system spoke to someone on the radio, and within minutes, he was hauling up buckets of water. It gave Shaun time to catch his breath. He felt lightheaded. He drank as much water as he could, but he felt nauseous.

Five men dosed the walls and waited for a few moments before they checked the integrity of the space again.

"Looks good," Abraham said, "but you definitely have to work on your trajectory. Or it will be too slippery to walk up, and those above will slide down with such speed it's liable to kill them."

Dizzy, Shaun crouched for a second. "Okay."

The steam vapors dissipated. No longer were his shoes sticking to the ground, but the smell was still there. It was cool enough for him to advance. He couldn't believe it. If he spoke, it would echo. The face of the wall was smooth, like a polished diamond. Abraham was right, he needed to change his angle.

Shaun took up his stance: right foot forward, left foot back. He started drawing the energy from the icosahedron. He separated his hands to expand the width of the laser beam. He changed the trajectory and punched through the next two hundred yards, and the next two hundred yards. Shaun only rested while the tunnel cooled sufficiently to continue. He carved the tunnel like a snake slithering its way up toward the surface. His body ached. He ignored the pain and fatigue. He felt like he was running a marathon, and his body was about to fail him.

"How much further?" Shaun said.

"Not much. Can you keep going?" Geoff said, looking concerned. "You're lit up like a giant blowtorch."

Geoff hadn't left his side and he was now actually overprotective. He fetched him water and oxygen, and made sure the others gave him space.

Forty minutes passed, and Shaun wanted to wipe the sweat from his brow that kept dripping into his eyes. After each section, he needed longer breaks. The salt in the sweat dripping into his eyes was making it hard for him to see. They stung, he needed to wash them out. He wished he was wearing at least a singlet so he could use it to mop his face. "I'd really like to wipe my face and wash my eyes out," Shaun said, taking a fifteen-minute break.

Abraham reached for his back pocket and took out his handkerchief. Shaun remembered seeing him use it the night before and passed. Geoff came to his rescue and poured water over his head and in his hands.

"Two more ten minute bursts should do," Abraham said.

Shaun went through the motions of drawing the power of the icosahedron and directing it into an explosive, iridescent blue laser beam. He glowed with the energy. He didn't tire from the energy coursing through him. What was draining him was keeping it merged into one beam and holding it steady. Shaun felt it burst forward, heating like an uncooled nuclear reactor. The unassuming sapphire spun furiously in his pocket. He wondered why it hadn't burrowed a hole into his leg. He trusted the power of the gemstone, and he needed to trust himself. Shaun had never felt this good about himself before – for the first time in his life he had a deep sense of purpose, and his life had meaning.

Shaun sat on the smooth floor of the tunnel and gulped back the water while Geoff doused his head. The workers finished cooling off the section for Abraham to inspect.

"Another fifty yards, and we'll be punching through the surface," Abraham said, squeezing Shaun's shoulder. "Prepare yourself. You're nearly done. Delilah was right about you. Good job, son."

Abraham gave instructions for an encrypted radio message to be sent for gun supplies, and for a message to be sent to the soldiers on the surface, telling them to secure the area because they were about to breach.

"Ready, Shaun?" Geoff said, taking away the empty bottles of water.

He didn't have the energy or confidence he could even stand. "Good to go."

The sapphire spun to life. He wondered if he should hold it in his hand. He thought next time he will. At the moment he was so weak he was liable to drop it. Shaun concentrated on maintaining the laser beam, and it filled his vision. Soon the tunnel that would lead him and Rachel to freedom would be complete. He put everything he had into the last burst.

Geoff stood behind Shaun, ready to cool him, and the workers were ready to cool the new section down. Shaun could hear Geoff shouting that Gil on the radio had wanted to know how the hell they were going to reach the surface in the next ten minutes. *Everyone will want to know what happened,* Shaun thought. It made him uncomfortable.

Lost in the power's noise, Shaun increased the force of the energy against the last layer of bedrock. He wished he had used earmuffs. He gave an extra push, and the beam spiraled as it burned through the rock and soil. The last section was big enough to drive a tank through.

His cramped arms dropped. His vision blurred, his mouth was tingling. A weight pressed down on his shoulders. He was finding it hard to remain standing, and his legs cramped. Silver stars filled his vision.

"I need to sit..." He struggled to speak. "Water."

Geoff handed him some water. He gulped. Puked.

His muscles were cramping. His legs went out from under him as he collapsed.

The icosahedron sapphire, the tiny powerful reactor in his pocket, was still. Its warmth left his body, and the sensation of being surrounded by a peppermint sheet disappeared. Curled on the ground, he shivered. Every muscle and bone in his body felt like liquid. He, too, was shutting down. His eyes closed. He could hear Geoff and Abraham calling for help. "Take him up."

"No, take me down. Please, not without Rachel," Shaun mumbled. He felt himself being lifted by two men, perhaps one was Geoff – he could smell Geoff's perspiration. His head felt like it would burst as they jostled his body and carried him through the new section before they cooled it down.

The smell of burning rubber, someone's shoes were melting; the smells were fading as he drifted beyond consciousness.

21

He was alive. A musty, earthy smell replaced the burning rubber. The jackhammers in his head had stopped, but every muscle in his body was on fire and cramping. He felt his back against a hard mattress. He listened to the sound of whispering voices. A rhythmic breeze was blowing the hairs on his arms, face and head. He felt clean and wondered if he was lying under a window. Or if he was outside under a date tree. He was afraid to open his eyes, scared he was not underground with Rachel.

Like tearing off an adhesive bandage, Shaun flung his eyes open, expecting to see the sky. His gaze met the underside of a bunk bed. A cannula was in his arm, transporting clear liquid from a bag that was duct-taped to the side of the upper bed. A boy hung over the edge of the top bed. He looked familiar. Shaun raked his memory for clues. It was the skinny water boy. He was waving a piece of cardboard in Shaun's face.

The old woman with the invisible crumbs on her apron, was sitting on a stool by his head. She squeezed out water from a cloth into a bowl on her lap, and gently placed the damp cloth on his forehead.

He didn't make it. He hadn't completed the tunnel. If he had, Abraham would have given the order to take him up for medical attention. They must have lowered him down the supply shaft instead. What little energy he had, now drained away with disappointment. He didn't finish the job. He failed.

Shaun smiled at the boy before thanking the woman. "Thank you."

Geoff must have been only a few feet away because no sooner had he spoken, than Geoff appeared from behind the gray felt curtain.

"You're a fool," he said, smiling.

"Sorry, I didn't finish the tunnel. I'll complete it tomorrow, for sure," Shaun said in a weak voice.

Abraham pushed back the gray curtain separating the kitchen. Behind him was a soldier with a Red Cross band around his arm. Shaun put his hands flat on the bed and tried to lift himself up. He searched the soldier's neck and chest for signs of an eldritch necklace.

Concerned for his safety, he kept trying to push himself up off the bed, but he was too weak.

"Take it easy," Geoff said. "It's all right, he's one of us," he said, patting the soldier on the back.

"You did well," Abraham said, leaning against the bunk railing. The water boy screwed up his face and made a show of fanning the smell of Abraham's armpits in Shaun's direction.

"I didn't finish it."

"You did. And because of you, we can now start bringing the soldiers down. We will insert the army from above over the next two days. They'll hole up in the warehouse area. They will be in place ahead of time, thanks to you," said Abraham, bending down to shake Shaun's hand.

Shaun's shoulder and arm muscles were jelly. He could barely manage to take hold of Abraham's hand.

"You've given us time to prepare, son. We need the compound and thanks to you we now have an even greater chance. The bunker is a city, it is the safest place to be. When this is over, you are welcome to stay. Once the Leviathan's dead, people can come and go as they please."

Shaun didn't want to know about Abraham's plans, or to stay. He felt like an imposter because he just wanted to leave with Rachel. He felt good that he helped, but he had to find Rachel and get out. He was spooked. Finding her family alive and returning to Casey's estate was the priority, and he needed to somehow convince Rachel they must leave. He felt like an old man – he wanted to hold Rachel in his arms and sleep for days. He didn't think he had the strength to move. What would happen if he didn't return for harvest day? Will they notice him missing? He assumed they would.

"I thought you would take me up," he said to Geoff.

"I did," Geoff said. "Then we brought you back with the first group of soldiers. We lowered you down the shaft strapped on a spinal board. Do you think you could widen the first group of tunnels and connect them to the new exit?" Geoff asked. "It was a tough climb down the laddered shaft sections."

"Probably, but I need time to recover. I'm pretty wiped out. Tomorrow. How long was I unconscious?" Shaun said.

"Okay, men. Give him some air," said Delilah.

"Four hours," Geoff replied, as Delilah shooed him away.

As if he was a good luck charm, Geoff, Abraham, and the soldier touched Shaun on the shoulder. Delilah drew the gray curtain to separate the two areas and sat on the edge of the bed beside him.

"Who are you? Where did you come from?" She waited a few seconds for him to answer. "Did you come through the portal when the others ascended?"

When she mentioned, portal, Shaun thought she knew about Kevin, but he realized Delilah was referring to the portal she had witnessed in Giza.

"Were you at the Lion's Gate? Are you from the gods?" she asked.

"No, and no. We're trying to get to the Lion's Gate," he said.

"I dreamed of you and Rachel, you know. I knew there was something special about you when Reis told us you saw the Leviathan. And what you have now done for us... is a miracle. Everyone in the resistance thinks you are an angel from heaven. I wish you could have arrived sooner. But together we will destroy the Leviathan, we will take back the compound, and free those enslaved by the eldritch necklaces, and afterward, you and Rachel will be free to go."

"I hope it's that easy," Shaun said. He sensed she was reminding him the job wasn't over until the Leviathan was dead.

"Get some rest, you've got about two hours before we have

to get you back to your designated zone." Delilah rose from the edge of the bed and disappeared behind the curtain.

There was movement on the top bunk. The water boy on the bed above dropped his head over and smiled at Shaun.

"Are you really an angel? What is it like outside? Are we all going outside now?" The boy was full of questions. "Have the mushroom clouds gone? The other kids' said that's why we have to stay down here because we nuked ourselves. Is that true?"

"What's your name?" Shaun asked.

"Theo. Gil's my dad."

"There might have been a sandstorm when I arrived, but I think the sky's blue behind the dust. There's no mushroom cloud. But earthquakes have destroyed the cities and awakened a terrible giant monster and its army of ancient beasts called Ammit. They hunt in packs like dogs. You have to run super-fast to get away from them, so right now, living down here is safer."

"I know about the Leviathan. Is that why God sent you, to destroy the Leviathan and the bad necklaces?"

"No, God didn't send me. It's just a coincidence I'm here."

"Nah, God sent you. Every day we're aware of earthquakes. We're woken from our sleep by tremors. The adults fear earth-quakes. Are we going to have another big one?"

"I don't know."

"Delilah said we will soon gaze up at the sky again, and we won't have to live underground unless we want to. Will the Ammit and the Leviathan be gone? He's an alien, you know. I want to find his spaceship. God has sent you to defeat the

Leviathan," Theo said, nodding his head in agreement with himself.

"No, God did not send me to fight the monster. I'm here to help my friend find her family."

"But, you have special powers?" Theo said, flipping over the edge of the bed and standing next to Shaun. "Are you from the stars like Delilah?"

"You ask a lot of questions," said Shaun.

"My dad said we must question everything," Theo said, sitting on the stool.

"I need to rest, or I'll be a dead angel."

"So you are an angel. I knew it!"

Shaun had to smile at Theo. "I was speaking figuratively."

Theo ran off through the quarters, yelling. "Daddy! Daddy, I talked to the blue angel."

Shaun looked at his fists, remembering the blue glowing light and the power that filled his veins. He started putting his hand down to the pocket of his work shorts. Apprehensive, he stopped, worried the gemstones were gone. He pushed his open hand in his pocket and touched the pouch. He let out a sigh of relief.

He dropped off into a deep sleep and dreamed he was a cocooned caterpillar, held tight by silk that became tighter the more he tried to struggle against it. His body jolted him awake as if he was falling off the edge of a cliff. He was covered in perspiration, and Rachel was sitting beside him on the stool.

She was leaning forward stroking his face. "How are you feeling?"

"You did it. You're a miracle, Shaun. You're their blue angel, but you're my knight. How about I help you out of bed because we have to get ourselves back to our zone before we're missed?"

She kissed his forehead. He could smell the sweetness of her neck. He breathed in her goodness, allowing it to fill him. He reached out to her and brought her lips to his.

Ending the soft kiss all too soon, Rachel stood up. "Come on, we have to get you back upstairs."

"Delilah said I have two hours. Lay with me."

The curtain opened and the medic, Abraham, and Delilah came in. The medic stuck a thermometer in his ear and checked his pulse and blood pressure.

"You slept for two hours and fifteen minutes," Delilah said.

"No, really? It's like I only closed my eyes for a minute or two."

"The people of the Resistance want me to thank you," said Abraham.

"Can I take Rachel and leave through the tunnels tonight?" Shaun said.

Rachel answered his question for them. "You know we can't. I have to be here for the harvest."

"Mia can do the harvest," said Shaun, not making eye contact with Abraham.

"He has already chosen me," Rachel said.

"What? What do you mean? I thought it didn't make a choice until the day of the harvest, which is Friday?" Shaun said, pushing himself up off the bed. He was confused and didn't understand why she needed to be a martyr.

"Let's not talk about it now," said Rachel. "But we have to go back for Ari. So, blue angel or not, get your sorry ass out of bed."

Shaun knew there was no point arguing with her. He had to trust in himself and make sure he is ready to be there when she needs him. While blasting his way to the surface something had awoken within him, giving him purpose and he knew in his heart she was right. They needed to stay and help battle the Leviathan, even if it killed him. He would do anything to keep Rachel safe. She belonged here, these were her people, and she could start a life with them. He may never get back to Casey's estate, but as long as he was with her it didn't matter where he was.

He pulled back the sheet. His head was light, and he sat on the edge of the bed to wait for his head to stop spinning. Rachel handed him his white shirt and pants. He was reluctant to stand, not sure if his legs could hold him up. Rachel reached out and helped him. The blood drained from his head a second time, while Rachel and Geoff held him up.

"Let's get you to the upper decks," Geoff said.

22

Passing through the restaurant, he stumbled. Insidious energy wormed its way into his aura and crept through his groin up into his stomach. It entered his solar plexus when he stepped into the beautifully manicured gardens of the atrium. Instantly, he felt sick. He didn't think he would make it. He was sure someone would pick up his offbeat vibe and become suspicious. Holding Ari tight, Shaun took refuge in his and Rachel's auras until he made back to the apartment.

Since he had woken up, he was sensing energy around people and noticing a shimmer around their bodies, or else he was delirious from dehydration … one or the other. There was so much he didn't know. The awareness had dampened when he had taken back the eldritch necklace. He coughed in the elevator as if he would throw up.

~

SHAUN BRACED HIMSELF AGAINST THE TILES. THE STEADY SPRAY of water from the shower filtered through his hair and cooled his head. It was good to be back in the apartment.

He welcomed the fresh cold water.

It wasn't so bad in Olivet, the City of Ascension. His apartment was simple and comfortable. He couldn't imagine it was actually designed for people like him. It had everything you could need to survive and thrive. Delilah and Abraham were right. They needed to take control of Olivet. The people should be freed from the Leviathan and not restricted by colored pendants. Everyone should have the right to move freely between the underground city and topside. The Leviathan's control must end.

He switched off the shower, pushing the lever down. The last drops of water splashed on the tiles around his feet. He watched the water swirl into the drain. Something about the dripping sent his thoughts back down to the belly of the city. Where are the desalination reservoirs? He was sure Administrator Helen mentioned it on arrival? Zone two or three? He recalled the water dripping off the pipes below in the tunnels, and how Geoff said it was condensation. This place can withstand a nuclear blast. Is it condensation, or a leak? He needed to be sure. He must talk to someone.

Deep in thought, Shaun stepped out of the shower. He wrapped a fresh white towel around his waist. Everything was clinically white. He touched the bathroom wall with vivid memories of cracking it the previous night. It had been repaired. Not a hint of a crack.

"What's wrong, babe?" Rachel said, standing in the bathroom doorway watching him touch the wall. "Reis had it fixed before housekeeping arrived. I told him you were angry and lashed out."

"And he believed that?" said Shaun.

"He didn't question it," said Rachel. "You have a faraway look on your face, what's the matter?" Rachel sat on the edge of the repaired bath.

"Something is bothering me about the water."

"Does it taste strange to you?" she asked.

"No, it tastes fine. I'm just a bit overwhelmed," Shaun said. "Oh god, I sound like a crackpot."

"Like a what? You've expelled a lot of energy, Shaun," said Rachel. "Give yourself a break. The medic said your organs could have shut down from dehydration. You will feel like crap for a while. Take it easy. Forget about the harvest and the Supreme Master. Let's just enjoy this wonderful City of Ascension for a few hours. There's so much we can do. We can go for a walk in the park, visit the artifact museums, go to the gym, have a swim. There are two movie theaters – we could go watch a movie. Earlier today I checked out the schools, hospital, shops …"

"Yeah, I'm really not up to it. You've been busy. I thought you would not go out?" Shaun said.

"I had to blend in. Anyway, Ari can go to the childcare facility. It's so cute. Our swipe cards and eldritch necklaces give us access and credits. Because we're part of the breeding program, we have unlimited credit. Isn't it just insane?"

Shaun sat on the edge of the bath beside her and leaned his elbows on his knees. "Look, we're not here to have fun, we're here to find your family or have you forgotten?"

"I haven't forgotten. Maria checked the computers. They're not here. And we can't leave until we help these people. There is nothing we can do right now, so let's go the movies and eat popcorn. Just for a few hours, let's pretend nothing is happening. Just while you recuperate. You need to heal," Rachel said, fiddling with her eldritch pendant.

"I can't stop thinking about the dripping pipe in the tunnel and let's not mention you will offer yourself to a monster that hides behind a handsome, smiling human face. Nobody has explained what the Supreme Master intends to do with you, or what he is harvesting." Shaun paced the room, frustrated.

"It doesn't matter," Rachel said. "I'll poison him, so Reis and the soldiers can kill it. Calm down, Shaun. Rest and allow yourself to heal. We will get answers tomorrow. For a few hours, let's pretend none of this is happening. We are one of the lucky few given refuge in this magnificent underground city."

Drained, Shaun needed time to clear his head. "Fine, there is no point arguing with you."

Rachel went stiff and covered her stomach. "Shaun, it's back! Where's your necklace?" She stood up and frantically searched the room. "Did you leave it with Ari? I didn't see it when I took mine." She looked down at her pendant and the pink had darkened.

They were both startled by a loud knock on the apartment door.

"Find your necklace and put it on. I'll stall them as long as I can," said Rachel, shutting the door to the bathroom as she left.

Shaun quickly searched the pile of dirty clothes for his necklace. It must have come off with his shirt. He could have sworn he put it on Ari before taking a shower. His head was so foggy he was making careless mistakes.

"There you are," he said to the necklace. Reluctantly, he placed it over his neck. He pulled on a fresh pair of white slacks and shirt, and before he could pull the eldritch stone from under his shirt, and on display, an administrator and a soldier pushed their way into the bathroom. The soldier's stone was a dark ruby red, and the administrator's pendant was a dirty, burned orange. They were furious. Rachel was behind them with Ari.

"We have warned you three times not to take off your necklace."

The administrator looked at the soldier who unclipped the strap, securing his gun.

"No, don't!" Rachel said.

She had no time to stop the soldier, and Shaun's gemstones were under Ari's mattress. The soldier advanced on Shaun with his gun pointed at his head. Shaun raised his hands. The soldier turned the gun around and slammed the butt into Shaun's head, knocking him unconscious.

Shaun woke on the floor with a killer headache.

"Are you okay?" Rachel said. They were alone.

"Are they gone?"

"Yes, but they left a message for you. They said next time you won't get off so lightly. They need women for the breeding program, not so much the men. It's only by the grace of the Supreme Master that you're accepted into the breeding program. Next time you will be sterilized or terminated."

"We've got to get out of here!" Shaun said, getting to his feet slowly. His face hurt. His entire body ached like he'd fallen from a moving a train.

"Come on, Shaun, it's only two days. We have a plan, let's stick to it, and everyone will win. Let's go out, show our faces and make them believe we are in his control. Let's extinguish any suspicions the Supreme Master might have."

"Okay, Rachel, let's go make a happy family," Shaun said, dabbing the side of his mouth with a face flannel to clean up the blood from his split bottom lip, and soothe his eye. It would be black as the ace of spades in no time. "Come Friday, as you as soon have drugged that monster, we're leaving. I'll be waiting outside the door with Reis and the others, ready to storm in and kill it. I'll blast him to pieces."

Rachel gently kissed his lip.

Slowly, he changed into a clean shirt. His head ached and he really preferred to sleep. He had hoped to return to the apartment and lay in bed with Rachel for the afternoon until it was time to show their faces at dinner. It hadn't happened.

He slid his feet into his assigned loafers.

TOGETHER THEY ENTERED THE HALLWAY AND MADE THEIR WAY TO the elevator. He could easily forget he was in an underground bunker, and instead believe he was living in an elaborate, futuristic underground city, if not for the pain in his head and body.

Waiting for the elevator was Administrator Helen. Rachel and Shaun acted unemotional, detached. Rachel, as if nothing had happened, asked how to get to the theater and if it was alright to leave Ari at the child-minding center while they went to a movie and had dinner afterward.

"There are four terrific movies each month, two in each theater house," Administrator Helen said robotically to Rachel.

Rachel nodded her head as the administrator spoke. "They all sound wonderful," she said in the same robotic tone.

The administrator laughed. "The Supreme Master wants us to enjoy ourselves. It is okay to have fun, to be enthusiastic, to laugh. You just can't take off your necklaces. It will cause all sorts of bother. Please try to have some fun and keep your necklaces on," she said, looking directly at Shaun.

Rachel smiled. "Thank you! We will."

"The childcare will expect you," the administrator said. "You must be honored, Shaun, knowing your wife was chosen by the Supreme Master for this harvest. Once, I was selected, but I failed. I gave my eggs to storage to populate future generations. It truly is an honor."

Shaun wanted to tell the woman what he thought, but he bit down on his cut lip instead, restraining himself. The cut bled. He could taste it and licked it away. The energy of the eldritch stone was like a parasite inside his stomach, but he still had free will. Administrator Helen didn't.

He smiled at her. "How about I answer that when harvest is over? If you are not part of the breeding program, what do you do during harvest?" Shaun watched the woman withdraw into silence.

The elevator doors opened. Rachel entered carrying Ari, towing Shaun by the hand. Helen didn't get in. Shaun pushed the button to close the door.

"I think you just scored some brownie points," Rachel said with raised eyebrows and pursed lips.

With caution, in case the eldritch stones and the elevator had ears, Shaun said, "I would like to see her reaction when it's removed..."

"Sometimes, when I meet her eyes, I imagine a silent cry for help," Rachel said.

The child-minding center was beyond the atrium, down a laneway past the main restaurant, next to the leisure center. It was bright and colorful. They had cartoons painted on the walls. Kiddie music was playing. They entered a childproof gate and pushed a buzzer. The door opened. Through a glass window, he saw children climbing and laughing inside a jungle gym. It was heaven to see genuine emotions. A woman greeted them. "Sign in here, please." She tapped on the window behind her. A young girl and a boy were playing with a group of babies.

The girl of about twelve looked up and left the room. A side door clicked open. The girl took Ari from Rachel and went back into the baby's room. Shaun watched her sit Ari down on the mat with a group of babies who could sit and were learning to crawl.

THE MOVIE THEATER WAS A TEN-MINUTE WALK TO THE SOUTH SIDE of the gardens. They walked through laneways, browsing in the stores. The polished concrete floors were silent. There wasn't one person wearing high heels or any shoes that made a noise. There were couples and families browsing. It was like any other day in a shopping arcade, and people were quiet and courteous. It was more like a library, Shaun told Rachel, than a busy shopping mall.

Rachel bought the movie tickets, scanning their access cards. "I have to admit, I am excited to watch this movie. It's two years old. I wanted to see it when I was in the army, but never got around to it. Are you sure you don't mind it has English subtitles? You can get the headphones with the English translation if you like?" she said, standing at the counter checking if the headphones were available.

Everything was self-service. You just had to scan your access card or eldritch necklace. Nobody else was selecting headphones and Shaun didn't think it would be a good idea if he did. He didn't want to stand out any more than he already did. The Supreme Master probably had subliminal messages programmed into them, anyway. Rachel was excited, and he would not burst her bubble. They've been through a lot, and this place was the closest thing to normal they had seen in a long time. He never thought he would go to the cinema again. They followed the people into the theater and Rachel chose seats closest to the middle.

No matter how much he focused on Rachel, an uneasy feeling festered in his gut. "Rachel, can we move closer to the exit?" Shaun asked.

"Yeah, sure, babe." Rachel carried her popcorn and moved toward vacant seats near the exit.

When did she start calling me babe? The more she wore the necklace, the more she referred to him as "babe." It was as if she was becoming gentle and subservient. Rachel was never subservient.

SHAUN KEPT HIS EYES OPEN AND READ THE SUBTITLES FOR AS LONG as he could before exhaustion governed his actions. His eyes fluttered, and like a gentle wave, sleep rose to meet him.

He saw a guiding light and followed it. He was on a journey heading toward the ocean and the coast stretched out for miles. Calm, inviting turquoise water became one with a cloudless sky. A sailing ship revealed the horizon. It looked lost, separated from its fleet. He looked up and down the coast and saw the remains of prestige motels and resorts. Water gently lapped against his feet. He didn't recall walking along the sand to the water's edge. The ocean pulled back, and his feet sank into the warm sand. The water rocked back and forth, covering his ankles. The rhythm was hypnotizing. He wished Rachel was beside him. He watched the white sails of the sailing ship glide across the horizon.

His feet sank deeper into the sand. The water no longer lapped against them, it was receding. The sailing ship's mast was disappearing as the ocean rose, as the sky turned to night. The ocean concealed the stars. A tsunami covered the length of the whole coastline. He couldn't make out where it started or ended, and it was coming toward him fast. There was no escape. It arched high above him. He turned away. He looked behind him and saw himself sleeping next to Rachel in the movie theater. She was laughing, enjoying the movie. She didn't know what was coming, and he was sleeping. He had to wake himself up.

Rachel suddenly screamed! People jumped from their seats, running for the exit. Rachel jumped up. She was shaking Shaun, trying to wake him up. He moved around lifelessly. Shaun wanted to tell her to run, to leave him behind and save herself. He saw the people piling up against the closed emergency blast doors. There was no way to open the heavy doors. Shaun struggled to understand what had started the mad panic. Why were they running, why were they panicking? They had no reason to be afraid.

Shaun looked up at the beautiful colored water; it was turning into black ink, like the dye from an octopus. He hated octopuses. They were tough and rubbery. Shaun turned away from the murky ocean and tried to run, but his feet were stuck in the sand, and he had sunk up to his knees. Frantic, he looked at Rachel inside the theater. She wasn't leaving – she persisted, struggling to move Shaun from his seat. She dragged him off the chair and dropped him on the floor, between the rows of seats. People were frantically climbing over seats to get out, while he slept on the floor as if nothing was happening. Why wasn't he waking up? Shaun slapped his face. It stung from the spray of the ocean. "Wake up, dammit! Wake up. Run, Rachel. Forget about me. Run!" Shaun heard his words, but nothing came out of his mouth.

Shaun pulled at his legs, trying to free himself from the sand. It was useless. He yelled at the ocean towering over his head – he demanded the sand to let him go, and he pleaded with himself to wake up.

He screamed at the top of his lungs, "Wake up! Let me go, let me go!"

He turned back to Rachel. The theater was underwater. Bodies floated in the depths of the water. He saw himself, his arms, legs and hair floating lifelessly. Shaun turned away from the macabre scene. They were all dead. Rachel too. Drowned, sealed in by the blast doors that were meant to keep them safe.

Shaun stared down the wave about to crash on him and yelled, "Why, God? I put my trust in you, and you take away the one thing that gives me life." The murky water cleared, and he could see through it. He heard the sounds from the theater of people laughing. He kept his focus on the tower of water, waiting for it to thunder down on him. The wind was strong underneath the arch. The spray of water stung like needles and tasted like sand. Shaun accepted death. He would be taken, crushed by the wave. He continued to stare hard through the water and saw the maker of the tsunami, a monster. It was the Leviathan. Shaun couldn't tear himself away from the hideous creature. The wave broke, pounding him into the sand.

Shaun woke up. He pushed himself out of his seat and stood up, panting. His heart was pounding in his throat, and he was steaming with perspiration. He looked around the theater. The people were laughing and enjoying themselves. Nothing was out of place except him standing in the way of the people behind him.

"What's the matter, babe? You've spilled popcorn everywhere. Sit down, Shaun. The people behind you can't see."

Shaun wasn't listening. He went to the exit and checked the blast doors. All doors were unlocked and opened. He went back to his seat. *I'm losing my mind*, he thought.

23

"Do you mind if we skip dinner? I'm not hungry? I'm really tired." His head was foggy. It was like looking out at the world through a dirty old window. "An early night would be good if that's all right with you?"

Rachel took his arm as they left the theater. "Sure, babe, whatever you like. So what did you think of the movie?" She smirked. "It's all right, I know you slept ninety percent of the time. Did you volunteer to work in the recycling area tomorrow? I don't know how you do it frankly. It must be disgusting. I remember putting the garbage out when I was a child, and it was gross. That was just for a family of four. I can only imagine what it must be like after catering for hundreds of people."

Shaun was mystified: *Why was she talking like that?* She'd never been precious or precocious, but she was acting weird, like a type of Stepford wife from the 1970s. Her necklace was deep pink. The Supreme Master had a powerful hold over her right now. Maybe the Supreme Master was courting her energetically for the harvest. Shaun didn't want to think about what that meant, but he could see her eyes were glassy, and she wasn't blinking.

Shaun nodded at everything she said. "Whatever you say is fine with me, Rachel."

Shaun had volunteered to help the recycling team. He might even start early; he wanted to talk to Abraham or Reis. He wondered if it would be dangerous to take her necklace off while it was so rich in color.

Back in the apartment, Shaun waited for Rachel to fall into a deep sleep, and her necklace glowed a faint pink. Careful not to wake her, he slowly slipped the necklace over her head and tiptoed into Ari's room and gave the little fellow both of their necklaces to wear. Making sure they wouldn't choke Ari during the night, Shaun tucked them in Ari's singlet pocket, which had a picture of a bright yellow duck. He kissed Ari on the cheek. It was so soft.

"Thanks, little guy. I wouldn't leave them with you if it weren't important. It won't be for much longer. I have to be sure Rachel remembers who she is when she wakes and what she needs to do. We can't lose her to the eldritch stone and the Supreme Master, because once he has his tentacles hooked in our souls, we will never leave. Thanks, Ari."

SHAUN WOKE, STARTLED, SURPRISED HE HAD FALLEN ASLEEP. THE images from his terrible nightmare at the theater had been haunting his waking thoughts. He needed to talk to Abraham. It was six o'clock in the morning, less than forty hours before harvest day. He needed to keep his shit together.

Rachel had not moved. She was lying on her back. He slipped out of bed, quickly dressed, took his necklace from Ari, and left the apartment. It was strange how quiet everything was. He took the elevator down to the ground floor of the atrium.

It was like being on the streets of any town in the early hours of the morning. Two workmen wearing mustard yellow stones nodded at him while they pruned the park trees with hand shears. A few early risers had taken to the track for a brisk walk or a jog, most wearing blue or green eldritch stones: medical and research. A man was wearing a rare-colored eldritch stone; Shaun had noticed only two men wearing them during the church service. The stone was black-brown with sparkles of silver and gold. They dressed in black suits and Reis said they had the power from the Supreme Master to rule certain Zones of Olivet like a mayor. Shaun dug his hands into his pockets and hunched his shoulders forward as if walking deep in thought. As he passed the man in black, Shaun's eldritch stone pulsated with light, as if sending out a signal.

"Excuse me," the man in black said.

Shaun pretended he was insignificant, and the man was probably talking to someone else even though no one else was near. The only soldier on guard was sitting erect on a park bench.

"Excuse me, sir?" the man in black said, slightly raising his voice.

"Hey, you! I think the mayor is talking to you," the security guard said, standing up and stepping in Shaun's path.

"Sorry," Shaun said, driving his hands further into his pocket, gripping his gemstones. The mayor came over and sized Shaun up. He tried to stand side-on, so he wasn't facing the black-brown sparkling eldritch stone. He thought he saw it blink. It felt like a prehistoric reptilian eye was studying him.

"You're up early for someone in the breeding program? Don't most of you like to spend your time in bed?" the man said.

The security guard, as if on cue, laughed. "You have it made," he said, slapping Shaun on the back.

Shaun wanted to shrug off the soldier's touch and punch him right between the eyes. The soldier's movements were forced, like a puppet.

"What happened to your face?" the mayor asked.

"I fell down the stairs to the recycling zone. My wife has been chosen by the Supreme Master for this coming harvest. I thought I could do some extra volunteer work to show my gratitude," said Shaun.

"Good for you. So you understand it is a great honor." The brown in the mayor's pendant disappeared, and the black intensified. It reminded Shaun of the obsidian stone he had placed in Alex's grave.

The pendant blinked, the sparkles flickered. "Who is Alex?" The lines around the mayor's head flickered like he was a televised image. It morphed into that of the Supreme Master, the face he had shown in the worship hall. The face bubbled with lesions as it decomposed into a reptilian creature that reminded him of a movie: *Predator*. The head flickered quickly back to the form of the mayor, who coughed as if choking on a hair.

Shaun, uncomfortable, moved from one foot to the other. The Supreme Master had been inside his head, or his eldritch stone had transmitted his thoughts. His necklace glowed like a pink diamond. "A friend, he died."

The mayor got the coughing under control, and the brown returned to the eldritch stone. "Move along. Don't let me keep you. Well done."

Shaun went into the restaurant kitchen and out through the back door to where the recycling was collected. He picked up a bag and started down the metal stairs. He swung the bag in the air and let it fall into the compost mulching pile. He nodded to the fellow workers, and when he thought they weren't looking, he hurried down the corridor and went behind the bales. He stopped and peered around the bales, making sure he wasn't being followed.

24

He rushed to turn the wheel, opening the airtight door and just as quickly closed it behind him. Abraham's son, Doron, was pointing a gun at his head. He lowered the gun, stepped forward and turned his necklace over.

"Well, if it isn't the Blue Angel. You're up early. You're still wearing your pendant." They hurried through the few corridors and sealed doors to the sleeping quarters. Doron took Shaun's necklace and headed to the first row of bunk beds. Gently, as not to disturb the sleeping child, he slipped the necklace over the boy's neck. Shaun was so tired and so grateful to get the necklace off, he could have cried.

They entered the radio room. Gil wasn't working the radio or sitting at the computers; his chair was empty. Shaun looked at the screens of maps and radar: he was confused about how they could even work so far underground. Blue ethernet and black coaxial cables snaked under the bench feeding the different systems. The computers monitored and recorded radio transmissions while searching for new signals. Abraham and Delilah were talking in hushed voices crowded over a map as Shaun and Doron entered the meeting room.

"Morning, Shaun!" Abraham said, genuinely pleased he was there.

"Morning," Shaun said without the heartfelt enthusiasm.

"Thanks, Doron. You best head back to your post," Abraham said.

Delilah had a quizzical expression. "Coffee?"

"That would be good, thanks."

"You look troubled." She cautiously handed him a cup and poured the coffee from the old percolator into it.

"He is probably eager to get started on widening the tunnels," Abraham said, lifting his tin cup up to Delilah for a refill while studying Shaun's face. "Have you come to open the lower sections of the tunnels? I'm sure you could have it all connected in the next twenty-four hours. The soldiers started coming down last night. A few dozen are already hauled up in the back of the supply area. We should easily have a hundred men in there by the end of the day."

Shaun waited for Abraham to finish.

"No, you haven't come to work," Delilah said, putting the percolator down on the side bench.

"No, I haven't. I will come back to dig later. I have to get back before Rachel wakes."

Delilah sat on a metal stool and sipped her coffee. "What's wrong?"

"It's Rachel. She's acting strange. She's behaving like a Stepford wife," Shaun said.

"Like what? What the hell's a Stepford wife?" Abraham said.

"It's from a film. Like decades ago, when a woman acted all proper, perfect manners, obedient, almost like a robot, emotionless. It's not like her. Rachel is argumentative, fiery, and passionate."

"What's wrong with that?" Abraham said with a cheeky grin.

Delilah shook her head and suppressed a smile before giving Abraham a playful swipe. "Let me fetch you both some breakfast," Delilah said in her best American accent. Delilah swung her hips in jest, entering the scullery, leaving the men alone.

"After tomorrow night, Rachel will be okay. This starts happening to the woman in the breeding program who is selected by the Leviathan. It's a kind of conditioning ... a courtship, you might say. It numbs them from the reality of what really happens to them. But we won't let anything happen to Rachel. Our pharmacist has confirmed the potion is ready. It's lethal to a man and would knock out an elephant. It will work on the Leviathan while it's in its human disguise."

"How is the Leviathan –"

"Supreme Master to you," Abraham interrupted. "If you accidentally call him Leviathan, he will know you know what he really is, and he will have you killed. Don't forget it!"

"Noted. How is the Supreme Master getting in and out of the Olivet?" said Shaun.

"We're not sure, but there are tremors every time he comes

and goes. At first we thought they were aftershocks from the big quake, but Reis and his team noticed the changes in the eldritch pendants, and the people, before and after the tremors. That's how we know when he's gone, the light of the eldritch stones dim, and there are mild behavior changes in the people. When he returns people panic a little in response to the tremors, but when he leaves people hardly blink. He mainly stays in the Primus where the breeding rooms are. His suite is sealed by a heavy steel door sporting a giant emblem of an inverted ammonite. You would have visited the Primus on your arrival."

"No. I've seen the door, but not sure it was in the Primus. They took me for a generalized medical. I didn't go into a Primus area until during the breeding program induction. They showed us the breeding rooms were in the Primus suite," Shaun said.

"The sorting room is on the upper floor of the penthouse. It has its own internal elevator," Abraham said. "We think it sticks out the side of Tower A. It isn't on any of the maps, and the building materials are foreign."

"It was dark and cold in the sorting room. I had my eyes closed, but the place smelled bad. It smelled like a septic tank. I smelled nothing that bad during the induction."

"It doesn't matter. I'm sure you're the type of guy that would put up a fight. Whoever told you to close your eyes probably saved your life, or you'd be like all the others up there," said Abraham.

"It was Reis Levin," Shaun said. "He recognized Rachel. They served together."

"Thank him sometime. Reis was the first to discover the secret of why the children didn't wear the pendants until after the age of six. He was in the elevator, and a baby was fascinated with his necklace, so he took it off to let the baby wear it and play with it. When no one came to reprimand him, he told Delilah."

"If a micro-virus can't get into this facility, how is the Supreme Master getting in and out? There must be a breach in the bunker?" Shaun asked.

"The only breach we know of is the one you made yesterday. What's this all about, Shaun?"

"Where are the reservoirs?" Shaun said rubbing his head in confusion, not sure what he was looking for.

"There are two water systems. Gray water drives turbine generators for electricity. A desalination system provides clean drinking water. There is a reservoir for each tower, both in Zone three, floors fifty-six to seventy-one. There is a much larger, third water turbine generator and desalination system for the residential apartments, parks and businesses in the atrium, in Zone seven, floor eighty-eight," said Abraham.

"How does a desalination system work?" Shaun said, taking the percolator and refilling his cup.

"It removes salt and impurities from seawater to produce fresh drinking water. It's called a reverse osmosis process: seawater passes through a pre-treatment filter that removes large and small unwanted particles," said Delilah, rifling through the scrolls of blueprints in the metal box.

"Where is it?" Shaun said.

Delilah unrolled the plans she had been looking for and

placed her coffee cup at one corner and a ruler along the top to stop the corners curling. She held down the last corner with her hand. It was a line drawing of the city. "We are here," she said, pointing to a void that extended beyond Tower B. "They used this area during construction of the first part of the city. They planned to reconstruct the area as an extension of the city, so the lower class could afford a bed. This area does not exist, we don't exist."

"One of the three desalination systems and reservoir is up here, Zone three, and extends beyond the tower," Delilah said, tapping the plans. "It supplies water to Zones one, two, three and four." She pointed to the images beside each tower's outer wall. "The other desalination plant and reservoir is in Zone seven, below the atrium. This reservoir supplies all the other areas."

"What are these pipes for?" Shaun said, pointing to the drawings.

"They supply seawater to the desalination tanks on the upper and lower levels," Abraham said, looking frustrated.

Shaun trailed his eyes along the pipes that went through the void area and out to the Gulf of Aqaba, which channeled in from the Red Sea. "We're what ... half a mile from the gulf?"

"I know what you're thinking," Abraham said, putting his hand up, "but we don't have the gear to swim in and out."

"No, I wasn't thinking of swimming out of here. But what about the Supreme Master, could he be coming through the desalination pipes? Can we block and stop him?"

"See this here? This is closed. The valve automatically opens when water in the reservoir reaches below a certain level.

He is way too big, in his natural form, to travel through the pipes. And in his human form, it would take thirty minutes, and he would need a good supply of oxygen tanks. It also wouldn't explain the tremors," Abraham said.

"You've got oxygen tanks for digging. He could definitely get the gear he needs. Is there a manual override to the valve?" Shaun asked.

"Possibly," said Delilah.

"How wide would you say those pipes are?" said Shaun, getting annoyed. Nothing made sense. There were no answers because he didn't know what he was looking for. A leak? But its just condensation?

Abraham put his hands on his hips, flustered. "On the ocean side there is a locked grate covering."

"Can you check the grate is locked and in one piece? Let's say that he is accessing the city through the pipes. He can shift his monstrous mass from over a hundred feet high to the size of a human. Why not a fish, a shark, a stingray, or even a goddam octopus? Is there any way to sabotage that lever so it can't be opened?"

"Why would you want to do that? It would be suicide," Abraham said. "I don't understand your thinking, Shaun. Where are you going with this?"

"Just hear me out. If we could do a manual override maybe we could shut him out," Shaun said. "I think it lives in the Red Sea."

Delilah looked at Abraham intently and then shrugged. He raised his eyebrows questioningly. Without one word spoken between them, they seemed to come to an agreement.

"Look," Abraham said. "It's possible you're right, but as a collective group, the Resistance has agreed to execute the plan we've been working on for months. We have thought of every scenario. We're so close Shaun, less than thirty-six hours, and you're free. We will all be free."

"Shaun," Delilah said, getting up from the stool, "Abraham's right. Why don't you go back to Rachel and we'll see you in an hour or so? It's all right if you don't want to widen the laddered sections of the tunnels. We have an opening to the surface; the soldiers are already coming down. What you have done is enough."

"Is it possible for the reservoir to burst?" Shaun said.

Abraham scratched his head and took his handkerchief from his pocket and blew his nose. "Anything is possible. They can seal every level in each Zone in such an event. The atrium is like a big air tank. Every floor can become watertight within seconds. They can block individual sections in an emergency, but it's a highly unlikely event. Somebody would have to sabotage the reservoirs internally. The only people that have free will to do something like that are those in the Resistance."

"I can't imagine anyone wanting to do that." Delilah said. "We're all on the same side down here, we all want to get out of here. Go back to Rachel, Shaun. Go give that baby of yours a cuddle."

"Why don't you tell us, Shaun, what's really troubling you, otherwise leave and cool down," Abraham said.

Shaun looked at them both and wondered how much to tell them.

"You're hiding something," said Delilah.

"Ari is not ours. We found him at the side of the road in an abandoned car. His parents were dead. A pack of Ammit was chasing us. He would have died if we had left him. After that, Rachel made out to the soldiers he was ours, but he's not really."

"We know. Maria told us the DNA tests didn't match you or Rachel. Don't worry, she changed it. The authorities won't find out, and for now he is your responsibility," said Abraham. "You found him because God wanted you to find him. You are here because God wants you here. Don't think for a minute, that Ari is not your responsibility. Go back to Rachel, Shaun, unless there's something else you've been hiding?"

"I had a bad dream. I dreamed of dozens of people drowning. The theater was like a big tank of water, and the people were floating, dead. The Supreme Master was behind a tsunami rising out of the ocean."

The couple looked at each other again, and then Delilah said, "Now we have the truth. We will have the pipes and reservoirs checked for cracks and tampering. We will make sure your dream doesn't become a reality. You should have told us about your dream sooner. Yesterday was tough – you were extremely dehydrated. You drank gallons of water. Enough water, in your mind, to possibly fill the theater. Shaun, it was probably just your subconscious responding to your day."

"Come on, Shaun, I'll walk with you," Abraham said.

Shaun couldn't argue with the logic. Yesterday, he was drained. It made sense. He was overreacting. He needed to go back to the apartment, snuggle into Rachel and sleep.

Shaun emptied his cup and put it on the metal table.

"It'll be all right, Shaun. If you're up to it, we'll see you after you have a nap and a late breakfast. Okay?" Abraham spun the wheel in the middle of the steel door and opened it and waited for Shaun to step through.

"Make sure he gets back up to the restaurant kitchen," Abraham said to Doron.

"Will do," Doron said.

RACHEL WAS ASLEEP IN BED. SHAUN WENT INTO ARI'S ROOM AND slipped his gemstones underneath Ari's mattress, before he gently removed his and Rachel's eldritch necklaces from Ari's pacifier pocket.

Wearing both necklaces, Shaun quietly eased himself into bed beside Rachel. He flipped his eldritch stone over to his back and placed Rachel's over her head while she slept. Gently, he kissed each of her eyelids until she slowly woke.

Rachel woke with a smile and kissed him back. "I have an exciting day planned," she said.

"And what is it you've been scheming?" he said, pulling her close.

"Now don't you get any ideas," she said. "Not while there's a baby in the next room about to wake up. What is the time?"

"Eight o'clock," said Shaun.

"Ari must be starving," she said, throwing back the covers.

"You both must be," he said, getting out of bed.

"I can't believe I slept in. Give me a few minutes to feed Ari, and I'll be ready to go to breakfast," said Rachel.

"No need," Shaun said. He turned her toward him. He could feel her chest against his. He kissed her softly on the lips. His lip was sore from yesterday's run-in with an administrator and her soldier. The pain was a small price to pay for the passion of Rachel's returned kiss.

He held her hand and led her into the small dining area. On the dining table he had arranged a platter of fruits and some mixed pastries.

"Shaun!" She pressed her lips hard against his. "How sweet. You did this while I was sleeping?"

"I did an early shift in the recycling unit. Afterward, while passing through the kitchen, I grabbed a few things for you." He pulled the seat out for Rachel, and she sat down to breakfast.

Shaun collected Ari, changed his nappy and made a bottle. He popped it in the microwave for twenty seconds. He opened the door on the fourth beep, then removed and shook the warm bottle of formula milk. He was getting the hang of changing and feeding Ari. Shaun tested the warmth of the milk. He sat opposite Rachel and watched her eat while he fed Ari. Her pendant color was light; the Supreme Master must have his eye on somebody else for a while. The idea of the Supreme Master infuriated Shaun, but he had to keep his emotions under control. Tomorrow was harvest day. He should be sedated by the eldritch pendant by now; he should be showing very little emotion, if any. He needed to be very careful.

He talked to Rachel about helping in the recycling unit and watched her face closely for a reaction, wondering if she knew he was referring to the tunnels. He wanted to find out how much she remembers about why they are there. "What was the best thing that happened yesterday?" he said.

"There were so many great moments yesterday. If I had to pick one, I would say being at the theater with you even though you slept most of the time. I missed you while you were working in the recycling section," she said with a smile.

"Do you know where my gemstones are?" He was taking a risk mentioning them, but he had to see if she remembered.

"Gemstones, what gemstones?"

His level of hope dropped. She didn't remember. "The little pouch of gemstones my mother gave me."

"I don't remember your mother," Rachel said with a puzzled look on her face. "Your parents died before we met, Shaun. Only my parents attended the wedding, and our friends in the college."

Shaun didn't know if she was making up her response or not, but Rachel seemed like she was living her made-up life story. "Rachel, do you recall when we met?"

"Of course, silly. We met after my service in the Israeli army, at Oxford. I fell in love with you the first time I saw you."

He searched her eyes, looking for her fire, but they were glassy and cold. He could see his own reflection. It frightened him to see her spirit suppressed. He had to restrain himself from picking her up and taking her down into the tunnels just to get the hell out of there. "I volunteered for the afternoon shift today, as well. Sorry. I thought I would catch a few hours of sleep before heading back to the recycling unit."

"You really have good work ethics, Shaun, something I

admire about you. I had so many things for us to do today, though," she said looking disappointed.

"How about after the harvest tomorrow? It'll be Saturday, and we can have the weekend together. We could ask Reis and Maria to babysit Ari."

"It sounds great! I'll ask Maria today," Rachel said, eating a strawberry.

Shaun handed Rachel Ari and kissed them both on the forehead. "I'll see you tonight."

He went into Ari's room and grabbed the gemstones from under the mattress and slipped them into his pocket. He had to be careful in the tunnels today. If anything happened, Rachel wasn't going to come running after him. He just hoped that during the harvest, she would remember what she had to do.

He reached for the door handle to leave the apartment. He paused and turned back to Rachel. "I just had a funny thought. Do you remember when we went riding on my brother's motorcycle?"

"Of course I do, we were on our honeymoon. We stayed at Casey's estate. Now stop asking so many questions, you have work to do!"

He smiled at her. She was still there. Just playing some game he didn't quite understand or like, but he was sure it had something to do with the Supreme Master watching over her.

Before he could open the door, there was a loud startling knock. Immediately, he glanced down at his chest, making sure he had his pendant on. He was jumpy today. He couldn't get the image of the leader's head changing out of his mind. Cautiously, he opened the door.

It was Geoff. "Good morning. Ready for work?" Geoff said, fiddling in the pocket of his pants. "Here, before I forget. I was told to give you these." Geoff handed Shaun a yellow plastic medicine bottle with a white lid.

Shaun unscrewed the plastic lid. Three tablets tumbled in his palm.

"Doc said the white tablets are magnesium, and the other is a super vitamin."

"Why do I need a vitamin and two magnesium tablets?" Shaun said.

"It's to prevent your muscles cramping."

Reversing back into the apartment, he grabbed a glass of water and took the pills. He smiled again at Rachel as he walked back out.

"Have we met?" Rachel asked Geoff.

Geoff looked unsure, as though he was waiting for some hint from Shaun as to what he should say. "Yes ma'am," he said.

"We met him on arrival," Shaun said.

"Oh, yes, that's right, I remember now."

25

Shaun flexed his jaw and clenched his teeth, heading for the elevator. For the first time, he paid attention to the bulkhead doorframes. In the event of an emergency, they would slide down within seconds and seal off the floor from the atrium. But what about the transparent ceiling above, would it hold? If Abraham had not shown him the layout of the city, he wouldn't have recognized them for what they were.

"Is it hot? Or is it just me? Do you think something is wrong with the air conditioning?" Shaun said.

"Seems normal to me," Geoff said.

"It's stuffy, and reeks like a crowded train. Don't you sometimes wish you could open a window and get some fresh air? Don't you find it claustrophobic down here?"

Geoff scratched his beard. "No, not really. Back home, it was cold, and the snow was thick, we couldn't go out for days," Geoff said, scratching his beard.

"Has anybody had a meltdown from being cooped up down here?" Shaun asked. "If not, I could be the first." He pulled at his collar, and untucked his shirt.

"One or two each month – mostly new arrivals. But they're quickly eliminated. Two days after my arrival, a man was shot during a reflection service in the worship hall. He removed his necklace and started calling the Supreme Master an alien, claiming the city was a giant spaceship. He demanded to be set free. I thought he was mad, why would he prefer to be outside? I thought he was a mad fool. I believed there was nothing but death outside, that the ancient Egyptian Ammit were waiting to eat your soul. I've seen them hunt people down, killing and eating whole families. It's terrible! But at least when you shoot them, they bleed and die. I thought being in here was the best option. Boy, was I wrong," he said, more to himself than Shaun. "We now realize the medical center segregates the sick and the elderly on arrival. My father and my older brother were sent to the back waiting room of the medical center."

"Yeah, I've seen it," Shaun said, listening intently.

"In the medical center my father and brother were lined up with a bunch of others who were old or sick." Geoff reached out and swiped his access card in front of the sensor again. "I haven't seen my father or brother since. Before the necklace had a stronghold on me, I asked Delilah, who worked in the administration section, to find out what section my dad and brother were assigned to. She checked the admission records on her computer. There was no record of them; they didn't exist. She told me it was best to drop it. Something in her eyes spoke to me, she wasn't like the rest. She had emotion in her eyes. Delilah invited me to join her for dinner to meet some of her friends."

There had been something bugging Shaun. There were no old people. The last old person he had seen was in the medical center when they arrived.

"If you haven't noticed, you have to be under the age of forty. I'm thirty-two. My brother was forty-one. Delilah and Abraham are forty-one. Luckily, they discovered the secret of the children a few months before their reassignment," he said, making air quotation marks. "That's what the soldiers call it, reassignment. It's murder, that's what is happening, murder!" Geoff said through clenched teeth.

"Maybe they're returned to the outside to fend for themselves," Shaun said, watching Geoff rapidly slapping his card over the elevator sensor.

"Let's hope so. But Gil asked the soldiers on the outside if they've seen people leave the city, and they haven't seen anyone leave, except soldiers wearing the pendants."

Shaun felt a tingle move over his chest. The stench in the lobby intensified. His ears were ringing. The color of his pendant intensified. Geoff's didn't seem to change. It didn't have the same outward glow or vapor.

"Geoff, should you be talking about this now?"

He is going to draw attention if he doesn't calm down, Shaun thought feeling his heart thumping.

A tremor, a wave of high-level static energy entered Shaun's body. A dreadful feeling washed over him, he couldn't help thinking something very bad was about to happen. A nervous sweat dampened his unshaven upper lip.

The elevator doors slid open. The tremors stopped. *Had he imagined them?*

Geoff widened his stance, bracing a hand against the wall of the lobby. Shaun studied the inside of the elevator. The back wall bulged and a reptilian face, covered in lesions, pushed out from the wall toward Shaun and sniffed. Its tentacle-like beard flickered in the air around him making his skin crawl. The tentacles turned into barbs.

Geoff quickly removed his hand from the wall and stepped away. He shook it as if he had been touched by something evil. Shaun blinked, the monster was gone and the elevator was empty. Shaun encouraged Geoff to move forward. "Get in before anything else happens," he said, pushing Geoff into the elevator.

With one hand Shaun held the doors open with his other he pressed it against his chest. The pendant sent shock waves of electricity into his heart. Shaun forced himself to look down the corridor. An apartment door opened ten feet away. Holding his chest Shaun let go of the doors and rapidly pushed the close door button afraid a hideous monster would exit the apartment. A woman stepped out. The sight of her gave him some comfort until she turned in his direction. She was pregnant and had the face of the monster. She turned her back to Shaun, waiting for someone else to exit the apartment. He doubled over as the pain in his chest increased. Her three-year-old son, Josh, rode out on his tricycle and headed down the corridor away from the elevator.

"That's far enough," she said to the toddler. "Now come back. You can go from here to there and no more. Okay?"

"Okay, mommy." Josh waved to Shaun.

"What's wrong?" Geoff said.

Shaun stepped back against the elevator wall. The doors shut before Shaun could return the wave or respond to Geoff. It was hard to breathe. Every breath was sharp. It was like he was continuously being stabbed with a stingray's barb. He dropped to his knees in pain.

"Hey, are you alright?" Geoff asked.

Shaun couldn't answer. He could feel the tentacles of the Supreme Master searching his most inner thoughts. He had to disengage from Geoff, he didn't want to so much as glance at Geoff, in case the Supreme Master could read his face and find out about ... Shaun focused on building a brick wall in his mind. He picked up a brick and used a spatula to scrape mortar from a wheelbarrow, slapping it onto the brick and laying it down, and continued to quickly complete his first row. He kept the focus on the next row and the next row until the brick wall became a strong barrier, and the Supreme Master couldn't see him. He used this same trick to block out the pain when his mother was dying. The memory of her passing was more painful than the electric shocks to his heart the Supreme Master had induced.

THE ENERGY RECOILED.

Shaun took in a big breath and straightened up. He zigzagged out of the elevator, stumbling. The muscles in his face released the tension caused by the pain. Entering the common area of the lower floor of the atrium, his expression was emotionless.

As soon as he entered the kitchen, he was roughly pulled aside by the head chef. "You need to get busy. You need to lighten the color."

"Wash your hands and keep washing them until I tell you to stop," the chef said.

Shaun did what he was told, grateful to be leaning against the sink. Pain traveled down the side of his head. He struggled to think straight. He was woozy and leaned heavily against the stainless steel sink. It was like he was drunk, or how he had felt as a kid after his dad had beaten him around the head with a shoe one time too many. He allowed the cool water to run over his wrists. The sensation was refreshing. Watching the water trailing over his wrist, he felt the energy of the Supreme Master step back and wait for a few seconds idling in the shadows of Shaun's memories. Shaun sighed. The Supreme Master moved out of his mind. Shaun vomited seawater into the sink, and his pendant returned to pale pink.

Geoff gave him a hand towel to dry his hands. "You're not in a good way."

"He'll be fine," the chef said. "Get him down to Abraham, and get that necklace off him."

Shaun stepped away from the sink. "What's happening to me?" he asked, drying his face and hands. He could hardly hold himself up. He had slowly allowed himself to care and feel when he had found Rachel again, but now, he was weak and vulnerable most of the time. Maybe he was better off without her.

"The Supreme Master is assessing you for the male contribution of the harvest. Now, stop asking so many questions while you're wearing that thing. No emotions remember. Got it?" chef said.

"What do you mean?" Shaun said as chef jostled him from the kitchen.

"Do you recall what the Supreme Master looked like at the service?"

"Yeah," Shaun said, nodding.

"After the harvest, there will be another service, and he will have a new human form, yours," Chef said, frowning at Geoff. "Get him downstairs now!"

Shaun wasn't sure what the cook meant. Something blurred his eyes. It was hard to focus. Gingerly taking the stairs, he said over his shoulder, "What does he mean, Geoff? Is the Supreme Master going to possess my body? Will I need an exorcism? I knew a priest; well, I think he was a priest. Doesn't matter, he died," Shaun said, laughing. "No need to be so rough!" He stumbled over the doorframe bumping into the soldier.

"Hey, it's you! I've meant to ask you something," said Shaun, sounding intoxicated. "What the hell is your name? Shorty shortass?" Shaun laughed at his own joke.

"What's wrong with you?" said the soldier.

"He's not himself. We've got to get the necklace off him," Geoff said.

"Do you want to know my secret?"

"It's the necklace," Geoff said.

"It was my old man who released the virus that caused the death of billions of people, including Rachel's father. He beat the shit out of me, so I beat the shit out of kids smaller than me. My soul's polluted, damned. I was so twisted with anger until I found Rachel again." He vomited.

"It's the influence of the Supreme Master."

"He sounds drunk," said the soldier.

"I think the Supreme Master has the hots for me. Or he is just suspicious. Something has captured his attention," he said, looking up at Geoff. "Mr. Blabbermouth here..."

"He definitely sounds drunk," said the soldier.

"I know, right? I sound like my dad," Shaun said. "He was a drunken fool!" he said, spitting the word *fool* in Geoff's face.

"He was fine when I picked him up. I don't like this. We need to get him to Delilah. He's losing it," Geoff said.

Shaun tried to push past Geoff to open the door. "I need to get back to Rachel and get out of this shithole. This whole place creeps me out." Shaun pushed Geoff and the soldier aside with new strength.

"My name is Yehuda," said the soldier, taking Shaun's necklace and putting it over his own head. "No more talking." Yehuda grabbed Shaun's arm and pulled it over his shoulder, partly carrying him along with Geoff to the next connecting sealed door. Abraham opened the connecting door from the other side as if expecting them. Yehuda hovered at the entrance, holding Shaun up with Geoff's help, and Abraham stepped aside for them to enter. The water-boy, Gil's son, Theo, was sitting on a top bunk reading a book to the little trike rider who liked to ride his bike up and down, up and down the rows of bunk beds. Yehuda removed Shaun's eldritch necklace from around his own neck and placed it over the younger boy's head, tucking it down under his shirt.

The boy patted his shirt and smiled up at Yehuda. "Is it the blue Angel's?"

Yehuda smiled back at the boy and said, "Yes."

Shaun collapsed to his hands and knees. "I must have the flu. A virus to end all viruses." He attempted to laugh. He wiped his mouth with the back of his hand. "I cannot drill today. I was fine until the elevator. Then, bam! It was like something reached inside me, examined my organs, one by one, then rifled through my mind."

"Geoff, give him two minutes," Abraham said, "then bring him through to the tunnel. Yehuda, get back to your post."

Shaun, struggling to his feet, accidentally pushed Geoff against the edge of the bunk beds.

"Sorry. What the hell were those tablets you gave me?" Shaun said. "Are you trying to poison me? To get my gemstones? You can have them. They've been nothing, but trouble."

"Give up the self-pity, Shaun, it's unbecoming. You're a man now, take some responsibility," Delilah said, stepping out from behind the gray curtain. Then Delilah whispered, "The Supreme Master has chosen you as the male offering. He will inject you with a toxin, to pacify you, so you will give yourself freely. We were afraid this might happen."

"Like pheromones?" Shaun said.

"I suppose, yes. Then he'll eat you from the inside out. He will assume your form for thirty days before he takes a new form at the next harvest. Each form lasts a moon cycle. While you are alive, he'll harvest your organs. By the end of the harvest, your skin will drop away from your bones like a onesie, and it will be the last thing he will take. He will slip into it like a glove. You'd better hope he doesn't skin you first and then eat you. It's horrendous. He has done that twice. There will be nothing left of you. Pray he goes for Rachel first, and she administers the lethal injection before he transforms and devours you," Delilah said.

Geoff no longer needed to hold him up. Delilah's words were sobering. Geoff entered the kitchen, leaving him with Delilah. He had been whining like a child. Tomorrow he would be served to the devil. Delilah held the curtain open, looked over her shoulder and said, "Oh, and Shaun, the magnesium is because you easily dehydrate while you are creating the photon laser. Give yourself a few minutes. Come have something to eat."

Shaun followed her into the kitchen. She tapped out the code on the handleless door and Abraham opened it. "Come on, let's get this show on the road before he croaks it," said Abraham.

"He's not ready yet," Delilah said, closing the door behind her.

"You'll be right in a few minutes," Geoff said. "Now that the eldritch pendant is off your neck, and when this is all over, you will feel a hell of a lot better. Everyone will."

"I hope so, because right now, I'm ready to die. Heart is racing like I've had half a dozen shocks from a defibrillator. I'm feverish, and I haven't even begun generating energy from the icosahedron to widen the tunnels."

"The what eye-saw-hedon?" Geoff said.

"Never mind that, sit," the elderly lady, who had the invisible crumbs on her apron, said to Shaun. She prepared a bowl of mashed boiled eggs with butter and salt. She poured a tall glass of freshly-squeezed orange juice. "This is all produced down here. Isn't it incredible? Absolutely incredible, isn't it?"

"How did you get down here? You're the oldest person I've seen in the city," Shaun said.

"My husband, God rest his soul, and I were here before the Supreme Master, and my husband showed me this unpopulated section of the underground city. This is where the work crew stayed during the construction period. He worked down here for years. As soon as they discovered the virus, they rushed to complete it, forgetting about this area. A lot of good men died, but they finished the underground city so others would survive. My husband was an incredible man. He was one of the original workers. He died for me to live," she said, crossing herself. "After the Leviathan and its eldritch system took control of the underground city, my husband refused the necklace. He saw how controlled the other men in his crew were – it turned them into emotionless, mindless robots. My husband was shot and killed. The last thing he said to me was to take off the necklace and hide. Nobody came looking until Abraham and Delilah showed up with a group of scared men and women with their children wearing the necklaces. Anyway, we'll have enough time to chat after all this business is over. You're our Blue Angel, and you've got a job to do, you and your marbles," she said, wiping down the front of her apron. "We're relying on you."

"Marbles?" The hairs stood up on the back of his neck. He felt a chill run through his chest.

"Yes, your little friend calls them magic marbles," she said. "Eat."

Shaun ate the eggs and drank the juice. He said nothing. *Was she talking about Alex?* Tears pooled in his eyes. He thought he was immune to tears. He kept his focus on the bottom of the cup of mashed eggs. Shaun got up without looking back and copied the pattern of knocking he had heard Delilah use to rap on the door a few minutes ago. A soldier he had never met opened the door for them.

He walked quietly beside Geoff and Abraham through to the warehouse. Before he entered, he could hear a beehive of activity and murmurs. There were perhaps over a hundred soldiers hunkered down at the back of the supply area, by the racks. They must have been descending all night.

"Is that the blue angel?" he heard someone whisper. He felt embarrassed and his face turned red. Shaun hurried past as someone patted him on the back. He didn't deserve this. He's never had to fight in muddy trenches, or put his life on the line to save others. These men were the heroes. He was here for a selfish reason. He was here for Rachel because he was afraid to lose her. *I'm not their Blue Angel, I'm an impostor,* he thought. Shaun took the hard hat with the light attached and put it on, hoping to conceal his presence. He had already stripped off his breeding zone whites and replaced them with filthy shorts and a soiled singlet. He would hate to work in the mines shoveling coal as an everyday job. *It's a tough gig,* he thought. Following Geoff and Abraham, he felt small and mortal.

Soldiers arriving from above passed him by.

"Only a few more will descend," Abraham said, looking over his hairy left shoulder at Shaun.

Shaun had trouble concentrating on what Abraham was saying.

"I have ordered them to wait until you open up this end of the tunnels. Maybe we can get a small truck load of soldiers down here afterward." Abraham waited for Shaun to fall into step with him. He slapped Shaun on the back. "You'll be right."

Groggy, Shaun tripped over some hoses on the way down the tunnel. Getting up, he saw the pipes running overhead. He couldn't take his eyes off them. His stomach somersaulted. He felt panicky and his stomach was full of jittering worms. He was jumpy, scared like a lost child.

"Geoff, wait up, something is wrong with these pipes," Shaun said.

Geoff stopped and waited.

"Abraham," Shaun shouted ahead, "has anyone checked these pipes."

Abraham didn't hear him and Shaun saw the man's pace quicken as he passed the junction where the cave had been sealed. *So it's true*, he thought.

"I told you, its just condensation," Geoff said.

There had been a lot of soldiers in the warehouse, preparing for tomorrow's takeover. No matter how well-executed tomorrow is, he will probably die. "Geoff, if anything happens to me, can you take care of Rachel? Make sure she is safe."

"Will do. Let's catch up to Abraham."

"We'll have the last man down in ten minutes," Abraham said, looking up into the hole that the ladder disappeared into. "We weren't sure if you were coming back, so we got as many soldiers down as we could. So, sit tight."

"So that's why you sent Geoff," said Shaun.

"You've got me pegged," Abraham said.

26

Shaun doubled back a little over half a mile until he reached the junction where the sealed cave was, and where he thought the pipe might be leaking. He followed the pipes down the unused side tunnel, tapping the pipes as he went, listening for a change in sound. They sounded dense, full. *Shouldn't these be empty?* A light was bobbing up and down, reflecting on the wall in front, as if someone was walking behind him. He assumed it was Geoff.

"Aren't these supposed to be empty? Does it mean someone has recently opened the valves to fill up the desalination tanks?" Shaun said. No one answered him. The light bounced off the walls and ceiling. Shaun quickly swiveled around, ready for a fight.

"What tanks?" Geoff said. "Come on, we have to get back."

"Answer me quicker next time, dammit." Shaun kept

following the pipes and he walked for another fifty meters before he heard water dripping into a pool.

"Shaun! Come back."

He ignored Geoff. He kept tapping the pipes. He ran a hand along the cold belly of the pipe. He stepped into a puddle, stopped and looked down at his feet. He tasted the droplets of water on his fingertip. It was salty. The pipes were wide enough for two men to scuba dive shoulder to shoulder out to the ocean, or for a great white, or any other ocean creature for that matter, to pass through the pipes. The overall size of the pipes couldn't fit the Supreme Master in his natural form, but if he can change into a man, then he can surely change into a man with gills, or a shark, octopus, or sting-ray.

He strained his ears, listening. There was a difference in the sound in this part of the tunnel, it had a hollow tone. It wasn't insulated, the bedrock maybe wasn't so thick. He knew he was sensing, more than he was hearing. The constant rhythm of water splashing was coming from further ahead. Suddenly, he saw his helmet's light shimmering on the floor before he waded into a cold body of water. The droplets couldn't have made a pool this size.

"There is a leak down here! Get Abraham." Shaun kept inspecting the pipes, advancing further until the water was up to his waist and the pipe disappeared into the wall. Dozens of trickles had merged into a steady stream cascading down the rock face into the pool.

Geoff caught up with Shaun and stopped at the edge of the water. "What's happening?"

Shaun touched the muddy wall and rubbed the mud between his fingers. "It's leaking on the other side of this wall."

He generated energy from the crystal in his pocket to make an opening big enough to inspect the damaged part of the pipe. A cool peppermint sensation traveled through his veins, restoring every cell in his body, and he released the energy through the fingertips touching the wall.

"I don't think that's a good idea," Geoff said.

Shaun could hear by the sound of Geoff's voice, that he was backing away.

A hole in the wall expanded to the width of his hand. Shaun peeked in. A pipe had buckled, and the metal had expanded; long, thin parallel cracks scarred the pipes. He could smell the ocean. There was more than a busted pipe on the other side. Water gushed from the hole Shaun had created. He clapped his other hand over the hole. "Geoff, run!"

The wall partly crumbled below his waist, knocking him off his feet, pinning him under the water. Glowing with power, Shaun pushed the energy out and burst up from under the rocks and water. He moved quickly and was on Geoff's heels when he heard the wall behind him give way. Shaun had unintentionally opened the floodgates.

"Close the bulkhead doors to the supply room," Geoff yelled as he ran. He was a big fellow and was struggling as the water rose around his ankles.

The soldiers could drown if they didn't lower the bulkhead doors. Shaun had no idea how much water was behind him, but the sound was like the wave he saw in his dream. The ocean had risen over time in the sea caves, and the only thing holding it back was that precarious wall.

Abraham and a couple of men were in the opposite direction, waiting for the last few soldiers to descend. *I must warn them.* Shaun sprinted as fast as he could, the water splashing around his ankles. He couldn't bear to think about Rachel being left alone to defeat the Leviathan on her own. His curiosity had sealed their fate. He would never see Rachel again. It made him furious.

Geoff, out of breath, running and yelling, "Lower the doors, activate the bulkhead doors. Now!"

"Abraham, get out of the tunnel – ascend!" The water rose up to Shaun's knees.

The force of the water knocked Geoff over. It pounded Shaun into the ground, and it was just like the tidal wave he saw in his dream. He tumbled along the ground headfirst. His helmet was washed off. The water jostled him from left to right, but then suddenly he couldn't feel the ground or a single drop of water. He wasn't gagging on salty water or struggling for air. It was like he was in a dream, floating in a cloud. A transparent blue shield surrounded his body. The gushing water had risen to the height of the passageway and was about to flood from the junction into the main tunnel.

Geoff banged up against him. Shaun grabbed hold of his bulky frame and latched onto him. Geoff hung on. Shaun expanded the shield creating an orb to enclose Geoff who was out of breath. He gasped in air as the sphere stretched around his head and body.

Shaun found his feet and they dragged along the floor for a

second or two before he could gain traction. He pulled Geoff up as best he could.

"Pull everyone into the shield. We've got to get ahead of the water and warn the others." He strengthened and thickened the outer shell of the hermetic shield. He magnified the energy from the oscillating sapphire and the water swirled over and around the sphere, he was no longer being forced forward by the torrents of water. Shaun and Geoff ran toward the bulkhead doors. Abraham, two Resistance workers, and five soldiers were running a hundred yards in front of them.

The bulkhead doors were closed, trapping Abraham, the workers and the recently descended soldiers. The water raced toward them, knocking them off their feet. Shaun and Geoff could do nothing while the water was above their heads. The powerful surge was crashing into Abraham and the men slamming them against the bulkhead doors. Shaun and Geoff were seconds behind. Shaun reached for one man, Geoff reached out for Abraham and pulled him into the sphere. Shaun pushed the man behind him then grabbed two soldiers. Geoff and Abraham grabbed the other workers. Shaun focused his energy on expanding the shield out to protect them all from drowning, while Geoff and Abraham continued to haul in the men.

Abraham shouted, "Increase the size of your bubble until the edge touches the walls! Create a barrier, a solid wall, Shaun, and drive the water back."

Three bodies floated in the water: two soldiers and the water boy, Gil's son Theo.

Shaun reached out for Theo with one hand. He was so close, he could almost touch him. He needed to keep one hand up to channel the energy from the icosahedron into the surrounding sphere, which he was quickly turning into a massive wall. He pushed his hand through the sphere one more time, reaching further into the water, and Theo lifelessly smacked up against Shaun's blue luminous wall. Shaun grabbed for Theo's skinny arm. It was warm. Shaun yanked the boy in through the wall of the blue shield. A soldier worked on Theo straight away, compressing his chest and blowing air periodically into his mouth.

"Geoff. Over there," Shaun said, indicating with a jerk of his head. "I have to concentrate on building the energy to hold back the water." Shaun pushed more energy into the wall as Geoff reached out again and grabbed for the soldier's jacket as he bounced against the shield. Abraham and the others tried to help him, but it was too late. The water rocked back and swept him away.

"Focus on the integrity of the shield, Shaun. Push that goddam water back where it came from," Abraham said.

Sounds of coughing and choking were coming from behind him, and Shaun glanced over his shoulder. Water spilled out the side of Theo's mouth as the soldier turned him on his side. The boy coughed some more.

"Take it easy, son, you will be all right. You're a tough young lad," the soldier said to Theo.

Geoff and the men braced themselves against the bulkhead door. The soldier picked up Theo. Shaun discharged a mammoth blinding blast of crystal blue energy and forced back the torrents of water. His arms stretched wide; he felt exhilarated as his body surged with power. He held the ocean water back and pushed it down the tunnel as he walked forward. Most of the water went down the tunnel toward the shaft and ladders. He stopped at the junction to seal the passageway.

The sphere kept the water at bay. Shaun had his left hand out in front to maintain the shield and he pushed the energy from his right hand. A blue laser exited from his hand in a spiral and drilled through the dense water to the ceiling. The laser beam sliced through the rock, causing an avalanche over the entrance to the passageway at the junction that led to the cave. They looked through the water; the rocks piled on top of each other in slow motion, creating a barrier, sealing the passageway, once again, from the main tunnel. Shaun released another burst of energy that spiraled through the water and fused the compounded pile of rocks together. But there was still a lot of displaced water in the main tunnel and once it hit the back wall near the ascending ladders, the force would drive the water back at them.

He turned to Abraham. "Do you think the rock fall will hold that passage?" Shaun said, shaking.

"Yes, I think it'll hold," Abraham said. "What the hell happened?"

"There was a leak and a cave-in. Are you sure it'll hold? I can't tell," Shaun said uncertainly.

"There's only one way to find out," Abraham said.

Geoff looked at Shaun. "Collapse the shield."

"What, are you crazy?"

The soldier repositioned his hold on Theo, ready for the unforeseen.

"All the water in the main tunnel that I've pushed down

beyond the junction is up to the roof. It's only held back by the shield. It'll surge toward us again," Shaun said.

"We have to try or this will ruin our plans," said Abraham.

"Water is down to the ascending ladder, it's flooded," Abraham said. "Yes, the water will surge back this way when the shield drops. It will be deep, but we can work with that?" He spoke to the soldiers. "We can use the water. We can use it to cool the melted rock after Shaun widens each section. If we swim to the first rung of ladders and climb to the top where you started yesterday, you can work your way downward. We can have most of this section drained before you're ready to join up with this lower section," Abraham said.

"We will need more manpower, a pump, and hoses, from the warehouse behind that bulkhead door," Geoff said.

"One problem at a time," Abraham replied.

Shaun prepared himself to reel in the energy and drop the shield quickly. *Here goes nothing.*

"WAIT! Reduce it slowly. If it doesn't hold, it will still protect us. If it does, it will reduce the force of the surge. We should huddle up against each other." Geoff suggested.

The soldier adjusted the boy's weight in his arms. They all huddled together.

"On my count, reduce the shield, slowly, slowly. He's right," said Abraham, "it will reduce the force of the surge dramatically. ONE!"

Shaun readied himself. *What if it doesn't work and I lose control of the whole shield? I'll need to re-establish it super quick to at least protect Theo and the soldier.* Shaun stood closer to them.

"TWO!"

He didn't like the responsibility. The countdown made him nervous. *If Kevin can start up a plane stalled in mid-flight, I can create a hermetic shield underwater.* "Hold on to each other. Get ready to hold your breath if this doesn't work, and I must reconstruct the shield super quick."

"THREE!"

"Yes! Thank Christ for that," Geoff said.

The shield was holding with every inch, as Shaun slowly reduced the size.

27

Slowly, they were being poisoned by carbon dioxide. It was like being inside a giant plastic bag as the air was being sucked out. Geoff mopped his brow and looked like he would pass out. They huddled together, back to back, six men and Theo – standing room only. The integrity of the hermetic shield was stable. The water was settling beyond the blue energy, just above Shaun's waistline, but Shaun's strength was waning. His outstretched arms were heavy. He moved his neck from left to right, up and down to ease the tension in his muscles. It was pointless. He gave up and let his head drop forward. It was becoming difficult to keep channeling the life force of the icosahedron.

Abraham wiped his brow and put his hand on the soldier's arm. "Does your radio work?"

"Yes, sir, what's your plan?"

Abraham, squashed up against Shaun's back, twisted his

head around to face Shaun. His breath was hot and stale. Shaun turned his head slightly away.

"How are you holding up, Shaun?" Abraham said, panting. "Expand the shield one more time from floor to ceiling, wall to wall, and encompass the bulkhead doorway, so those on the other side can open up. We need more men and equipment. Can you do that, Shaun? Can you drive the water back to give us twenty feet, or so?"

It would be difficult, but Shaun would not quit now. Theo was on the edge of passing out. "Yeah, I can do it. Just tell me when," Shaun said, panting.

"And we need oxygen," said Geoff.

"We'll radio ahead for them to prepare the equipment. We'll step out and catch our breath. Do you think we can we re-enter the sphere on our own?" Abraham said to Shaun.

"No, it's a hermetic shield. I must pull you in," Shaun said.

"Get on the radio," Abraham said to the soldier. "Tell them what we need, and to be ready to open the bulkhead doors partly on our command. And get someone standing by with oxygen for Shaun. And for all of us." He stopped for a moment, trying to catch his breath.

"Shaun, you'll have to pull the first man through the shield, and then he can reach out for everyone else," Abraham said. "Make sure you expand the parameters of the shield enough to accommodate two rafts. We'll use them to get back to the end of the tunnel. We'll use a pump to pump this seawater to cool off the bedrock in each new section you create."

"Well, that sounds easy enough," Shaun said, sarcastically. His muscles ached. He was out of breath and gulped the CO_2.

He wanted to lower his arms and sleep. Everyone was sleepy. Maybe if he held the stone in his hand, the energy wouldn't have to travel through every atom of his body before being expelled through his hands. Maybe he need not keep his arms up, but he dared not to put them down. He was afraid the shield would collapse, drowning them; or worse, that it would definitely wrap around them and suffocate them all. He didn't want to be responsible for Theo's death. When this is all over, if Shaun made it out alive, he will practice and find out what the gemstones can do when it's not a matter of life and death.

"I can do it." He kept his focus on the tunnel of water in front of him. His mind was playing tricks, and he felt like he was in Disneyland on the ride, It's a Small World. He blinked his eyes. Focus, dammit!

"Whenever you're ready, Shaun." Abraham's speech was slurred.

Okay, let's do this. He tuned the power of the icosahedron, generating a greater force, and the tiny reactor's speed increased in his pocket, releasing scintillating energy. The continuous steady flow of light around him amplified, shooting through his body, down his arms and out of his hands. He upped the ante even more and pushed the shield outward, driving the water back. Immediately, the shield expanded and collided with the ceiling and walls. His ears were ringing, it was difficult to hear. "How big do you need it?" Shaun stepped forward, driving the water toward the ceiling. His vision was blurring. He blinked rapidly, trying to focus. He bent his head to his shoulder and whipped his eyes and face from side to side. The salt in his sweat was stinging his eyes.

Abraham was holding Geoff up. "That's perfect, Shaun."

The soldier was on the radio, and the door slowly cranked open. From the radio, Shaun heard the utterance of blue and angel and thought he must tell them to stop calling him that. He stayed focused on expanding the shield away from the doorway. He wondered if Doron and Cowan had been playing with a football when the bulkhead doors slammed closed. Shaun glanced over his shoulder. The radiating heat from Abraham's and Geoff's body was gone. The soldier with Theo was the first to step from the shield and into the safety of the warehouse. Then Geoff, Abraham and the two others left Shaun alone within the energy field. He turned his head back to the front and stared at the water, half expecting the Leviathan to be hiding behind the wall of water like in his dream. Keep it steady, he told himself.

"Where's that oxygen?" Silver stars sparkled in the water. He looked back over his shoulder to see two teams of soldiers holding military, black motorized inflated boats. A soldier reached out and touched the hermetic shield and was knocked off his feet as if he had touched an electrified fence. The next soldier stepped up. Shaun reached out with one arm and took a firm grip on the next soldier's forearm. The soldier went rigid, paralyzed with static energy. Shaun waited for the current to earth, then yanked the man forward through the shield. Shaken, the man moved quickly to secure an oxygen mask to Shaun's face. Shaun greedily breathed in the fresh air.

"Slow it down," the soldier demanded. "I'm Eitan Jacobs. Slow down your breathing, or you will pass out and we'll be in trouble."

Shaun calmed his breathing.

"That's better. You're doing well. How the hell are you doing it?" He shook his head in amazement and left Shaun with the oxygen.

The next few minutes, while they brought in the rafts and soldiers, seemed like forever. The bulkhead door was being lowered. A raft nudged him in the back.

Eitan started to put a harness around Shaun's waist. "You're weakened. This is so we don't lose you when the shield drops and the water crashes down around us. Do you understand?"

"Yeah," Shaun said.

"Then I want you to climb into the raft. Can you lower your arms?"

What would happen if he dropped both arms, would the shield come down, too? It would stay up, he decided. He just had to consciously project the energy outward like before, but he didn't want to take any chances. If only he had had time to practice, he wouldn't feel so impotent. "I'm afraid to," Shaun admitted to Eitan. He felt the hard rubber tip of the boat against him. Gingerly, he made his way to the side of the raft with Eitan's guidance. Shaun kept his arms out, maintaining the shield. He sat down on the edge of the boat. His legs were like jelly as he lifted his right leg up, then his left over the thick edge of the black rubber craft and climbed in.

They shut the bulkhead doors. The men in the boat were holding on to the sides, ready for him to reel in the energy and drop the shield.

"Make it quick," said Eitan.

The men looked like special ops, dressed in black fatigues.

Shaun wondered if Geoff and Abraham were among the men in the boats. Probably not, he thought, they had looked exhausted. He dropped his arms. The shield stayed in place. He felt like a loser for a few seconds, then, like a magnet, he drew in the icosahedron energy. Shaun was a mass of blue light, hidden behind the recoiling light that was traveling through his body into the tiny reactor. The shield disappeared.

The water surged forward, pushing the boats up against the bulkhead doors. A tower of water pounded down on top of the rubber boats. It bounced Shaun out of the raft into the churning water and he felt the harness around his waist go taut. It was like being at the bottom of a waterfall, the water kept pushing him under. Eitan hauled him over the edge of the violently tossing raft while the deep green water settled into the surrounding space. The raft rose up to the ceiling and dropped slowly as the water rhythmically rocked and became calmer.

He noticed the second boat was carrying a crate with the pump and hoses. Shaun continued to glow as the oscillations of the crystal in his pocket slowed down.

Shaun rested against the side of the raft while a medic tried to check his vitals and give him a round of injections. The needle for the first injection broke. The medic had to wait for Shaun to stop glowing before he could complete his assessment. He could smell the rubber and tasted the seawater. He welcomed the opportunity to rest.

Then he spotted Geoff and Abraham traveling on the second raft with the equipment. They gave him a casual salute as their boat took the lead and raced toward the ladders, the first point of ascension.

28

Boat one had arrived first and two soldiers were climbing to the first platform when Shaun's boat arrived. Shaun was dreading the long climb up. Eitan and two men from Shaun's craft jumped into the water to help Geoff and Abraham who were preparing to hoist the crate with the pump and hoses up the supply shaft.

Shaun continued to rest against the side of the raft while the medic put another IV in his arm. "What's in the bag today?"

"The final cocktail to get you back on your feet in the next fifteen minutes," the medic said. "You'll be right as rain soon enough. We'll just float here and let the others do the heavy lifting."

They dropped cables from above. Eitan and his men reached for the hooks on the end of the cables and fastened them to the middle ring of the harness around the wooden crate. There were two other separate cables dangling down into the supply shaft. Two soldiers secured the cables to the harnesses around their torso. Simultaneously, they were hoisted up by the two soldiers who had gone ahead.

"How is he doing?" Eitan asked the medic.

The medic removed the cuff from Shaun's arm after checking him for the second time and said, "His vitals are good. I'll just remove the IV, he's had twenty minutes. He's ready, sir."

"Good to go!" Shaun's arms were dead weight. He didn't think he could climb up to the fifth landing.

"Put these fatigues on, they will help regulate your body temperature," Eitan said, tossing Shaun a waterproof duffel bag.

Shaun undid the clips and unrolled the top of the bag and pulled out the fatigues. He struggled with the long-sleeved black compression top and pants and getting his boots back on without falling off the boat. He thought he looked like a Navy Seal, but certainly didn't feel like it. Eitan helped him put the harness back on.

"You ready?" Eitan gave him the thumbs-up waiting for his response.

Despite feeling like crap, he returned the thumbs-up. "Ready, Eitan."

"I need you to wade to the opening of the supply shaft, but don't enter the shaft until we get the all clear from above. It would be a disaster if the cables lifting the equipment broke," Eitan said. "Be careful when you stand up in the raft."

"Thanks, you really know how to generate a sense of security!" Shaun slid over the side of the black edge and joined Eitan in the water. He drew in a sudden deep breath. The water was chilly.

Eitan waded ahead of him and grabbed the cable. "I will connect this to your harness. Hold here when they raise you."

"What for?"

"It will take some pressure off your jewels. Otherwise, it will hurt when the cable tightens." Eitan slapped him on the back and looped the rope through the rings of the harness. He spoke into the radio, and they lifted Shaun out of the water.

It was dark inside the shaft. He could see the lights from below and above. He created his own blue iridescent light from the sapphire and felt energized. From below, he heard Eitan call out, "He's glowing and flying like a blue angel."

I hate being called an angel. It sounds so cheesy.

It took minutes to reach the fifth landing. Shaun unhooked himself from the cable and helped to hoist up the medic and Eitan and Abraham – not that they needed the help. The two soldiers who had been first up to the fifth landing slid down the cable and stayed with Geoff, who had remained below to make sure nothing happened to the hoses and boats. They activated the pump, and the hoses snapped to attention ready to cool off each new section Shaun carved into the bedrock with his laser beam and so expanding the laddered shafts into sloping tunnels wide enough to drive a jeep on.

The clock was ticking. He kept working, channeling the blue laser beam. His body radiated light like a super nebula.

"More of an angle, Shaun!" Abraham shouted at him. "We don't want a giant slippery slide."

Shaun changed his trajectory and burrowed into the

bedrock, creating a moderately curved descending tunnel that joined the upper level with the lower level. It was like a subway winding down from the surface to the main tunnel and Geoff below.

The soldiers followed closely behind Shaun, cooling off each section by pumping the water from below. Steam trailed behind him as he worked on each section. He imagined the series of tunnels looked like a giant ant farm. Shaun pulled back on the energy slightly as he neared the last section and Geoff and the soldier. He didn't want to blow them out of the water or incinerate them with the laser beam.

It surprised Shaun to see how low the water was now. It was below his shin. He stepped in a raft and rested. For a few minutes, while the others took a break and assessed his handiwork, Shaun lay in the boat and thought about tomorrow night's harvest.

"Come on, let's get this over and done with," Geoff said, lightly slapping the leg dangling over the edge of the boat. The black ops suit was helping Shaun, because he wasn't as sore as yesterday. He drank the cocktail of electrolytes from the medic and went back to work. He drew on the icosahedron sapphire and blasted the energy along the walls to widen the tunnel. He walked in the middle, with the others behind him cooling each section. Passing the junction, the retaining wall he created out of an avalanche of rock, he felt there was something about the tunnel making him uncomfortable and curious. *It's nearly over,* he thought nearing the bulkhead doors.

Tomorrow morning, with Rachel, he can drive a jeep through the tunnel, out to the sunlight. He touched the smooth, ethereal blue walls of the tunnel as they hissed with steam and were cooled. They were like a polished diamond and appeared as mysterious as an underwater glacier. He couldn't believe what he had created. He was having a rare moment of thinking that he had done good. Soon the people of the city will no longer be under the control of the eldritch stones and the Leviathan. They will soon be free.

"Nice work, Shaun," Eitan said.

"It's a challenge. I have to work hard to control the energy so as not to disintegrate everyone around me. I don't think I'll have to expel that much energy at once ever again," Shaun said looking at the puddles of water that would eventually dry up.

Eitan took the risk and slapped him on the back. "Probably not."

"Raise the doors," Eitan said into the radio, and they raised the bulkhead doors.

The soldiers walking behind, with the boats on their shoulders, caught up to Shaun and as they passed, they patted him on the back or shoulder saying, "Nice job, Tekhelet Malak."

"What does that mean?" Shaun asked Eitan.

"Blue Angel."

"Before you leave, Shaun, I want you, Geoff and the officers to meet me in the map room," Abraham said. "We'll go over the plan for tomorrow before we all hunker down for the evening,"

Evening, Shaun thought. Surely it had only been a few hours, and now only early afternoon. "What's the time?" he said to Eitan as they entered the map room.

Eitan squeezed into the room and joined the other officers. "Just after five."

"Listen up, everyone," Abraham said to the soldiers packed into the room. "The next time we see Shaun, we will need to save his ass. He is the male chosen one, for the harvest," Abraham said.

There were murmurs among the men.

"Man, you just can't catch a break," Eitan said to Shaun.

"They will take him to the Leviathan's private rooms at the back of the breeding facility. We will enter the Primus suite from floor seventy-six once we have secured Zone seven, six and five. The others will continue moving up the towers and secure the zones above the dome."

"Let's pray the mission is successful, and Shaun is in his skin and alive when we get to him," Abraham said.

"Just take care of Rachel." Shaun could barely hold himself up. Without the life force from the sapphire, he was weary. He just wanted this over. Whatever they had injected him with was keeping him on his feet, but he could do with a top-up. The review of the plan was taking longer than he liked. He wobbled and regained his composure. He was standing among vigorous men ready for action, and he didn't want to look weak. These were the last moments of preparation, and they needed to get it right. He listened diligently as Eitan, Abraham, and the officers discussed how they would execute the plan: who would infiltrate Tower A, Tower B, and the atrium, and who would take down the Supreme Master after Rachel poisons him. It all sounded good, almost too good. He had to be ready for the unexpected; he had to be ready to save Rachel.

It was up to Rachel and the soldiers now.

Doron brought in a wooden box with handles and placed it

in the middle of the table. Eitan gave Doron a nod of permission to open the box. Doron started handing out eldritch stones. Geoff refused and moved away from the box.

"It's okay," Eitan said to Shaun. "They're fakes."

"I already have one," Geoff said to Shaun.

Shaun took the fake pendant. *That's why Geoff's pendant hadn't changed in the elevator. It was fake!*

They gave everyone in the meeting a fake eldritch necklace before they left the map room. Shaun headed in the opposite direction with Geoff. In the kitchen, the old lady, like clockwork, was preparing freshly-squeezed orange juice to go with the egg and lettuce sandwiches that she made just for Shaun. She made him feel special. He sat and talked with her and shared half his sandwich with Geoff.

"What is your name?" Shaun asked, realizing he didn't know.

"Everyone calls me Mama Bina. Next time I see you it will be when my granddaughter, Leah, is free."

THE LITTLE BOY WEARING SHAUN'S ELDRITCH NECKLACE HANDED it over to him. He gave Shaun a hug. Each hug reminded him of Alex. Did all children start off so innocently? Did he? He couldn't remember ever being like that. Well, maybe before his mother died, but never after. Shaun walked through the series of bulkhead doors to the recycling area and climbed the metal stairs back to the restaurant kitchen. The weight of the necklace was suffocating, and he couldn't wait to take the hideous thing off and put on the fake one. He passed through the atrium and said a non-emotional goodbye to Geoff at the elevator. He had to blend in. No emotions. It was incredible how much emotion we express through body language. He had to make conscious decisions not to look down, or walk fast, and not to frown or smile. Even his posture had an attitude. He dropped his shoulders and rode the elevator in silence, wondering when he could put on the fake necklace. His reflection in the polished doors stared back at him. He looked as clean as a whistle, but underneath the clean white garments, he felt filthy, and under his skin, he felt the hideous sensation of the tentacles of the eldritch stone seeping into his being.

The more times he took it off, the more he despised and loathed the Supreme Master.

29

Shaun called out to Rachel as the door locked behind him, though he knew the apartment was empty. He had hoped Ari would be there to relieve him of the burden of the necklace. Shaun didn't want to go through another one of the Supreme Master's violating assessments. He wished Rachel and Ari would return soon. Maybe they had gone to dinner without him, but it was a little early for dinner. They rarely ate until after seven. He would have to wear the necklace in the shower.

Shaun quickly showered and lay on the couch facing the apartment door. He waited vigilantly for Rachel and Ari to return. He fell into a deep sleep and dreamed of being in a cocoon again, trying to break free, when, suddenly, he felt like he was floating above Casey's house back in England.

He had drifted off and when he woke, he could've sworn he had visited Casey and Sophia. The dream had felt so real. Casey needed help, and so did Kevin. There was a knock at the door. "No way!" he muttered. He opened the door, half expecting Casey.

It was the administrator carrying a neat pile of clothes and shower wash. She handed him the pile. "Congratulations. You are officially chosen by the Supreme Master to be the male counterpart at the harvest. Tomorrow at half six, you must scrub your skin for ten minutes with this liquid, rinse off in the shower, then dry yourself with a fresh towel before putting on these special garments. You will need to present yourself to his private rooms five minutes after the evening candles have been lit." The woman walked away.

Barefoot, Shaun stepped out into the hall and watched her walk down the corridor. The elevator from the atrium dinged, drawing his attention away from the disappearing administrator. He had to be careful not to look suspicious. Rachel walked out of the elevator with Ari on her hip. He relaxed at the sight of them. Rachel looked good. She is playing the mother well – she's kind, caring, gentle and attentive to Ari – but she still had a non-emotional, robotic demeanor, like ninety percent of the people. She and everyone else were being programmed. He had known the first time he saw her that she was the girl for him, and he could not imagine life without her. He *had* to kill the Supreme Master.

"Are you out here waiting for us? You look exhausted," Rachel said. "I'm terrible."

She didn't look like she felt terrible. She looked like she didn't even know what the word meant anymore.

"I've been having such a wonderful day. I've met so many wonderful people that have told me nothing but good things about the harvest tomorrow night. So many of them said I am blessed. I was blessed the day I met you, Shaun."

"How can you say that?" Shaun said. "The day you met me, you lost your father."

"That was no fault of yours," Rachel said.

"Tomorrow at harvest. Do you know what will happen to Ari? Where will he go?"

"He will be with Sergeant Reis Levin's wife, Maria. She has volunteered and she will take very good care of him. After harvest, we will meet for dinner, and she will bring Ari," Rachel said in a matter-of-fact tone.

"Do you remember how long they said it would take?" Shaun said.

"They said that the Supreme Master's window of opportunity is during twilight. The women light the celebration candles and say the harvest prayers," she said.

The stone in her eldritch necklace deepened. "You will be fine. Maria will choose you."

Her stone's color was making him nervous. He tried to speak without emotion. He wanted to tell her about his experience in the elevator this morning. "I too have been chosen by the Supreme Master. I am to be the male counterpart of the harvest."

"What? What do you mean?" Rachel looked dumbfounded.

"The women today didn't tell you?" Shaun said.

"No. Tell me what?"

"It's good. It's an honor," he said directly to the pendant.

"I can't wait. Something tells me that this will be a very positive thing. Things will change tomorrow for us, I just know it,"

Rachel said, hugging him. Her eldritch stone faded to a soft pink. The Supreme Master had backed away.

"Go freshen up for dinner. I'll look after Ari," Shaun said.

"Yes, of course," she said, handing Ari to him.

Shaun put his necklace around Ari's neck. Instantly, he had a sense of loss. He missed the fiery Rachel. He missed the heated arguments. She was melancholic rather than full of unbridled energy, and there was no passion. He felt his heart physically ache. "We have to just get through the next twenty-four hours, buddy, and we'll have good old Rachel back, then we can get out of here," Shaun said to Ari. "How does that sound?"

DURING THE DAY OF HARVEST, RACHEL WAS DRIFTING FURTHER away. They strolled in the park with Ari, they visited the artifact museum, had a drink in the bar at lunchtime, and they even went to the theater again. Shaun couldn't wait for the candle lighting and the harvest to begin. The endless waiting was making him agitated. Rachel ran into a woman she had met the day before, and they agreed to have coffee. Shaun bowed out politely. He said he would take Ari back to the apartment, feed him, and put him down for a nap.

He tucked the necklace into Ari's nappy. While Ari slept, Shaun toyed with his icosahedron sapphire and played with the energy. He lost track of time. Two hours had passed, when he suddenly heard Rachel opening the front door to the apartment. Quickly, he put away his gemstones and took back his necklace.

"Did you have a good nap?" she asked him.

"Yes, Ari and I just woke up," he said.

"Oh, Shaun, you let him sleep for too long. He will be up all night." She picked Ari up and kissed his cheek. Ari wriggled excitedly in her arms.

"I'll just change his nappy and then go scrub up for the harvest," Shaun said, taking Ari from her. He noticed that she no longer took off her necklace.

Shaun peeled off the nappy and moved back as Ari let one go. Shaun quickly threw a nappy over the spray of urine and waited for Ari to finish. "You reek. How much urine can a little guy your size make?" Shaun said undressing Ari. He took Ari into the bathroom and gave the baby a quick wash under the shower.

"Rachel, can you come get Ari," he called from the bathroom.

Rachel took the towel off the rail and wrapped it around Ari and left the room. Shaun stripped off and stepped into the shower with the special stuff he had to clean himself with for the harvest. He squeezed the white plastic bottle and green goo poured into his open palm. "You've got to be kidding me!" he said to his eldritch pendant.

Reluctantly, he washed his body with the green slime courtesy of the Supreme Master.

273

30

While Rachel finished up in the bathroom Shaun switched his eldritch necklace for the fake one.

There was a thump at the door. They were here. Thump thump. This is it. He took in a deep breath. He looked back at Ari, wondering if he should take the real necklace back before opening the door.

"Showtime, Ari."

Ari started screaming. "Shh! Not now, buddy, you've been so good. Shh, it's okay. Shh." Shaun rocked Ari in his capsule. The person thumped the door harder.

Rachel, ready for the harvest, walked from the bathroom and opened the apartment door. It was too late to put the real eldritch necklace back on. He was wearing the fake, and he just hoped to god they won't notice.

"Have you both followed the instructions and washed in the special solution?" the administrator said.

Shaun wanted to ask if the wash was like a garnish to make him more palatable to the Supreme Master, but with a straight face, he said, "Yes, and I smell like seaweed." He kept rocking Ari, trying to get him to calm down.

"How do I look?" Rachel said.

"Wonderful," Shaun said. She, too, has lime-green special garments, but she truly was radiant. Whispers of a black haze trailed around the outside of her body and Shaun tried not to act startled. It was also around the administrator. So, maybe that's why Ari is crying, Shaun thought, he senses the dark energy.

"Hopefully, for your sake, you please the Supreme Master," said the administrator. "I will escort you to the Supreme Master's private rooms."

"What about the candle lighting?" Rachel said. Shaun looked at her sideways as he continued to rock Ari.

The administrator tilted her head inquisitively at Rachel. "Are you all right?"

"Yes, it's just a tremendous honor. I thought it was the woman's duty to light a candle, to purify her spirit and to say the harvest prayers." Rachel was avoiding eye contact with Shaun. She picked up Ari's bag and busied herself packing nappies and bottles. She zipped up the bag and faced the administrator, while Shaun picked up the capsule with Ari in it.

"Not this time," the administrator said. "We have excused you. And I have instructions to carry out, so let's go."

"WHY DON'T WE JUST WALK AROUND TO THE MAIN ENTRANCE OF the Primus? It's on this level," Shaun said, pointing away from the elevator as they waited in the lobby.

"I'm to take you to the private entrance, via the medical floor."

Shaun saw Geoff exit the elevator below them. He was walking toward the fountain in the atrium with a woman Shaun recognized as a Resistance soldier. More soldiers than usual stood at ease at strategic locations wearing the red eldritch necklaces. He just hoped they were wearing the fake necklaces ready for the takeover. Shaun was hot, his palm wet with sweat. He shifted Ari from one hand to the other, aware of Ari's weight as he gripped the handle of the capsule. He saw Eitan patrolling the park. As if sensing his presence, Eitan looked up and Shaun could have sworn he tilted his head to the side in acknowledgment. Suddenly, a woman rushed out of the elevator as the doors opened and accidentally bumped into Rachel. They fumbled, trying to help each other collect their belongings from the ground before apologizing without emotion and moving on.

Rachel stepped inside the elevator first. Shaun followed with the administrator on his tail. The administrator pushed the button for seventy-five.

The doors opened on the medical floor. Maria was outside the doors waiting for them. She quickly took the baby capsule. "I will take good care of him, don't worry. We will meet you afterward for supper," she said.

They walked to the Primus suite's private internal elevator and went down to the breeding rooms. *At least we'll be together until this is over*, Shaun thought, relaxing a little in the belief that he and Rachel would see this through together. Once they entered the private room, he would take off her pendant.

On exiting the private internal elevator, Shaun expected to move toward the atrium, which was at the front of the suite, where everyone had gathered during the induction. But as soon as they stepped out, a woman and a man wearing the pink eldritch pendants were waiting.

"Please go with your escorts," the administrator said.

The escorts stood blocking the way to the main entrance and atrium, forcing them down toward a dead-end.

"We're supposed to go to the front," Shaun said, looking back. The administrator was still standing at the elevator as if frozen in time. "Where are you taking us?"

The dead-end was an illusion. It was a T-intersection. The hallway continued in both directions.

From behind, the male escort placed his hand on Shaun's shoulder and gently guided him to the right. Rachel's female escort ushered her to the left. Shaun glanced over his shoulder. Rachel was being led down the hallway in the opposite direction, and she didn't look back.

"Wait!" Shaun said. "The Supreme Master has called for both of us."

The male escort was close behind him. "Yes, that is correct, but you still need to enter his private rooms via separate entrances. The male donor enters on the right and the female donor from the left. You will be processed separately."

Shaun shoved his hand in his pocket and touched the icosahedron sapphire to get his emotions under control. He wanted to grab the guy's hand on his shoulder and break it. Anger, fear and defiance were bubbling to the surface, and he felt like exploding. He didn't know how much longer he could contain himself and not ignite the power of the sapphire.

Shaun felt the man's breath as he spoke. "It's all about the energy. The coupling can only happen through the Supreme Master."

Shaun recognized nothing in his surroundings. There was nothing familiar from what he remembered of the induction tour. There was no one else around. It was bizarre.

They hadn't walked far when the male escort stopped Shaun abruptly. He glanced down the passageway and saw Rachel also had stopped. Shaun took his hands from his pockets and nervously rubbed them together. He was standing in front of a door, and he assumed Rachel was too. The male escort turned and stood next to the door and faced Shaun.

"You need to go in on your own."

Shaun watched Rachel step forward and disappear. "Do I knock?"

"No," the escort said, unlocking the door.

31

The ceiling was at least twenty foot high. A narrow metal staircase spiraled up to a mezzanine level. Shaun tilted his head back. There was a bed and a built-in aquarium that stretched the length of the whole back mezzanine wall. Shaun felt his heart skip a beat. He took a step back, away from the mezzanine. It was like the ocean was on the other side of the glass. He thought he saw a shark. How could anyone sleep with those predators lurking? It was freaky, but he wanted a closer look.

There was a bar directly next to him with four stools. Shaun took in his surroundings as he walked across the porcelain tiles that covered the entire ground floor. He stopped in the middle of the suite. Through the use of furniture and rugs, four different areas were defined: under the mezzanine there was a decked-out games area; a bar area was by the entrance; a library and reading area off to his right, with bookshelves; and a lounge area in the middle of the room. He browsed the gaming section. The smart television was impressive; there were miked-up headphones, lounge chairs, ancient pinball machines. He pressed the buttons along the sides of the latter, and the flippers banged loudly in the silent room. On the pool table, the balls were set ready for a game. He wondered if the boy who had been removed from the chapel on Shaun's first night had come here and used the games room. *Probably not.* Shaun aggressively rolled the white ball scattering the colored balls across the table. He walked around the perimeter of the room and dragged his hands along the bookshelves and leather reading chairs on the right side of the room.

Shaun looked up to the mezzanine level. He couldn't resist going upstairs any longer. He climbed the stairs two at a time. The aquarium was impressive. Shaun realized that lying on the king-size bed would give a spectacular view of the underwater emporium, so he dropped onto the bed and watched a shark swimming toward him. It banged its nose against the glass. Jellyfish hovered, and stingrays glided through the clear water. Fish in a variety of colors scattered like an exploding rainbow. An alligator was swimming up behind the shark. *Oh, no way, it's an Ammit.* Shaun couldn't help but watch as the Ammit attacked the shark from behind. It swallowed the shark's tail before its elongated jaws clamped down on the shark's back, biting it in half. Shaun jumped up from the bed. The jellyfish and stingrays were hidden by the bloodied water. As the blood drifted and diluted, a sinking dark object came into view. It was the shark's head. Shaun searched for the Ammit. *Where did it go?*

He scanned the four areas downstairs in case the Leviathan was waiting in the shadows. He couldn't see anyone. Despite the plush and cleanliness of the apartment, it smelled of rotting fish. He noticed there was something different in the middle of the bookshelves. A glint of light was reflecting off metal. There was a connecting door on the far side of the room where the reading chairs were. He moved over there and saw a band of light coming from underneath a door. They had camouflaged the door, blending it into the wall of the bookshelves. There was a brass door handle, which he pushed down and outward. It was locked. He lightly tapped on it, hoping Rachel was on the other side. "Rachel, are you in there? Rachel, can you hear me?" Shaun pushed his ear against the door trying to hear any sounds from the next room.

"Shaun, I'm here. Are you okay?" Rachel whispered.

She sounded slightly worried, rushing her words, struggling to keep her voice free of emotions.

"Are you still wearing your necklace?" Shaun asked.

"Remember the woman who bumped into me? When I bent down, she slipped a small package wrapped in tissue paper into my hand. She said to open it when I was alone. I did, and it was another pendant with a note. I changed the pendants like the note said, and my head is clearing."

Shaun turned the brass handle and pushed against the door with his shoulder. It wouldn't budge. There was no key in the lock. "Rachel, is there a key on your side? Can you unlock the door?"

"There's no key or door handle," Rachel said.

Shaun thought about what the absence of a door handle

meant: the Supreme Master would have to enter the female room from the male side, so he will come for Shaun first. Once he had finished harvesting the male donor's organs, he would transition. He will become the mirror image of the new host, me, and only then will he pass through the connecting door to the female donor. Rachel will think the Supreme Master is me and give herself to him. He will come for me first. Abraham and Delilah were wrong.

"The Supreme Master will come for me first. Get out of here, Rachel. Remember why you came. Get to the Lion's Gate and find your family. Leave here, take them back to the portal, back to Casey's estate." He relaxed against the door, knowing what he needed to do. "I love you, Rachel."

"What the hell! Don't say that now! Shaun! Open this door, or I'll bust it down."

The sound of her fiery passion fueled him. Rachel shouted up against the door, "What do you mean, he is coming for you?"

"Rachel, listen to me. Did the woman give you anything else? Did anybody give you anything today?" He felt a new sense of calm as he waited for her to answer. The shadow moved under the door as she moved about the room. She had to have the serum for him to destroy the Leviathan. "Rachel, what are you doing?"

A small yellow envelope poked out from under the door. Shaun reached down and opened it. It held a small vial containing an orange solution, with a note.

"Where were you hiding that?" Shaun asked.

"I wasn't. It was on the table with my name on it when I arrived. I thought it was instructions. When the woman handed me the small parcel with the fake eldritch necklace, she said there would be an envelope, and I should open it. I was foggy from the eldritch necklace when she said it, but I've started to sober up. That's when I noticed the envelope on the side table. Shaun..."

Shaun read the message: *We are indebted to you, thank you. Squirt three or more drops into a drink for the Supreme Master. Three drops should be enough to kill an elephant, so don't worry if you don't get enough time to use it all. Plan B, use the syringe.*

"Where's the syringe? Rachel, where's the syringe?"

Rachel's shadow moved away from the door again. "Hurry, he could be here any second." The adrenaline was pumping. "Come on!"

Rachel pushed another envelope under the door. This one contained a syringe.

"I had already placed it under the pillow," she said.

"This monster will not sit down and have a drink with me, Rachel. I must stab him with the syringe first chance I get."

"Appeal to its ego. He'll be in human form. Mix a drink, Shaun, just in case."

"The harvest is not about mating and conserving eggs for future generations, Rachel. He will harvest our organs. Your ovaries are probably like caviar to him. We're food, Rachel. We're food!"

Shaun looked over his shoulder toward the bar and decided to mix a drink. It couldn't hurt. He couldn't imagine the Supreme Master drinking alcohol. *What the hell am I going to do?* Frantically he searched the cabinet and cupboards. There was a blender and a shaker. *Great,* he thought sarcastically, *so I can make a cocktail.* He opened the refrigerator and found kale, seaweed, and jars of what looked like human organs: hearts, lungs, livers, kidneys and entrails. He unscrewed the jar with the liver, it smelled of blood. *This is more like it.* Shaun mixed the seaweed, liver, and some intestine juice in a blender and poured it into a small shot glass. He squeezed the contents of the vial into the drink and stirred. He poured himself an enormous glass of water to keep himself hydrated.

32

Putting down the empty glass on the counter, he heard a thud from behind him. A door had opened and closed. His first thought was Rachel had somehow opened the connecting door, but the sound did not come from the side where Rachel was. There was a foul smell of rotting flesh and the energy in the room intensified. He didn't want to turn around. He hadn't found any other doors. The fake necklace projected beta waves so the Supreme Master would think they were sleeping. An elongated shadow darkened the bar. Shaun put his hand in his pocket and held the syringe ready to attack.

Composed, he picked up the shot glass and pivoted around to face the Supreme Master. He tried not to stare. The skin on the Supreme Master's arms was moist, translucent, sagging as if the bones and muscles were dissolving at a rapid pace. He looked frail. It surprised Shaun just how much the Supreme Master's human form had deteriorated in a few days. His overbearing personality during the welcoming service hasn't diminished; he was still taller than an average man. He had stretched the human flesh beyond its original host's size. Shaun understood now why it needed a donor, a new body each month. There wasn't much of the previous donor left. The actual form of the Leviathan was breaking through the human flesh, and the human flesh was falling off to the ground.

Shaun stepped forward carefully and offered the poisonous drink. "I found your private stash of seaweed and liver and added a dash of entrails. It looks like you could use a few nutrients. Your skin looks soggy. Been soaking in the bath too long perhaps? It looks like you haven't put your skin on properly. Maybe I should turn around while you fix yourself up?" Shaun enjoyed being a smartass – it energized him. He had missed being a smartass.

"Was that you?" Shaun asked, pointing up to the mezzanine level. "Take some time to put your game face on, I'll wait, I'm not going anywhere."

It took the drink with a hand that was no longer human. The skin was peeling back and dropping off to the floor, exposing wet slimy stumps of fingers that reminded him of slugs. Claws broke free from the knuckles. His authentic form was breaking free from its human constraints at a sped-up pace.

Shaun stepped back, keeping his distance, waiting to see what it would do. He didn't know if it was enough of a human form for the poison to work.

In a garbled voice, the beast bellowed, "PROSTRATE YOURSELF BEFORE ME!" It was difficult to understand. It took seconds for Shaun to interpret the words.

"NOW!" it screamed. Its eyes were bulging from their sockets.

Shaun looked up, keeping eye contact, and bent to his knees to kneel on the floor. He was eyeballing the drink as the Supreme Master knocked it back in one satisfying gulp. Shaun relaxed, expecting the poison to take hold. He stood up defiantly. The Supreme Master delivered a blow to the side of his head that knocked him straight back down to the floor. Before Shaun could move, the Supreme Master was on his back, pinning his face and shoulders to the floor. Its claws were digging into his head and neck. Skin fell from its arm, dropping onto the side of Shaun's face. Shaun didn't know if the poison would have enough time to work. The note didn't specify how long it would take.

"Get off me!" Shaun wrestled to free the hand that was holding the syringe. A sticky, reptilian claw-hand wrapped around his neck. The Leviathan was lifting him up off the ground. The toes of Shaun's shoes dragged along the slippery floor, hooking clumps of bloodied human skin. He dangled off the floor, staring into the hideous face of the Leviathan. It reminded him of the first time he saw a reindeer shedding velvet. It was terrible to see the red velvet falling from the antlers looking like blood trailing down the side of the reindeer's face. He had been five years old, and it was the only memory he had of a holiday to Canada with his mom and dad before she got sick. They said the reindeer was in no pain, but he never believed it. The Leviathan had completely transformed, and Shaun hoped it *was* in pain, big-time!

It no longer looked frail. Shaun was dwarfed by its shadow.

It was slightly unsteady, or Shaun was imagining it. The Leviathan held Shaun up to its face. Its breath stunk of rotting shrimp, its beard was a mass of wriggling tentacles that stretched out and covered Shaun's face. He tried to peel them off and away from his mouth. The Leviathan stabbed Shaun in the side and Shaun screamed. The tentacles tightened their grip over his mouth. Its claw, like a serrated knife, dragged up the side of Shaun's back. He cried out in excruciating pain. The blood soaking into his green shirt was warm. The Leviathan rammed its claw into his opened side as if trying to pick out his kidney. Shaun's cries were muffled by the suffocating tentacles, but still Rachel heard his pain.

Rachel violently banged against the hidden door, scream-ing. The Leviathan, amused by Rachel's emotional outburst, turned toward the door and laughed unnaturally. Shaun lashed out at the clawed hand around his neck with the syringe and punctured the back of the reptilian hand. He pushed down on the plunger, injecting the concentrated poison into the Leviathan. He prayed it was a lethal dose. Holding his breath and his mouth shut as the slimy tentacles tried to force their way into his mouth, Shaun choked, trying to draw in air. He felt like the caterpillar in his dream, trying to break free. *Where the hell is Eitan, Abraham, with the soldiers?* He wished they would burst through the door and shoot this asshole because the potion and the injection didn't seem to have any noticeable consequences.

The tentacles retracted from his face. The clawed hand around his neck opened, dropping him to the floor. Shaun coughed, gasping for air. Pieces of bloody skin surrounded him.

He clenched his side. The blood was leaking down into his pants. He focused on the icosahedron sapphire and ignited the energy from the stone.

The Leviathan picked him up like a rag doll and threw him across the room. He crashed into the bookshelves and fell to the floor.

"Do you treat all your guests like this?" Shaun said, coughing blood. He wiped his mouth with his forearm. The pain in his back was unbearable. *I could use some duct tape*, he thought. He might die, but he wouldn't go without a fight. He just needed to focus and channel the energy into a hermetic orb around himself. But the pain was so distracting he couldn't focus.

"What have you done with the eldritch necklaces?" the Leviathan said. His throat still sounded garbled. It picked him off the ground again. It came at him and pulled back the flap of skin on his back where its claw had opened him up.

"Arrrrgh!" Shaun fell to the floor. He was going to black out. "What are you serving for dinner?" Shaun said on the edge of consciousness. "Let me guess, kidneys? I think I'll pass, I'm a vegetarian."

The Leviathan tore the necklace from Shaun's neck and crushed it in his hand.

"Hey, that was pewter." The life was draining from Shaun. He wished Abraham would hurry and storm into the room. He didn't know how much longer he would live. He struggled to his feet and felt a surge of energy course through his veins from the gemstone that was spinning like a tiny reactor inside his pocket. The blue light was being expelled from his being.

Shaun had trouble hearing and understanding the garbled voice of the Leviathan. While ranting, it struck out at Shaun sending him crashing over the bar, knocking the blender to the ground. The Leviathan stumbled a few steps backward. It roared. The poison was finally kicking in. Its tentacles opened up like a flower, releasing a hideous stench and a terrifying scream. It reached over the bar, grabbed Shaun and threw him over to the other side of the room. Shaun landed on his back on the pool table.

Within seconds, the growing Leviathan pinned him down on top of the pool table with one clawed hand and tapped his clawed finger down on Shaun's sternum, dragging it down his stomach. But the claw didn't penetrate the hermetic shield that had formed and Shaun never felt a thing. The magic of the icosahedron sapphire was greater than the Leviathan's.

The blue shield tightly wrapped around Shaun, putting pressure on his wound, holding him together. Darkness was closing in, and his blood pressure was dropping. He had to finish the Leviathan off while it was off-guard, bewildered by the poison.

Unable to slice Shaun open, the Leviathan roared in his face and flipped the pool table. Shaun rolled off the table before he ended underneath it and scrambled to the stairs. He was glowing like a star as he pulled himself up the spiral staircase.

The thin blue hermetic shield thickened and deepened in color as energy poured into it. Up on the mezzanine level, Shaun dug his hand into his pocket and grabbed the stone. In his clenched fist, he felt the stone burrow into his hand. Shaun exploded with energy, releasing expanded magic bolts of electrifying energy at the Leviathan from above. It burned through the reptilian skin that stood nearly eight foot tall now, and it was still growing. Shaun felt the stone go sonic in his hand. It was crazy. The pain in his hand distracted him from the pain in his back. He opened his hand, and the stone had borrowed into his palm. They were now one. He threw the expanded energy bolts of lightning again and again, pushing at the Leviathan as it reached out for him. Within three strides it was up and over the security wire on the mezzanine. Hunched over, it advanced toward Shaun. With only a bed between them, Shaun exploded with energy from his entire body knocking the Leviathan back against the mezzanine security wire railing. It banged its head on the ceiling, its tentacles reaching out for Shaun as it crashed through the rail over the side to the tiled floor below, hitting its head on the stair railing on its way down.

Shaun could hear Rachel banging on the connecting door, cursing the Leviathan. He could swear she would kick the door down. That's the Rachel he knew.

The Leviathan got back up on its feet and let out a roar that cracked the glass of the aquarium. "Prostate yourself before me!"

Shaun stood his ground. The Leviathan was wider and uglier. It was little effort for it to reach up and knock Shaun off the mezzanine. He went flying over the stairs into the bar stools. The Leviathan turned to Shaun and kicked him and the stools across the room. Shaun struck the hidden door, though there was no pain from the impact; the shield held, protecting him. Scrambling to his feet he charged at the Leviathan. Jumping up and off the leather chairs he threw himself over the stair rails and raced up the stairs only to throw himself over the edge and onto the Leviathan's head, blasting its head with photonic power-balls. The Leviathan's claws and tentacles picked Shaun off its head. Shaun was only making it angrier, and it tossed him aside, up onto the mezzanine with such force Shaun hit the glass wall of the Aquarium and heard it cracking. Two sharks head-butted the glass.

The Leviathan looked up and laughed at Shaun, and derived pleasure at the sight of the sharks. It started moving toward the connecting door again. It was going after Rachel. Shaun jumped off the mezzanine onto its back, grabbing a fistful of its slimy tentacle-beard with his left hand, and power punched into its skull with his right hand. The Leviathan peeled Shaun off, tossing him like a bug. He crashed into the giant television and lay on the splintered screen for a few seconds, waiting for his vision to return.

Water spilled over the edge of the mezzanine. His vision turned to sparkles and cleared. Shaun staggered over to the exit and climbed up onto the bar and fired a concentrated continuous solid energy beam at the Leviathan, pinning it against the far bookshelves. Shaun's heart was racing with adrenaline. One knee buckled, but he regained his composure. The Leviathan pushed back the energy, knocking him off the bar. Shaun looked up, and there was a hole in the wall behind him. He stood up and pumped both fists at the monster. Shaun staggered, and his sight kept going black as he continued to lose blood.

The room shook. Shaun covered his ears as wood and stone showered around him. Bullets sailed past him and ricocheted off the hermetic shield. The door to the Leviathan's private rooms had exploded open, and soldiers stormed into the room. Rapid gunfire shredded the furniture. Shaun scurried across the room and hid behind the overturned pool table and hoped it was made from slate.

Abraham and his son Doron rushed into the room. The Leviathan lanced Doron through the chest with its claw. The Leviathan flicked Doron off to the floor. A few men grabbed Doron, pulling him backward out of the room.

Shaun couldn't stand by and watch the men being crushed like ants. No matter how weak he was, he had to die trying. Shaun stood up. Soldiers continued to enter the room with guns blazing. Bullets had no effect on the Leviathan's reptilian hide. The Leviathan used his claw like a sword piercing three soldiers at once. Everything was happening too fast. Shaun stood in front of the soldiers and expanded the shield to protect them. He yelled at them to back out. He would lure the beast into the atrium. The men took refuge behind the hermetic shield and backed out of the room.

Shaun cast the energy like a web around the Leviathan and lassoed it around its ankles. He heaved it off its feet. The Leviathan's head crashed through the wall, knocking out the secret connecting door. Rachel was only inches away from the Leviathan's head. Eitan came up behind Rachel and pulled her away. The life-force from the icosahedron embedded in his hand spiraled outward, strengthening his hold on the Leviathan. Shaun dragged the nine-foot beast out of the room and blasted his way down the hallway, out of the Primus suite's main entrance.

He had the Leviathan wrapped up like a spider's prey, although it kept struggling to sit up. Shaun jumped off the balcony and dropped ten floors toward the waterfall in the atrium below. He jolted to a stop three floors from the ground, dangling in midair. He looked up just as the Leviathan toppled over the edge, breaking free from the bindings. Shaun fell three floors landing hard in the bushes next to the waterfall. The Leviathan had doubled in size, and was falling toward him. He had no time to do anything but register he was about to be squashed like a bug. He wanted to yell for the bulkhead doors to be closed, sealing him in the atrium with the monster, but they were already in motion. Shaun could hear the torrents of water before he saw it. The aquarium glass wall must have exploded. The water, sharks, and every other sea creature the tank had caged, along with the Leviathan, tumbled toward him. It was a moment that seemed to last forever.

Numb, Shaun couldn't feel the physical weight of the Leviathan as it struggled to right itself. It broke free from the energy web completely. If it wasn't for the shield, he would already be dead. Dizzy, Shaun blinked and thought he blacked out for a microsecond, because he couldn't remember the monster landing on him. He mustered all the power from the icosahedron, and the blue energy around him intensified, expanding, turning white with power. Shaun held onto the power until he felt it would go atomic. Sparkles of brilliant white light behind Shaun's eyes intensified, as he let go, and the energy exploded outward from his body. It clapped like thunder as the energy went atomic, a blinding light filling the atrium. Shaun was peaceful at its nucleus.

The light consumed the Leviathan. Shaun couldn't see beyond the light. He needed to gain control of the energy and reel it back in before he destroyed the entire city. He could smell the park was on fire and as the gathered energy came toward him, the light diminished and the trees were set on fire. The energy flickered, and licked against the bulkhead walls like lightning. Pieces of what he assumed were burning fat fell from above. The dome had held. He had given everything he had. The Leviathan was dead. It had been a bloodbath and the blood dripping off the bulkhead security panels was a reminder of it.

Lying on his back, fatigued beyond anything he'd ever experienced, Shaun floated on the water that had cascaded from the aquarium above before they activated the bulkhead doors. Shaun felt peaceful, waiting for everything to settle. Everyone in the facility was free. Rachel would be free to find her family. They were all free. There was nothing more he needed to do. Shaun reeled in the remaining energy, closed his eyes and saw the cocoon from his dreams. He was a glory of color, wings expanding as he emerged from the confines of the cocoon and flew into a blue sky.

33

The familiar rhythmic beeping sounds of hospital machines brought back memories of his childhood fears. He was afraid to open his eyes, afraid he was lying next to his dying mother with his head resting on her chest. He waited for the rise and fall of her chest.

His body ached, but against his body were cool and fresh, crisp white sheets. He felt the bottom of the bed with his feet. He was tall, and he was an adult. *Rachel.* He opened his eyes, and light glared off the white walls forcing him to close them again. Reopening his eyes carefully, he tilted his head to the side. He smiled – Rachel was asleep in a comfy hospital chair. Eitan was standing by her, grinning down at him. Eitan bounced Ari in his arms while Ari tried to pull Eitan's neatly trimmed beard. Ari was giggling.

"Take it easy, Shaun. How are you doing?" Eitan said.

"I've been better. Is it dead?"

"Yes, thanks to you. And Shaun, thanks for taking care of my nephew."

Shaun looked at Eitan, then at Ari and recognized a similarity between them. They were family. "The woman in the car..."

"Was my sister, Carla," Eitan said. "Rachel told me what happened. I am so grateful you and Rachel saved Ari." Eitan took Ari's chubby fingers away from his mouth as he talked.

Shaun slowly pushed himself up into a sitting position. "What's his actual name?"

"Ari. Save your strength."

"Really? That's crazy," Shaun said.

"Why?"

"We didn't know his name. Rachel named him after her father." Shaun felt guilty about that.

"You've just about finished your last pint of blood. I assume you will leave for the Lion's Gate as soon as you can get out of bed."

"You've got that right. How is Abraham's son doing?" At the sound of Shaun's voice, Ari turned and stretched out his soft arms.

"You up for cuddles?" Eitan said wrestling to keep Ari from falling on top of Shaun.

Shaun pushed himself further into a sitting position, and the pain was bearable. Ari fell into his arms. Shaun kissed him on the head and held him tight. *It's only been four days, but it's like I've known him for years.*

Ari laid his head down on Shaun's shoulder and fell asleep while they talked quietly so as not to wake Rachel. "I suppose you're going to want to keep Ari with you?" Shaun's arm slowly became numb from holding Ari, but he didn't want to let him go.

"I talked to Rachel and she told me you two are willing to raise Ari as your own, but I think my sister would have wanted him to be with me."

"I understand. We'll never forget him." Shaun pumped his fist and turned his hand around. His skin had grown around the edges of the icosahedron sapphire as it nestled in the palm of his hand. It felt smooth and cool to touch. In a bizarre way, it looked like it belonged. He glanced up at Eitan.

"The doc said he can cut that out for you."

The stone was dormant, just a smooth polished jewel. He remembered the sapphire burrowing into his hand, but he couldn't remember if it caused him pain. The icosahedron sapphire was embedded in place in the palm of his hand. Shaun curled his fingers and touched the stone with his fingertips. He stared at Rachel, sleeping. He didn't want the power to be in his hand. What if he lost control and blasted a power-ball at someone he loved? "Can you get the doctor, Eitan? I need to have this removed."

Shaun let his head drop back on to the pillow. He watched Rachel and Ari sleeping. They were beautiful. He thought of his father when his mother had been alive. He wished things could have been different. Shaun had vowed if he ever became a father, he would never drink, hit, or emotionally abuse his son.

The doctor, wearing a dark blue operating gown, entered the room. Eitan took Ari from Shaun. "The good news is, you're alive," the doctor said. "The bad news, you're minus a kidney and you lost a lot of blood. We've replaced the blood, but not the kidney." The doctor shone a light to test Shaun's pupils for a reaction.

Rachel opened her eyes and gave Shaun a warm, gentle smile that filled her eyes and face.

"Technically, you died on the operating table for forty-two seconds. No smoking, no vaping, no soft drink, and reduce salt intake. Drink plenty of water, and you'll be fine," the doctor said, rolling Shaun onto his side to check the wound dressing.

"Arrrgh!" Shaun screamed through clenched teeth.

"You have a few stitches, thirty-six to be precise, courtesy of the Leviathan. I'll take them out in about seven to ten days."

Recalling the sensation of the Leviathan's claw dragging along his side and slicing him open, Shaun shivered. He wasn't going to be around that long. Callie can take them out back at the estate because once he enters the portal membrane, he will be healed, and the stitches will probably fall out or dissolve anyway.

"We've given you antibiotics in case of infection. The area will be numb for a few more hours, but once the local anesthetic wears off, you will know about it. Tell us before your pain reaches a three out of ten; we need to stay on top of it. It's harder to manage pain, the longer you leave it. We'll give you something to take the edge off for a few days only, painkillers can be addictive."

Shaun clenched his fist around the stone. He opened his palm and held his hand up to the doctor. "Can you remove this? It's too much power for anyone to have in the palm of their hand."

Rachel leaned forward and rubbed his shoulder.

"I have a few more soldiers to operate on. I'll take it out tomorrow afternoon, if that's what you want. Like it or not, Shaun, the way your skin is cradling that gemstone, I'd have said God intended for you, and it, to be one."

"I don't think I can be trusted with that much power."

"Everything will be okay, Shaun," Rachel said, pushing his hair back.

"How do you know?" Shaun said, taking her hand in his.

"Because we have each other."

A nurse walked into the room and whispered something to the doctor. "I have to go. If you want that removed, I'll do it tomorrow afternoon." The doctor left the room in a hurry.

"It's probably better in your hand then someone else's," Eitan said. "Anyway, you're the blue angel."

A male nurse wheeled a blood pressure machine into the room, walked it around to Shaun's left side, and wrapped the cuff around his upper arm. He nodded his head and smiled at Shaun. "It's an honor."

Shaun didn't know what to say or do. He smiled and clenched his fist around the stone.

"Can you glow whenever you choose?" the male nurse asked, pumping up the cuff and taking Shaun's temperature.

"Yeah, I think so," Shaun said, considering the idea.

The nurse cleared his throat. "You're a superhero, you know that? You're a bona fide superhero. Debriefing lectures have already started for those that were under the influence of the eldritch necklaces. We're all still dazed, but damn! The stories about the blue angel are right up there. You're a superhero in my book."

"It was a team effort. It's the military and the Resistance you should thank," he said, looking at Rachel. "We just showed up at the right time to help. And I think now it's time for us to go."

"You need to give your body time to heal," the male nurse said.

"Once I'm back with my friends, my body will heal in seconds. You think I'm a superhero, you should meet my friends."

A nurse popped her head in the room. "You're needed in room seven."

The male nurse quickly removed the cuff. "I'm sure we'd welcome any of your friends," the nurse said as he rushed from the room.

"Where are the eldritch necklaces?" Shaun asked Eitan.

"They're locked up in the artifacts room in a lead vault. We still haven't worked out how to destroy them. The metal is unfamiliar to the scientists; it's possible it's not from Earth. We're hoping, when you're well enough, you could blast the hell out of the eldritch necklaces, turn them to dust. The colored stones are lifeless. None are pulsating, but you never know, right? Best to get rid of them."

"Yeah, no worries," Shaun said.

"Just to let you know, the facility is under the joint control of the military and the Resistance."

Shaun watched Ari play with Eitan's dog tags. He would miss Ari, but they had to get to the Lion's Gate and find Rachel's family and get back to the portal before the pain in his back became unbearable. It was now the fourth day, and they had less than six hours to meet Kevin.

"I'll be back in a few minutes. I have to check on something. Can you mind Ari one more time, Rachel?"

"Definitely, but I can't promise we'll be here when you get back," Rachel said, taking Ari.

Eitan kissed Rachel on the cheek. "I won't be long."

Maybe the icosahedron sapphire should stay in his palm for now. He hadn't had a lot of practice with it, or a chance to understand its power or how to control it. He didn't understand its capabilities or the potential of the other nine stones, but he knew they came to him for a reason. If the other gemstones had even a hint of what the icosahedron sapphire had, he must learn how to use them properly, respect their power and protect them.

"Where are my gemstones?" Shaun sat upright, suddenly realizing he had nothing more than a gown on.

Rachel pushed him back down onto the pillows with one hand. "Relax, they're safe. I took them. I had them locked up in one of those bank vaults."

Shaun frowned confused. "Why did you do that?"

"The whole pouch was glowing. They worried me, I was concerned they might explode."

"What?" Shaun moved to the side of the bed and pulled out the intravenous fluid line. "I need clothes," he said to Rachel.

"I knew you wouldn't stay in bed for long," Geoff said, walking into the room with a clean set of clothes: dark blue tactical cargo pants, a blue t-shirt, a leather jacket and a pair of black military boots. He handed him his bowie knife, then gave Rachel's to her.

"Where did you find these?" Rachel asked, sitting Ari in her chair while she stood and strapped her blade holster around her waist. "That's so much better."

She was wearing the same outfit Geoff had given him, but he thought she looked way more sexy.

"I've organized a four-wheel drive for you and Rachel to get to the Lion's Gate. It's ready whenever you are. I've taken the liberty to pack a few supplies, including some painkillers," Geoff said, dropping the duffel bag on the floor. "It will take us seven and a half hours to get there from here, then another twelve hours to get you back to your meeting place in Jerusalem."

"What's the time?"

"Zero six hundred," Geoff said.

"We don't have that much time. We've got six hours, at best," he said to Geoff.

Walking back into the room with Reis and Maria, Eitan said, "Nineteen hours bouncing around in a four-wheel drive after losing a kidney is a long time."

Reis fist-pumped Shaun's left hand – he must have known the sapphire was in his right – then gave him a man hug and kissed his cheek. His wife was next. She looked different in everyday clothes.

"Thanks for trusting me with your secret," Geoff said. "I'd like to say that your secret is safe with me, but I think everybody in the city knows by now. You're a mystical angel sent to save us. With or without your crystals, Shaun, you are a bright light in this world, don't ever forget it. Anything you need, I'm here for you. Abraham is with Delilah, and they're got their hands full. They asked me to tell you that if you want to stick around, which they doubt, there's a place here for you and Rachel."

"Thanks, Geoff, and you're welcome to come with us. Once we find Rachel's family, we'll be heading back to Casey's estate, and you are welcome to tag along if you like. Hopefully our portal friend will wait for us."

"Why don't you join us?" Abraham said, walking into the rooms. "Find Rachel's family, go get your friends, and bring everyone here to this amazing city. We can clean up this world together."

"I'll think about it," Shaun said. The local anesthetic was already wearing off. Each time he leaned forward, a huge, acute pain radiated through the left side of his back. He couldn't help thinking it was the Leviathan's claw all over again. "How's Doron?"

"He'll be fine. He has a punctured lung. He was lucky. We lost a lot of good men, but it would have been worse if you hadn't protected them like you did and killed that beast." Abraham was swallowing his emotions. "I can't stand around and chitchat, I've got work to do. We've confirmed the sorting room is the entrance to a spacecraft. The scientists are ecstatic, they have a lot of questions that they want answers to. They believe it's been there for thousands of years. Well done, Shaun. I'll see you around maybe." Abraham did not wait for a response. Shaun watched him rush off down the hall.

Reis kissed Maria. He fist pumped Shaun's hand again,

kissed his cheek, and kissed Rachel's cheek. "Something tells me I won't see you two again, or at least not for a long time. Take care of each other." Reis followed Abraham out of the room and down the hall.

Shaun went to get out of bed when the old woman with the invisible crumbs, Mama Bina, walked in with Administrator Helen. Shaun automatically grabbed at his chest for his eldritch necklace – at the sight of her, his heart raced.

Mama Bina was carrying a food tray. "This is my daughter, Leah," she said with a proud smile. "You need to eat." She put the tray on a side trolley.

"You said your name was Helen," Rachel said.

"Sorry, have we met?" Leah said in a very soft, meek voice.

"No, I don't think we have," Rachel said.

"I only came to thank you," Mama Bina said. "Thank you, Tekhelet Malak." She rubbed Shaun's forearm and departed.

With Rachel's help, Shaun sat on the edge of the bed and changed out of his gown into the clothes. "Get that four-wheel drive ready," he said to Geoff. "We need to leave now."

Pulling on his pants, he noticed how stiff his body was. His stitches went below his waist, so it was hard to button his pants. He pushed his feet into the boots and Rachel laced them up.

"Like I said, nineteen hours in a four-wheel drive is a long time," Eitan said. He grinned broadly. "Anyone interested in a ride in a Black Hawk?"

"You have a helicopter," Shaun said, amazed.

"Technically, it's not mine, it belongs to the military, but I used to fly them all the time. Come on, I can get you there and back in under four hours."

Rachel stared at Shaun. "We still have to find my family and get back to Jerusalem to meet Kevin."

"Who is Kevin, and why is he so important?" Eitan asked.

"Maybe another time," Rachel said to Eitan. "When can we leave?"

"She's fueled and ready to go. But Rachel, before we go," he said in a gentle tone, "you need to understand that nobody has been found at the Lion's Gate since thousands disappeared in August, eight months ago."

"I understand, but I need to see the place for myself," Rachel said.

"My gemstones?" Shaun said.

Rachel gave Geoff a key from around her neck. "Take this and get Shaun's stones from the bank, vault forty-two."

"Meet us up on the helipad," Eitan said.

"I'm your man. I'll meet you topside," Geoff said, running down the hall.

"Hey, slow it down. This is a hospital," a male nurse shouted, nearly colliding with Geoff.

Shaun and Rachel said their goodbyes to Maria who was cradling Ari at the bottom of the bed. He had fallen asleep again in her arms. He looked so peaceful. Shaun knew he would miss him. He kissed Ari softly on the cheek, careful not to wake him, and Rachel did the same.

Eitan left the room and came back with a wheelchair. "Get in."

"I'm not getting into a wheelchair!" Shaun said.

"It'll be a lot quicker if you do," said Eitan.

Shaun got into the wheelchair allowing Eitan to push him down the hall. He was heading for the Primus private elevator.

"Where are we going?" Shaun said.

"It's okay, trust me." Eitan said.

Shun squeezed the arms of the wheelchair a little too tight and tried to relax.

"It goes straight up to the top, to a helipad for emergencies."

34

G eoff was already waiting on the helipad with the duffel bag. He gave Shaun the pouch of gemstones that were no longer glowing in the manner Rachel had described. Geoff placed the duffel bag on Shaun's lap, then took control of the wheelchair. Eitan ran ahead and prepared for flight. Shaun was pleased Geoff was coming. He didn't think Kevin would mind, and he thought Geoff would get along with everyone at the estate. Geoff helped Shaun up into the chopper and tossed in the duffel bag, but he didn't climb aboard. Instead he secured the door and waved. Shaun waved back and looked out the side window until Geoff was a just a dot on the helipad.

Eitan flew into the blue sky and over the border into Egypt. Rachel was rummaging in the duffel bag and found the painkillers. She gave two to Shaun.

He looked down at the terrain, relaxed and pain-free, admiring the clear water of the Gulf of Aqaba, and the pyramids in the distance. The resorts along the banks of the Gulf lay in ruins. It would've been nice to have visited before the world had gone crazy, before his dad had stolen the Emerald Tablet. If only things had been different. He had read about Egypt in his adventure books as a kid. He had imagined accompanying his dad on archeology digs and traveling to remote undiscovered places.

THE HELICOPTER WAS SILENT. THE LIGHT THAT SHONE THROUGH the window was dull. He had fallen asleep and it hurt to move now. The sun was low on the horizon and Rachel and Eitan were missing. He climbed out of the chopper, although he was stiff and couldn't stretch easily. "Rachel!" There was nothing but silence. "Rachel, Eitan!"

Shaun hooded his eyes with his hands. A pharaoh's head loomed above him. He was at the foot of the Sphinx. He walked up to the Sphinx, searching for an entry. He walked between its paws and called out for Rachel. *Where has she gone? Why did she leave me behind? Why didn't she wake me?*

Under the shade of the head, he rested before going through the entrance he'd discovered. He took off his leather jacket, leaving it on the paw, and proceeded down narrow steps that led into the bowels of the Sphinx. As the light from outside diminished, he drew on the energy of the stone. His hand glowed with light. Continuing further down the steps he entered a cold chamber, the chill pinching his skin with goosebumps. He wished he had left his jacket on. Shaun knew

Rachel wasn't there, the chamber felt empty. There were symbols on the walls and circles carved into the ground that meant nothing to him. He was lightheaded and went back outside to wait. She had to come back.

Heading back toward the helicopter, Shaun yelled into the ether. "Rachel!"

He could sense the lack of people, but most of all he felt the emptiness her absence created. It's like she had disappeared off the face of the Earth. He continued searching behind every boulder and in every shadow. "Rachel!"

Shaun thought it was probably late afternoon. The sun was glaringly hot, and his side was hurting. Kevin would have come and gone by now. Shaun made his way back to the helicopter and took two more tablets. Praying Rachel hadn't been dragged off by an Ammit, he searched the chopper for a note, anything that could give him a clue as to where she was. From the air he remembered spotting a backpack, before he fell asleep. He pushed the door closed and headed for the lowest point of the Sphinx. He struggled, climbing up to the top of the Sphinx. Nothing but stillness in every direction.

"Raaaa-chel!" Shaun collapsed.

THE SUN HAD DISAPPEARED, AND THE STARS WERE SPARKLING above. He thought he saw a bolt of light, a beam shining down from the heavens. It passed between the stars like a laser, making its way toward him in slow motion. It was beautiful. Shaun had passed out hours ago and wondered if he was experiencing delirium from the painkillers. Shaun lay on his back on top of the Sphinx, watching the laser beam traveling toward Earth. He sat up as the light expanded like the ripples of a nuclear explosion. It would connect with the Earth close by, or on top of him. It was probably just a hallucination. He kept watching it descend toward him, believing by now he was delusional. He struggled to his feet.

The beam of light passed the edge of the head of the Sphinx and smacked into the desert soil between the front paws. It saturated the area in starlight. He looked back up to the sky. The light trail was fading. On the ground where the light hit, Rachel was crouching next to Eitan. They both glowed in the starlight. As quickly as he could Shaun stumbled down. *This had better not be a hallucination.* Whispers of steam and vapors trailed off their translucent clothes and glowing bodies. Sand falling like snow settled around their ethereal bodies. Shaun was so stunned by her radiant beauty, he couldn't speak. He stepped forward slowly.

"Rachel?"

Jumping down the Sphinx's paw, he dismissed the pain and called out to Rachel. Disoriented, she slowly stood up, getting her bearings. She shaded her eyes with her hands, but was blinded by the blue spotlight that was fading. She was waiting, perhaps, for her eyes to adjust. When she saw Shaun jump from the Sphinx, she ran to him awkwardly and threw herself into his arms. Weak, he struggled to remain standing as she cried into his neck. She laughed and cried all at once. It confused Shaun. Was she happy or was she sad? Eitan was slowly standing also looking dazed, like a man who did not understand what was going on or where he was.

"Rachel, are you all right? What just happened? It looked like you just came from," he looked up to the stars, "the sky?"

"I found them, Shaun. I found everyone. I found heaven," Rachel said, stepping back from him and reaching out her arms as if to include the universe.

"You're not making sense." Concerned that he was still under the influence of the painkillers and dreaming or hallucinating, Shaun pinched himself. "There's nobody around. I've looked. Where are they?" he said, with his arms outstretched and walking in a circle. "And what's wrong with Eitan?"

"He'll be fine. He tried to stop me entering the portal and was transported along with me."

"Rachel, we're hours away from where we need to meet Kevin. You're not making any sense."

"There is another portal, right here," she said. "I went up there!" She pointed to the twinkling stars. "Up there is where we're meant to be. Up there is where my mom and brother are. Up there is home, our home," she said, sitting him down on the paw, running her fingers through her hair, messing it up a bit.

He sat next to her trying to process what she was saying. It was easier to imagine it was a dream. But he just saw her travel from the stars on a beam of light. He looked at the crystal in his hand, then back up to the sky. The beam had gone. The stars were twinkling in the normal way. "Rachel, start from the beginning."

"When Eitan landed, you were asleep. We got out and looked around. I waited for you to wake up while Eitan refueled with the reserve tanks. I kept searching the area. There wasn't a sense of another living soul, but us three. It was deathly silent. I checked on you and thought there was no point in waking you. I believed if my mom was here, she would have left a sign. I was right, Shaun. There was a message carved into the wall. The message was from my mom."

"How could you know it was from your mom," Shaun said.

"At first, I wasn't sure. Well, actually, I didn't know. It said 'you'll find me in the heavens among the Seven Sisters on the brightest star.'"

Shaun looked up, knowing he had just seen seven stars.

"The Lion's Gate is a portal, like Delilah said. We can't activate it from Earth. It can only be activated from the heavens. When Sirius, the Sun, the Earth, the constellation of Leo, and the great pyramids and the Sphinx line up, a portal will open for ascension, before the final cleansing of the Earth. The Sphinx was originally a lion that faced the constellation of Leo, Sirius, Orion's Belt, and the Pleiades."

"So how did you activate the portal?" Shaun asked.

"I was inside a chamber of the Sphinx when I found the message. There was a circle on the ground. I walked into the center trying to decipher the hieroglyphics on the walls and the portal opened. I did nothing to make it happen. They took me."

Eitan still disoriented. He sat down on the other side of Rachel and said, "I followed her into the chamber. I saw it happening and grabbed her arm. We were transported within seconds to ... up there. They took her away from me. I was guarded by men glowing like white crystals. I couldn't move from the spot, I couldn't speak. The energy was so intense, it was difficult for me to remain conscious. It scared me. I worried I could never return to Ari. Then I heard my sister's voice as if I was talking to her telepathically. Then Rachel was back, and we were being beamed down from the heavens, which took nearly ten seconds. It was incredible, Shaun." Eitan hugged him.

He's never had so many hugs from men in his entire life since being in Israel, and it's something he wished his dad had done.

"They led me to an adjoining room and I was enlightened by two elders," Rachel said. "Everything was glass, ice, or crystal, I don't know which one, but it was beautiful. There was one male, one female: I assumed they were male and female by their energy and tone of their voices inside my head. They communicated telepathically. Their mouths moved only to smile. They were pure white light. Everything was clean and fresh. Nothing was solid, everything was compressed light. They spoke with their minds and showed me us ... you, me, Casey, Sophia, Kevin, Jade, and Tim, waiting for the world to adjust itself after the return of the Emerald Tablet. They were watching to see what we would do. Remember when we first saw New York through the portal between Athanasia and our world? Remember, only a third of the people were able to get to their feet and move around? That's because the rest went up there," she said, gazing at the stars. "I'll never look at the stars the same way again. We're protected because we're destined to destroy the evil that has come through the negative realms. We must cleanse this world, or die trying. I wasn't permitted to go beyond the adjoining chamber, so my mom and brother came to me. They looked like white angels." Rachel teared up.

"Shaun, I thought I saw Sophia. She was ascending with the angels."

Shaun held her. "She'll be all right. She's tough. What happens to the Earth once it's been cleansed?" Shaun said. "Will it return to nature?"

"I don't know," Rachel said, "but we must gather the surviving humans and prepare them for ascension when it is cleansed."

"Let's get you two back to Jerusalem," Eitan said, regaining a sense of control.

"It's well past the meeting time. Kevin won't be there," Shaun said.

"We have to try," Rachel said.

They helped each other back into the helicopter. "Do we have enough fuel?" Shaun asked. "Are you sure you're okay to fly this thing?"

"Not quite. We should have enough fuel to get you close, and actually I feel invincible," Eitan said starting up the engine.

THE BLACK HAWK SOARED THROUGH THE NIGHT SKY, BUT TEN minutes out from Jerusalem, the fuel alarm went off. They quickly searched for vehicles. Rachel spotted a four-wheel drive vehicle and Eitan landed the helicopter as close as possible to the car.

"How are you going to get back to Olivet and Ari?" Shaun said. He knew Eitan couldn't go with them. He had to go back for Ari.

"Don't worry about me. I'll sleep in the chopper for tonight and refuel in the morning. You two get going," Eitan said.

Shaun and Rachel jumped out of the chopper and into the car.

"There are keys!" Rachel said, exhilarated. He hoped it would start and wasn't abandoned because it had run out of fuel.

Rachel turned over the ignition. The car engine labored. She turned the key into the off position and let go of it, waiting for a minute. Then she grabbed the key again and turned the engine on. The motor labored, coughed and revved into life. Rachel wasted no time and took off. She drove back to the exact street where Kevin had opened the portal days ago.

THE STREET WAS SHROUDED IN DARKNESS.

Shaun sat next to Rachel in the idling car.

"Kevin's not here. We should go back to Eitan and the city," she said with her hand on the gearstick, ready to reverse.

"No, wait, Kevin's been here," he said putting his hand over hers. "Listen." In the distance, there was the noise of a motorcycle. "Can you hear that? It sounds like it's heading toward us."

"Should we hide?" Rachel said.

She didn't wait for an answer, but reversed the vehicle into a side street and turned off the headlights. They waited for the motorcycle to come into view. The motorcycle's back wheel skidded as the bike came to a stop where the portal should have been. The rider didn't take off his helmet or turn off the engine, but Shaun knew it was Kevin, and so did Rachel.

Rachel turned on the headlights and pulled the SUV out from the side street. Kevin spun the motorbike around to face the car.

"Kill the lights," Shaun said to Rachel, getting out of the car.

"K, it's me, Shaun."

Kevin killed the engine. He kicked down the side stand, took off his helmet and hung it on the mirror. Shaun embraced Kevin. They held each other for a few seconds before they pulled apart.

"You're hurt!" Kevin said.

"Just a tad. I knew you would be back," Shaun said. "Did you bring the motorcycle through the portal?"

"Sure did."

"Where's Jade? Did she find her father?"

"She did, and she's waiting for Sophia and Casey to return to the estate."

"Where did they go?"

"Remember the guy that stopped out front of Casey's estate and climbed up on the roof of his car? He came back, and Sophia let him into the estate. Casey, Sophia and Tim have gone to help him bring back his family," Kevin said. "Jade and Joe worry about them."

"It's great to see you. Jade and I have so much to tell you guys."

"Is that Rachel in the SUV? Did she find her family?"

"Yeah, sort of, I'll let Rachel explain it. I'm glad you're here."

Kevin lifted his helmet off the mirror. "Let's do this. I'll open up the portal. Follow me."

"No worries, K," Shaun said, hobbling back to the car. He was in so much pain he was finding it hard to breathe.

Shaun sat in the car watching Kevin open the portal. Rachel started the car and turned on the headlights, putting Kevin in the spotlight. Kevin put on his helmet and doubled back on the motorcycle. Shaun heard him revving the bike like a badass. Kevin took off at full throttle and rode straight into the portal, Rachel sped up and was right behind him. They disappeared from the face of the Earth. The healing qualities of the portal embraced Shaun instantly. All his concerns faded away in the bliss. All pain evaporated. It healed him.

The car landed hard on the front lawn of Casey's estate in the UK. Rachel slammed on the brakes, skidding to a stop. Shaun checked his wound, touched it: totally pain-free. He opened his palm, expecting the icosahedron sapphire to be gone, extracted from his palm, fallen to the floor, but he could touch the smooth faces with his fingertips. It was now part of him.

Rachel climbed out of the car. "Where is everyone?"

- The End -

GET FREE SHADOWS OF DOUBT: BOOK ONE IN THE EMERALD TABLET SERIES

Building a relationship with my readers is the very best thing about writing. I occasionally send newsletters with details on new releases, special offers and other bits of news relating to the Chronicles of the Supernatural and The Emerald Tablet series.

If you sign up to the mailing list I'll send you Shadows of Doubt and other free stuff: You can get the novel, for free, by signing up here:

https://dl.bookfunnel.com/7ap4hxiq3u

The Emerald Tablet Serial:

Shadows of Doubt: Book One

Immersion: Book Two

Convergence: Book Three

Chronicles of the Supernatural:

The Emerald Tablet Omnibus: Book One

Realm of Lost Souls: Book Two

The Devil's Harvest: Book Three

Separated by Evil: Book Four.

(Book four is due to be released in July 2021)

Author Note

Enjoy this book? You can make a big difference.

Reviews are the most powerful tools in my arsenal when it comes getting attention for my books. Much as I'd like to, I don't have the financial muscle of a New York publisher. I can't take out full page ads in the newspaper or put posters on the subway.

(Not yet, anyway).

But I do have something much more powerful and effective than that, and it's something that those publishers would kill to get their hands on.

A committed and loyal bunch of readers.

Honest reviews of my books help bring them to the attention of other readers.

If you've enjoyed this book I would be very grateful if you could spend just five minutes leaving a review (it can be as short as you like) on the your favorite online bookstore, Goodreads which you can access through my website as well as books one and two in the series. https://jmhartwriter.com/buy-now/

Thank you very much.

ACKNOWLEDGMENTS

I would like to thank my supportive family and friends for their encouragements. Thank you, to the invaluable editor, Stephanie Smith, proofreader from BookBaby.com, and cover designer Juan Padrón, and JMH World Publishing's ARC team who have been a tremendous support throughout the process. No book is complete without the vital service of editors, proofreaders, and great book cover designers.

ABOUT JM HART

Now semi-retired, JM (Jeanette) moved to a peaceful county town south of Sydney, to focus on her grandchildren and writing.

JM Hart is the author of The Chronicles of the Supernatural Series: She makes her online home at http://jmhartwriter.com You can also connect with Jeanette on social media. Click Links below.

If the mood strikes you send send her an email at author@jmhartwriter.com

facebook.com/JM-Hart-Writer-208264706568204

twitter.com/JMHartWriter

instagram.com/jmhartwriter

goodreads.com/goodreadscomjmhart